The Mobster's Girl

by

Tabitha Devine

Meet the Cousinhood

Cover Art by *Teddi Black*

The Wild Rose Press, Inc.
PO Box 708
Adams Basin, NY 14410-0708
Visit us at www.thewildrosepress.com

Publishing History
First Edition, 2025
Trade Paperback Print ISBN 978-1-5092-6386-8
Digital ISBN 978-1-5092-6387-5

Meet the Cousinhood
Published in the United States of America

Dedication

For Jessica, who believed before anyone else did.
For Marisa, for her honesty and insight.
For Ally, who saw what this could become.
For my family, who gave me the space to dream.
And for every reader who finds a piece of themselves in these pages

Chapter 1

Madison Bryant sat at the slanted design desk and clutched her phone to her ear. Her fingers hurt from how hard she squeezed the phone as she tried to understand what her landlord, Gloria, said.

"What do you mean it says insufficient funds?" she whispered. She hoped none of her fellow interns had heard what she said. Her eyes darted around the room. No one was looked except for her friend Sabrina whose face was a question. Madison shook her head and angled her chair towards a corner in the large open space.

"I tried it several times and it wouldn't go through. Maybe you hit your limit?"

Madison's landlady was so sweet, but she didn't take any mess and no matter that she was the granny to several grandkids, she wouldn't think twice to enforce her renters' rules. She didn't bend them for anyone.

"It's set up to come straight from my account and I'm sure this is just a misunderstanding. I'll call the bank and have them fix it." This didn't make sense.

"That's what I figured," Gloria said in a kind voice. "You've never been late before and haven't caused me any trouble. As long as you get it fixed today, I won't charge you the two-hundred-dollar late fee."

"Great. Thanks." She hung up and looked around the room again. She got a few strange looks, but she tried not to pay them too much attention. She couldn't leave to call the bank now as the head of HR at the fashion house would come around to tell who was in the top four and would move to the final round.

Madison knew she did good work. She was consistent and placed in the top three for all the projects she had completed so far and was sure one of those spots was hers. But if she left now, they would give it to another. They had let interns go for smaller infractions. Anastazia's House of Fashion looked for the best of the best and those who wanted it the most, and she did. Lucky for her, today was the last day of the internship and the workday was close to the end.

She pushed the bank app on her phone to check the balance and would have fallen down if she had not been already seated. Her account had been drained. This had to be a glitch. She had painstakingly saved enough money to cover her with an extra cushion and now it was all gone.

Madison chanced another look around the open concept room and then dashed to the bathroom in the hallway. The bank would be closed when she got out and she needed to call now if she was to get this sorted. She hoped it wouldn't take long, but she'd sooner have her fellow interns think she was stuck on the potty, then to have to pay the two-hundred-dollar late fee if she had to wait until tomorrow.

She pulled up the notifications on her phone. She kept it on do not disturb when she was at work. It was clear, someone had accessed her account.

Madison waited to be connected to a live person. "Hello, this is Madison Bryant. I'm calling because I believe there was a mistake made to my account as I didn't withdraw nor authorize anyone else to remove funds from my account."

"I see, let me collect some quick information to verify the account and then I should be able to help you," the bank associate said.

"Ok, great." Madison's shoulders drooped as she gave them the needed information. They would get things sorted, and the money would go back to her account and if she was lucky, she would be able to avoid the two-hundred-dollar late fee.

"Ok, I found your account right here. And it looks like you have a joint account, and it was this person that removed the funds."

"Shared with who? Oh, my dad. But he would never take out money. He only put things in." He hadn't put much in since his stroke when he could no longer work. Her dad had set up the account for her so that he could give her money that her mother wouldn't have access to. Her mother wasn't even to know.

"It looks like it wasn't your dad. There's a note in your file. Someone came in with a Power of Attorney for your dad and it looked like it was verified by the bank manager and the money was taken. It looks like it was for an Elaine Bryant. Do you know them?"

"That's my mom."

"Oh well, then there you have it, the POA gave her access to the account and she used it," the bank associate said.

Madison ended the call with a nasty taste in her mouth and a stomach that was twisted and turned like it was up for an award against a hurricane.

The call had left her ripped apart at the seams. Her mother had gotten around the setup her dad had in place and used his stroke to get access to Madison's money.

She could just imagine her mom's face when she got the money. How had she even found out?

How was she to come up with the now fourteen hundred dollars she would need, because there was no way she would be able to drop it off today.

She knew one way to make the money, but she didn't have any stripping gigs lined up. She had taken a break to focus on her internship and hadn't needed extra money since she had her savings to cover her.

None of the places she worked would take on a last-minute extra. They had their schedule set weeks in advance. She could get in if she subbed for someone, but if they were on the schedule they were sure to have gotten someone to cover their shift by now.

Madison pushed out of the bathroom, her head low, and stumbled back to her design station. There was no way anyone would switch with her since she didn't have any gigs scheduled. Even though today was the last day of the internship, she had worked hard. With early starts and late finishes she looked forward to a week off.

Her butt had just hit the seat when the head of HR, Kristy Washington, came by. Everyone looked like eager prairie dogs, all at attention on the edge of their seat, and Madison was no exception.

"We are so lucky to have you all here at Anastazia Stewart's House of Fashion. As you know there are twelve of you, but only four will go to the last round. You all did excellent work, but there were four who stood out and will move to the next round." She looked around the room and took a deep sigh. "No need to drag it out." She took a manila folder from under her arm and opened it up.

If possible, Madison slid even farther to the edge of

her seat. At this point, she was in a chair sit without the chair. Her body tingled at the chance that they called her name, but it was dampened by the heavy weight on her shoulders. What could she do to cover her rent?

"The top four are Madison Bryant, Kara Ward, Sebastian Mason, and Sabrina Anderson. These are in order in case you are interested. We will pick the top candidate at the fashion show, after the designs have had a chance to walk the runway." She closed the file. "As you can guess this is a big occasion and opportunity to further your career. You have three months to come up with and execute your designs to be worn at the show. Each of you will be assigned a model and be able to take measurements. Congratulations."

Madison felt like her heart would explode. She was in first place. Hard work had gotten her there, and her work ethic and killer designs would keep her there. She already had an idea of what she wanted to do. But she couldn't focus with her mind on how she could keep her apartment.

She could feel the eyes of the eight on her. But it was the looks of the three that burned her skin. She now had a target on her back, and she needed to bring it. That didn't faze her. Not only did she know her seamstress skills were superior, but her ideas were out of the box and her attention to how the fabric moved when worn set her apart.

"Everyone can pack up their desks. I'd like to see the four of you in my office after you all are done." And with that she left the room.

Madison swiveled her chair back to her desk to collect the dressmakers' tools of the trade, her pincushion and her granny's old silver butterfly seam ripper that worked better than the new tools, design pencils, and sketch pads she had brought in with her. She didn't pack the sewing machine as the fashion house let them use theirs, as they would use them if hired.

Her fellow competitors threw their tools into their bags, but Madison didn't follow suit. She placed all her tools in her design satchel in the right spot, wiped her desk down and turned around. The slowness of the motion helped ease the tension that related to her money problem, but it was only a slight relief.

The other three hadn't bothered to clean their desks and waited for her. Her mother hadn't taught her much, but her granny when she had been alive had taught Madison all she knew, which included how to sew.

Madison followed behind the others on the way to Kristy's office. The door was open, but no one wanted to be the first to go in.

Kristy looked up from her desk. They all stood around in a semi-circle around her office door and she took pity on them. "Come in. I know it's the end of the workday and a nine-month internship, and I'm sure you want to go home and celebrate, so I won't keep you long." She handed each of them a sealed envelope.

"Inside you will find an instruction sheet on the basics of what we will look for to serve as a guide when you create your designs. There is also an expenses tracker included. We expect you to do your best to shop on a budget as that will also account for who goes on to be an Anastazia Stewart design associate. You will also have access to the design rooms and the fashion house's tools if needed and can meet your models here for fittings should you wish. Your model information and agency measurements are also included. You of course will fund the designs yourself."

Madison planned to do it all out of her apartment. If she still had an apartment to go to. This issue of money weighed her down like a ton of last year's fashion pieces. She couldn't be as excited as she wanted to be with a thunder cloud that hung over her head.

She still hadn't been able to come up with a solution. She could see if they needed extra people at the restaurant where she sometimes worked part time, but even if they did, the tips would be nowhere near what she could earn at a club.

Madison would be lucky to get the late fee in tips.

"Again, I want to say congratulations to you all. Fashion week is huge, and AS fashion has promoted the race between four up and coming designers. Lots of eyes will be on you, so don't hold back. The last thing is I wanted to see if you have any questions?"

"Yes. Is there a certain budget range we should stay in?" Madison asked.

"I would say no more than ten thousand, but you also don't want to go too low. It will show in the quality of your fabric," Kristy said.

"Do we need to submit our fabric samples for approval?" Kara said.

"No, you can surprise us."

"Can we re-use designs from previous competitions?" Sabrina asked.

"You could, but we expect to see new creations."

"Can we modify existing clothes?" Sabrina asked.

"No, it must be your own original work."

"Do we also need to provide the accessories and makeup?" Madison asked.

"No, you will be able to use what we have in house,

but feel free to make or buy your own if you think that works better with the design." Kristy looked around. "Any more questions?"

They all shook their heads no.

"I know this can be a lot, so if questions come up later, feel free to contact me."

"Thank you," they all murmured and turned and left. A ripple of excitement went through them. Madison's was blunted by her money troubles. She turned to Sabrina as they headed out. "We made it," Madison said.

"Yeah. Congratulations on being in first place," Sabrina said.

"Thanks, but we both know how things could change." Madison lifted her bag higher on her shoulder.

"Yeah, but it's doubtful you will slip from first place."

"I don't know. I won't take it for granted and think I can coast. I have to work as hard as everyone else." Madison pushed through the front door of the fashion house.

"I can't go out and celebrate with you tonight. I have to work." Sabrina headed for her car.

"Yeah, no worries. I have some things I need to take care of." Like her place. She needed to figure out how she was to fund her design.

"So, I can't give you a ride." Sabrina stopped outside her car.

"Oh, ok. That's all right. I need time to think. See you later."

Madison headed to the bus that would take her to the train that would take her out of the city and into the neighborhood where she lived. For now. She racked her brain for what would get her the fourteen hundred dollars.

There was no way her mom still had it, and even if she did, she wouldn't give it back. She had learned that the hard way after too many piggy bank raids.

Her mom was the epitome of a trophy wife, but one on a middle-class budget. She would do whatever she could to get her hands on more money to buy more lavish outfits or whatever she had seen someone else wear, eat, or drink. Her mother wanted to keep up with everyone.

The bus jostled her side to side, and she held her design bag close. All she had done in the internship led to this moment. She had had an idea of what she wanted to do if selected, but now she wanted to do something different. Something wilder. If only she could free up some mental space to work on designs.

Madison boarded the MARC train and sat down. She had taken a seat alone until a man decided to sit by her even though there were plenty of other open seats. She looked at her phone, willing it to tell her how to get the money she needed and to keep the guy from talking to her.

She wasn't in a relationship and didn't have any plans or time to even if she wanted to. But she wasn't a good liar and didn't like to tell the guys she was in a relationship to get them to back off. They then said, "Oh, your man doesn't let you have friends?" It would just become a headache.

She'd prefer to be honest and let them know she wasn't interested, boyfriend or not. She could move to another seat, but she didn't want to seem rude. It was something she tried to work on. To put herself and her feelings in the top space instead of as an afterthought.

A message popped up on her screen.

—Sabrina: Hey, I know you weren't planning on working, but something just came up with Randy that I need to do. Can you sub for me pretty please—

Madison's shoulders relaxed, and she took a deep breath in relief.

—M: Sure, yes of course I can sub for you.—

Things were looking up.

****

Madison changed her clothes and headed to the hospital to visit her brother, Henry. He had been in a regular room but had been moved back to the intensive care unit that day. He just couldn't seem to catch a break. The breast cancer had spread, and he would get sick between bouts of chemotherapy. He had to fight off pneumonia now. Last month it was bronchitis.

He had used all he earned as a pro NBA star. He received some medical assistance, but it wasn't enough to cover all of his bills. Madison did her part to help out with the extra expenses as best she could. But her brother still hadn't learned how to manage his money, so she paid his bills directly when she made payments.

Inside the room, he was hooked up to tubes and wires. The doctors said his kidneys were failing, and he would need a transplant. Madison was a match, but each time the operation was scheduled, Henry came down with an illness and it needed to be postponed. Maybe she couldn't afford to take a week off.

That would be selfish when Henry needed so much. She sat down beside his bed and touched his hand. He took after their dad. Henry had the same toasted brown skin color and the height. He was asleep but woke up. They weren't super close, not because they didn't get along, but because he was ten years older than her. So, they were always in two different stages. It was only now that they started to connect when he had received his diagnosis.

"Hey, how are you feeling?"

"Not too—" He coughed. "—bad." He did his best to sit up and she rose from the chair to help him.

"Here." She picked up his water from the beside table and handed it to him. She also plumped up his pillows so he could be more comfortable.

"Thanks." His voice was raspy with sleep and dryness. "How was work today?"

"It was good. I moved to the next round."

"Congratulations, I know you've worked hard for this since you were little." Henry fist bumped her hand.

"Thanks."

"Weren't you supposed to take a week off?"

"I am."

"Then why are you dressed in your bartending outfit?"

Madison looked down at herself. Her family didn't know she stripped. She had picked up after a dare in high school, and it had come in handy in college and for her master's program.

"Oh, that." She knew she should have worn a jacket over top, but it was too hot in this July heat. Baltimore was oppressive. "I'm subbing for Sabrina."

"She always could tell you a story and get you to do what she should be doing. What was it this time?"

"It had to do with her brother Randy, and it helps me out too." Madison was offended that her brother assumed she was a pushover. She was helping a friend out. It wasn't like Sabrina took advantage of her kindness.

They didn't hang out as much as they used to. She

knew Henry believed Brina was jealous of her, but who wasn't jealous of someone else? She was jealous of how close Sabrina and Randy were. They were only two years apart, so much closer than her and Henry's ten-year difference.

The idea popped to tell Henry that her mom took all of her savings, but she didn't want to burden him with it. Especially when he was still unwell.

"Any news on the transplant?"

"No. With this latest flare-up of pneumonia, it's on hold again, but they say it should clear up within two weeks, and as long as I stay healthy, knock on wood, it will be a go." He put his hand on hers. "I really appreciate you giving me this kidney."

She turned their hands around so that hers was on top. "Of course I would do this for you. I'd do it for anyone."

"Even for your mom?" He gave her a look.

He had her there. She and her mom didn't get along, not that she didn't try on Madison's part. "I'm not that cruel that I wouldn't help her out too. It might make her a better person if she had a piece of me in her."

"You were made from the two of them. You know that, right? Basic biology and all that. I'm sure even those getting a masters in fashion design had to take biology at some point."

"I did take it and the only thing I can think of is that she has to be mixed together in equal parts to become a decent human being. There needs to be some dad in there. I mean we both turned out great."

Henry's chuckle turned into a coughing fit, and she jumped up to pat him on the back. Once it eased up, she gave him the water back, and he took a few sips.

He held the cup in his hand. "I know if I die, you will go no contact with her, and I don't want you to be alone with Dad sick."

"Don't talk like that, and I'm not alone." Henry always looked for the best in people. He was too optimistic when it came to her relationship with her mom. Her father and Henry made it seem as if it was Madison's fault her mom got riled up when Madison came around.

"I mean besides friends. Someone special in your life."

"I've seen what that does to a person, and I wouldn't want to put that on anyone else, especially kids." Madison wouldn't ignore her kid like her mom did, but if she got married and her husband ignored her for the kid or ignored the kid for her, either way it wouldn't be good. Although all marriages didn't have kids and there were plenty of unmarried people that did have kids. But she didn't want to be taken advantage of. She hadn't seen any healthy marriages to go off of.

Her mother had taught her that love was finite. There wasn't enough for everyone to have it, and she didn't want to have a kid and have that end up for them. In marriage, all Madison could see was how her mother took advantage of her dad, and she didn't want to be in either position.

"Our parents are our parents, and they did their best. I know your mom and our dad made mistakes, but she's been much better now, hasn't she?"

Madison didn't have the heart to tell him that her mom had taken her savings, and she might lose her apartment. "Yeah. You seem tired. Let me let you rest, and I'll come back and see you after my shift. I'll let the nurses know to expect me." She took the water before it slipped out of his hand.

"You don't have to."

"I know." She got up and went to the door. By the time she turned around, he had fallen asleep. "But I want to."

Chapter 2

"Hey Zoe, I'm in for Sabrina. Do you need help?" Madison entered behind the bar to punch in.

"Hey." Zoe stopped her swipe across the bar top that she had wiped down to give her a quick side hug. "It's been a long time."

"I know. We need to get together for another ninety-day fiancé watch party." Madison set her bag down on a barstool. "Yes, as soon as—"

"Your internship is through." Zoe gestured with her cloth. "Girl, I know. How's it going? It's almost over right?" Zoe turned back around to grab clean glasses from the crates.

Madison leaned against the bar. "Yeah. I found out today that I made it to the top four, and my design will get shown at fashion week."

"What?" Zoe set the glasses down and gave her a full-on hug.

"That is awesome. Congratulations. You deserve it." Zoe went back to the crate.

"Thanks." Madison looked down.

"Anytime. I could use the help to get the bar set up." Zoe leaned forward. "Brenda is the other bartender on the schedule."

They both rolled their eyes.

"So, I don't mind, but you know she will have an attitude and say that you've gotten her tips."

"I'm fine with it if you are."

"Of course, I am. I'm happy for the help. I wish everything wasn't a competition here."

"True, but that's how they set it up. They like it when the girls try to outdo each other."

"I know. I can't believe they fall for it."

"Me either, but at the end it all relates to money and what gets you the most."

"True." In that way she and Zoe were pretty similar. If they could, they helped each other out.

It was nice to have another person to talk to besides Sabrina.

"So, if you have time to help behind the bar, I'll take it."

"Sure." Madison stood and grabbed her bag.

Madison dropped her things in the back and slid her tracks to the DJ for her sets, then walked back to the front. She had on her usual jeans and tank that she always wore when she stripped. She walked past a table and then there were hands on her ass before someone grabbed her arm.

"Well, well, well. What do we have here but the high and mighty Madison. I see you're back to slumming it. On your knees."

Madison looked into Eric's face. She didn't care for him and yanked her arm out of his grip. She turned to stride away and then his hand was on her again.

"Did you hear me? I said on your knees."

"Did you see me? I'm walking away." This club was disgusting. It allowed patrons to tell the women to get on their knees whenever they wanted for whatever they wanted if they were caught on the floor out of their string bikini "uniforms." The management knew if they wanted her to come in and get a cut of the money that she made they didn't make her follow that rule.

She might strip, but she wasn't a whore. She walked to the bar. Eric was on her heels. From the corner of her eye, she could see one of the bouncers stop Eric as he reached out to grab her again.

"I'm surprised Eric tried that on you. It's not like he's new. He should remember he's not allowed to touch," Zoe said.

"Yeah, but he does whatever he wants." Madison finished. Eric was attractive in a pretty boy way with the asshole attitude to match. He didn't understand why she didn't fall over him like the other girls did.

They only did it because he was rich. Though he didn't tip well after the first time. Madison wasn't interested in any of the carrots he dangled in front of the other girls or the shitty way he treated them.

They didn't have a lot of time to talk as she helped mix drinks and served the customers. Things had calmed down when her body started to tingle. It was like the wind rushed through her, which was strange. She had never had this feeling when being watched before. There was someone who approached her. He was attractive in a dangerous kind of way. There was an aura that surrounded him. It screamed bad boy. Tall, dark brown hair.

A muscular body, but not too much. Like he liked to keep fit and lift weights, but he didn't try to hit any weight records. A body she wanted to feel against hers which shocked her. She couldn't quite see the color of his eyes, but his look seemed deadly, and like his eyes were trained on her.

Maybe it was the air with which he carried himself.

Like he owned the place. He was confident and cocky. Arrogant. That was it. And there was an immediate attraction to him and there was a pull in her sensitive places. A feeling she wanted to act on.

"What can I do you for?"

"You and me and a private room."

"For?"

"Blow job."

"Shot or drink?

"Neither. I'd like one from you."

She met the new guy's eyes, a smoky gray in color. Hers narrowed. She wasn't sure if it was a joke or not. Everyone had stopped talking. There was what appeared to be a bodyguard standing behind the newcomer. The man's suit was expensive and the way Eric's now-terrified eyes were bouncing back and forth between her, the man, and his bodyguard, she wasn't sure what would happen if she pissed him off.

"Cute, but I only serve alcohol," Madison said.

"Then I guess I'll take a red-headed slut."

Madison looked at him. Her hair had streaks of red, that gave it an auburn look under the overhead lights, but Zoe's was all red. She figured he didn't want the shot or the drink but another innuendo that he wanted her. She had never had this pull before in any of her failed to become real relationships. And she didn't like the word slut, but the way he said it made her hot.

"One moment." She walked down and whispered in Zoe's ear.

"I think that guy down there thinks I don't only serve drinks. I need to do my set. I'll try to get back out after I'm done." Madison walked away with the bouncer who came to collect her. The eyes of the man were hot on her back, but she refused to turn around.

****

Dante watched the little minx walk away. She said she didn't serve, but what why did she go with the bouncer?

He would find out soon enough. Zoe walked over. She had worked for him for a while. He still hadn't figured out her deal. She was happy to bartend and pick up extra shifts or do special events, but she wasn't interested in some of the other activities they offered. But he liked her and knew she would give it to him straight and tell him what he wanted to know.

"You asked for me?"

"No, I wanted her."

"Madison doesn't serve; she was helping."

Dante was tired of people telling him what Madison did. He would decide what Madison did.

"When she comes out, I'd like to see her in my office. Where did she go?"

"She went to do her set. I don't know if she planned on staying—"

He knew the face he made had cut her off. He didn't care what Madison wanted or expected. The girls who worked at the club all knew the deal. True, it wasn't typical to ask a bartender for something explicit, but Madison was different and that made him make an exception. Before he could let Zoe know, the music changed, and he turned his head to the stage.

He was enthralled as he watched Madison walk out in some of the highest heels he had ever seen. Her outfit didn't reveal much. She had on hot pants with no hint of butt cheek and a racer back tank that covered her stomach. What she didn't show didn't matter as she worked the pole.

He watched, entranced as her body moved. She walked around the pole and did a flair. Then she took it to a flatline scorpion into a star, followed by a superman and ended in a superman pose.

She moved from the butterfly move into more inversions than he had seen before. Different variations on splits and handstands and sits that inch by inch brought her down to the floor in a wheelbarrow and she began her floor portion.

That's when the money flew onto the stage. He couldn't pull his gaze away from her. She knew what she was doing. She didn't need to take her clothes off. What she did was more than sexual enough. It was hotter because she wasn't naked.

Some of the girls just took off their clothes and twirled around on the pole, but it seemed Madison took a whole new approach. She made good use of the floor, pole, and her body. She also knew how to use her face. There were no dead eyes there.

As the music faded, he was able to tear his gaze away from the stage. He watched as she walked off, and they cleared the stage of all the money that had been thrown out for her. The music changed and she came out again, but she wasn't alone.

She was in the background. He didn't know who had put her there. She was better than the other girls she was with. He would have preferred not to have the other girls there.

The grumbles of the other patrons mirrored his own thoughts. One by one, each of the other girls left the stage until Madison was there on her own. She performed some amazing tricks. He was spellbound until she was finished. Dante headed for his office and made sure to tell one of the bouncers to send her up.

****

Dante was sat at his desk and looked over the books when there was a knock at the door. He looked up to see his dad come in and close the door behind him. Dante loved his father, but he didn't like the way he liked to interfere in what he was doing. He wasn't a boy anymore who needed his pops to look over his shoulder to check on him and advise him of the moves he should make.

"Son, I wanted to talk to you." His dad sat down without prompting and leaned back in the seat. Crossed one leg over the other and connected the opposite ankle and knee.

Dante didn't bother to ask what. He was pretty sure he knew what it was. His dad didn't need Dante to speak to start a monologue on anything mafia related.

"Don Calo and us talked, and we think it's time you boys take a more active role in the business. You boys each have your little area, but if you guys are to take over, you wouldn't know what to do. The Don has Lucca, but you're like a second son to him. You and Lucca get along; you could be his right hand when he takes over."

Dante took a deep breath and bit his tongue before he spoke. He had told his dad in what had to be a billion different ways that he didn't want to take over or move up into any more of a leadership role. It wasn't what he wanted for himself. Especially with the job offer at the brokerage firm on the table.

His dad would without a doubt have a fit if he knew he had plans to leave the family. It was rare for someone to leave on their own.

"Dad, I don't want to be Lucca's right-hand man. I want—"

"That's my boy." He slapped his hand down on his thigh. "You want to be the top. I knew you had it in you. I was worried when we sent you boys to college that you would all get soft."

College hadn't made them soft. But it had shown them a different world. And for Dante, it was a world he was more interested in being in. There he had been seen as a whole person. Not just as the numbers guy. His teachers pushed him hard and encouraged him to continue to learn.

It had been a struggle to get his dad to let him go to get his master's in business and finance. But his uncle, Don Calo, had prevailed because it helped them to grow their real estate businesses as well as their other holdings.

He had already been cleaning up his businesses within the family and had branched out to doing other people's books. He also worked on others' investment portfolios. He was a businessman at heart. He loved to invest and increase his and his client's portfolios.

"Dad, college can't make you soft. Look at all the improvements we've made so far and that have increased the family bottom line."

"True, but you think we don't know that you shun our ways. The protection money side is steady. I've checked the books."

"You fucking checked up on me?" It just slipped out. The forbidden word. His father had cut out the tongues of men who had disrespected him with "that street language." He wasn't immune to punishment.

"Watch your mouth. I won't hesitate to correct disrespect."

Dante nodded his head. "Sorry."

"Have you been in the field?"

"I have been. I checked on some of our other properties."

"Good boy." His dad slapped his thigh, and placed both feet on the floor. "Have you acquired any new money-laundering clients."

"No, but I have feelers out."

"Well, work on it. The amount of money being washed has decreased. If I didn't know any better, I would think you were trying to clean up the business and get rid of the family way."

Dante knew not to look guilty or to divert eye contact. He kept his back straight and his face relaxed. He didn't flinch at the penetrating stare his father was giving him.

Then there was that call he had gotten. He needed to do something with the information.

"Dad, I can't talk right now. I'm expecting a dancer to come up that I need to talk to."

His dad took the hint. He couldn't outright tell his dad to leave, but this was the next best way.

****

Dante listened to footsteps approach before his door opened. He watched as Madison walked in. She had changed back into what she had on at the bar. He allowed his eyes to roam over her body again. Her skin flushed at his look. He leaned back in his chair.

"Take a seat." He inclined his head at the chair closest to his desk.

"I'd rather not." She stood rooted by the doorway.

He studied her face. "Then I guess it is good that I don't care what you want. Take a seat."

Her jaw clenched before she released a huff and sat down. She was pretty, not as leggy as he liked them but her golden-brown skin, so different from his own, drew him to her. An inner light and glow that he had first believed had been the stage lights, but it was her own natural glow. An innocence that was strange to find in a strip club, let alone in a stripper.

"See that wasn't that hard, was it?" He leaned back in his chair and angled it towards her.

"They said you wanted me downstairs."

"I told you I wanted you, but you said you don't serve. I think you might be confused how things work around here." He leaned forward over his desk. "I didn't even audition you." Her breath hitched when he got in her space, and he could see her nostrils flare.

"I don't work here. I'm a sub for Sabrina. I spoke with Enzo, and he told me it was fine, and I didn't need to follow certain rules."

"Well, I'm back and things have changed." He sat back and picked up a pen that he rolled between his fingers.

"Fine." She stood up. "I won't be back then."

"You won't get paid for tonight either." He placed the pen down and rested his back against the chair. He wanted to know what she would do next.

She whirled around and the fire blazed in her deep brown eyes flecked with hints of gold. He liked that. There was passion under her cold controlled exterior.

"What?"

"You heard me."

She stalked over to his desk. "You can't do that. I earned that money." He liked her angry. Would that passion translate to the bedroom? She had either forgotten who he was or didn't know he was a Bianchi. Most people wouldn't dare talk to him like that for fear of what he'd do, but she seemed unbothered by the fact that she stood in front of a mobster. Maybe he had been away too long.

He stood up and moved towards her. He was surprised when she didn't back up. "I can do whatever I want. You didn't earn that money. You were working here illegally if you don't follow our rules. I do know of a way that you can get that money and maybe more."

"I bet. I'm not interested. You can tell Enzo I won't be back."

She reached for the door and pulled it open. He didn't believe she would leave. He was intrigued when she walked out and didn't bother to close the door behind her. Did she not know who he was?

He went back to his chair and waited until Enzo walked in like he owned the place, which was part true. All of the cousins were partners in the various businesses, but one was always in charge and this was Dante's. His cousin seemed to have made himself real comfortable while Dante had been away.

"Why are you sitting here? Aren't you downstairs at this time?" Enzo pulled out a chair to take a seat. And adjusted his suit sleeves.

"I came up to speak with one of the dancers. She was supposed to come back up. She told me to tell you she wouldn't be coming back."

"Which one?"

"Madison."

Enzo shot forward in his chair. "Dammit, Dante. Didn't she tell you not to touch her? Everyone knows she's off limits. I can't believe no one told you...I guess you just decided to ignore it. What did you do to her?"

Dante didn't care for the aggressive move or the fact that Enzo had questioned him. Especially when it had to do with a business he had majority in. "Why can't anyone touch her?" Dante leaned over his desk. "Is she yours?" His hand gripped the edge of his desk. The little he had learned from Madison told him she would have said if she belonged to Enzo. He had never fought with his cousins over a woman, but he wanted Madison and he didn't want to share. He would explore the reasons why later.

"You didn't seem to care before. What did you do to her?" Enzo stood up and paced around the room.

"I didn't do anything to her. I made her an offer. She didn't accept it and she left."

"You know I'm going to talk to her."

"Fine. I didn't pay her."

Enzo whipped around and stomped back over to the desk. "Dante, what the… You know how much she brings in when she spotlights for us? We just lost that. You better hope I can get her back."

Enzo stormed out of the office and slammed the door behind him. Dante didn't like it. While he had been away to check on other business holdings, he had lost touch with il Signore, which was his pet project.

He should know what the deal Madison appeared to have made with Enzo and why. It was only if they were serious with a girl that they didn't make her follow certain rules if she worked for them. But he hadn't known that Enzo was serious with anyone.

Maybe he had stayed away too long. He had seen the other patron approach her when she had come in. She had caught his eye from the moment she walked in. The way her body moved. Fluid and like sex in motion, but what intrigued him the most was that she didn't seem to be doing it on purpose. She didn't notice how eyes and bodies turned to follow her movements.

She was confident in her body, and it showed.

Chapter 3

Madison could combust; she was so hot. It was like she had walked into a fire. She had been ignited from the inside out and the outside in. She didn't even feel the weight of her dance duffle as it swung across her body and her feet ate up the ground between her and the bus stop. How could he do this to her? Who was he? And where was Enzo? She had been so pissed she hadn't bothered to look for Enzo.

Or to tell Zoe she was leaving. Her shoulders slumped. At least she had those tips. Enzo always came around when she was there, so she figured he might have been out for him not to come to her sets. She needed that money.

How was she to pay her landlady that night when she got home? She had hoped with what she had made from her sets, she could slip it under her door and cross her fingers that she wouldn't need to pay the extra two hundred dollars.

Madison also needed to work at il Signore as a sub. They had the best splits of the places she worked, and the customers were always generous with their tips. They even let her bartend before and after her sets.

She wouldn't build her nest egg back up anytime soon at this rate.

She knew Enzo from high school. He had always been nice to her and she trusted him, and he hadn't given her a reason not to.

Until now.

He had been dependable and trustworthy with payments, and he made sure the patrons followed the special rules they had for her. And this other guy had come and screwed her over. She looked up and noticed she had passed the bus stop.

As heated as she was, she could have walked the five miles to her place no problem, but she wasn't headed to her place. She wanted to go to the hospital. Madison turned around and headed back to the bus stop.

She took a deep breath and willed herself to look happy. She didn't want to cause her brother any distress. He was already asking where the money was coming from and how she got so much from just bartending tips.

She also viewed it as bad for not staying to help Zoe out. She hadn't even told her she was leaving.

"Madison, wait."

She looked up to find Enzo sprinting towards her. "Did you bring my money?"

"No—Wait, listen." He held his hands out in a pleading fashion. "Dante is majority owner in the club, and I was in charge of it while he was out on other business. He has the final say on what goes on, and he says he doesn't want the deal."

"You know I'm never coming back, right?" She was screwed. She wanted to throw her hands up in the air and scream. She should be celebrating not in this mess.

"Listen, I know it looks bad, but Dante says he's willing to make a deal with you if you come back."

"I know what kind of deal he wants, and you know I'm not going to take it, so there is no point."

"No. I told him that, and he said it wasn't that."

Madison's gut told her something was wrong, and she should just go see her brother, but if she could get her money. It would be the last time she stepped into that bar, but it would be worth it to go back and miss visiting hours.

"Ok."

"Let me take your bag for you."

"No need. I won't be staying long."

****

Dante waited for Enzo to bring her back. That was where the profit spikes had come from. It had been Madison moonlighting at their club. Even with the normal club split, they made five thousand more on nights she was there. He was a businessman first, and he couldn't let that money slip through his fingers. Not with the information he had learned from the call he received. He would need that money and more if he was to beat the clock. Now he just had to figure out what type of deal he could offer where they would both get what they wanted.

The door opened and Madison came in behind Enzo.

"Enzo says you have an offer for me?"

Right to the point he liked it. "Yeah. Enzo, you can leave."

"I'm not fucking you if that's why you want him to leave."

"Enzo told me. It's just this deal is between the two of us. Take a seat." Enzo stood rooted to the spot before Dante gave him a look, and he left and closed the door. Would she tell him off again? She stared him down before she lifted the strap from between her breasts and set her duffel down before she sat in the chair.

He showed her his palms. "See, we can work

together."

She crossed her legs at the ankles and pulled them under the chair. Interesting. He was used to most women crossing their legs when they were together. Not this demure gesture.

"Are you going to tell me what the deal is or not? I have someone waiting for me."

A man? His chest tightened. There was something that drew him to her. He wanted to make her his. Well, at least until he was done with her.

It shouldn't take long. It never did, before he got bored and moved onto the next one. They were all the same, wanted to be seen out with him and for what he could give them. The women that he was around weren't real, and he didn't show the real him to them either. The man behind the mafia ties. He had presumed Monica did, but she didn't. In the end, she was just like everyone else who had come before her and would come after her.

Enzo said Madison had come to him and needed money bad, but she didn't say what for. She didn't look like she was on drugs. Was the money for her? Or the money had to be for someone else. Maybe the one who waited for her.

"You got a man?" Had her boyfriend sent her to work on the pole? It seemed like she wanted to be there and wasn't forced. Hell, some of the girls him and his cousins were seeing worked the pole, but it was to get money for themselves.

"If it's a deal I'm going along with, that won't matter."

He gave a slight nod of his head. She had him there. He would have a guy find out. Maybe they were on a break. He just wanted to fuck her for a while and be done.

Hell, with her attitude she might be a bad lay and just starfish. But the memory how she worked the pole replayed in his head.

"I'll give you the money if you're exclusive." He leaned back in the chair and picked up a pen, his thumb poised over the button. He studied her face for her reaction.

"No. I'm won't follow the rules of the club." She stood. "This was pointless."

"Under the same deal you made with Enzo. No one touches you." His grip on the pen tightened.

She lifted her bag halfway over her head before she stopped. "Does that include you?" Her voice was breathy.

He opened his hands up again. "I won't touch you until you ask me to."

"No problem then. Will the split be different?" She sat back down in the chair.

"No, the same one." He leaned forward. He had her.

"I just can't work at any other club. For how long?" Her ponytail swung as she cocked her head.

"What do you mean?" He hadn't planned that far ahead. He leaned back in his chair. He had only been thinking of how to get her to come back.

"For how long does the arrangement last? I don't want to give up my other jobs if I can tell them I will be out for three months or so." She pulled out her phone.

"Why do you think it's only for three months?"

She looked into his eyes, and her pupils dilated. She was feeling what he was feeling. "They will get bored when they can see me every day and won't pay as much as they do now."

Dante steepled his fingers. "You think so?"

"Yes."

"But you said they never know when you come in?"

"For the most part if I'm a sub for someone. I used to come twice a month."

"Why'd you stop?"

"Some people didn't want to accept that I didn't follow club rules. I don't know if you noticed what happened when I first came in with Eric. Besides." She leaned forward and lowered her voice. "There were rumors the mafia ran it, but since you said you're the owner, I will take the deal."

Dante choked. This girl didn't know who he was. Or who his father was. Eric. That was the name of the prick he wanted to kill. Would have killed on the spot. Nice and slow. If the bouncer hadn't intervened.

From the moment he'd seen her, he had wanted her for himself.

"Can I have my money now please?"

Dante held out the wad of cash but didn't let go of it.

"I do have another separate offer from this one if you're interested."

"Nope." She pulled the money from his grip and stuffed it into the back of her jeans. "Tell Enzo to let me know what my schedule will be for the next three months and I'll be here." She turned for the door, but looked back over her shoulder. "By the way, I have a day job."

"Enzo told me you need money. I have a way to help you."

"I won't sleep with you or anyone else to earn money." She turned around to leave, and he jumped out of his seat and stopped her from opening the door. He had seen interest flash across her face, when she mentioned not sleeping with him and also in the middle of their conversation on the floor. He had her caged in between his arms. She backed up into his erection, and he sensed her stiffen.

"Are you going to take the money away from me?"

"No. I want to help you earn more." He moved closer to her body, and she inched forward as close as she could to the door with her bag in the way.

"And I said, I'm not interested." Her voice hitched.

"Come on, don't be like that. I know you feel this between us." He dipped his head. Her ponytail tickled his nose. "I'm not the only one." He wanted her to admit that she experienced something too. He didn't believe in love at first sight. That was only in the movies. Lust was a given, but there was something in the way she spoke to him. The fact that she didn't know he was a Bianchi.

He didn't think it was an act.

"Even if there was something, it doesn't mean we have to act on it." Her voice was throaty.

"So you admit that you feel this?"

She turned her head, and desire was there in her eyes. "I didn't say that."

"Let's make a bet—"

She shook her head. "No need to. I'm not interested in your challenge."

"You scared?"

"Peer pressure doesn't touch me. I don't need to prove anything." She turned her head to face the door.

"One kiss."

"No." She let out a huff. "Can I go now?"

"You know you're real difficult. You don't have to make everything so hard."

"If I didn't make things hard, we wouldn't be here."

Dante couldn't stop the laugh. She had jokes. It made him want to find out more, which was dangerous. He didn't care. He should let her go. He leaned in more and caught her scent of cinnamon and honey and spice.

He hardened even more if that was possible.

"You're not going to let me go are you?"

"All I ask for is a kiss. You say no and I back off." She turned to look at him over her shoulder again.

"One kiss?"

He whispered in her ear. "One kiss."

She shivered. "And then I can leave? You won't try to do more?"

"I won't do any more than what you ask me to do."

"That won't be a problem." She turned around in his arms.

****

Madison didn't know why she was giving in. No, that wasn't true. She knew why. She had got the feeling of a spark when their eyes met, and his closeness did something she had never experienced before. Only read in her romance novels. She didn't think it was real but wouldn't dare ask any friends to confirm. They teased her enough because she was inexperienced. She knew she should set some boundaries, because it was clear he was a man who was used to getting his way. But she wanted it. She wanted something for herself. Someone who wanted her. Something to take her mind off the bills and being the sole caregiver to her brother and their parents. She wanted to feel like a woman. To see if those romance novels had it right. Give herself something to look back on. Anyway, it was just one kiss.

She took a deep breath and let her shoulders drop now that she had made her decision. "Ok."

"Ok," he repeated.

"I'm ready." She stood still. How were you even supposed to stand when you waited to get kissed?

"Good. Do you have a man?"

"No, but would it matter if I did?"

"It would. I don't cheat or help anyone else to cheat."

She tilted her head to the side. "Then aren't you going to kiss me?"

"Yeah. I'm going to kiss that smart mouth, but there is a lot that goes into a kiss before lips even touch."

She had never heard that, but she didn't know from personal experience so less she look stupid, she would have to take his word for it.

"Ok, well I'm ready whenever you are." She closed her eyes and puckered her lips. But nothing happened. She cracked open one eye to find him staring at her. She opened the other eye as heat crept up her neck. Was he just teasing her? He didn't want to kiss her. Just wanted to see if she would let him. She was stupid. She was wasting time here when she could be with Henry.

"Look, this has been fun and all, but I gotta go."

He moved towards her, and she backed up. Her bottom hit the door, followed by her back.

"I want your eyes open when you're kissing me." He cupped her cheek. He slide his fingers into the hair at the nape of her neck. "I want to be clear that it is me that makes you feel good." His other hand did the same and she couldn't help the whimper that escaped as her head lolled back and exposed her neck. "That's it, Madison."

Before she could change her mind, his lips came down on hers. Not in the crushing punishing way she had expected. It was soft and gentle. Close to tender the way he nibbled the corners of her mouth. When he licked one, she gasped and that's when things turned. His tongue slipped into her mouth, and his lips applied more pressure.

She didn't know what it was, but she opened her mouth wider. She wanted to let his tongue explore her mouth. He moved closer to her, and she could feel his arousal hard and thick on her stomach. And she came alive and pressed into him. Her tongue tangled with his as she copied him move for move.

Madison's hair fell to her shoulders and down her back and some part of her realized that he had let her hair down, but she was in a fog. One of his hands slid down her neck. Traced down her shoulder and stopped at her hip. He pulled her in closer and then moved both hands to her rear.

Hands. Where were her hands? They were in between them. But instead of doing what she put them there to do—push him away after the peck—they fisted his shirt and pulled him closer to her. She wanted to feel his skin, and she lifted the shirt higher until she could get her hands underneath.

Dante had the same idea, and her eyes sprang open. She hadn't known she had closed them until his hands slid up her ribcage and cup her breasts. This wasn't his first time, and he was quick to unclasp her bra and had her breasts free in seconds. The air was cool on them, and her nipples were quick to bead under his fingers. She followed his lead and mimicked what he did to his nipples.

He pulled her tank over her head and his shirt was quick to follow. They were chest to chest, and it still wasn't enough. She needed to feel him all over. She cupped his manhood through his pants and then her fingers, with a mind of their own, undid his pants.

He had the same idea earlier than her as her pants were pushed down her hips. She cried out when he kneeled in front of her to take her pants off. She missed his lips, but they soon found hers. But these were the ones between her legs.

She tried to push his head away, but he wouldn't let her. He placed a kiss on her panty-covered mound before he slid her panties down and then lifted her leg over his shoulder. With the movement, she was exposed to his eyes.

And underneath her embarrassment was desire. She got wetter, and her muscles down there clenched the air. She wanted more. She wanted to be filled. When his tongue touched her folds, it was like an electric shock from her clit to her nipples, and her hips jerked forward. He took another slow lick, parted her folds until he touched the bundle of nerves at the apex of her center. And if possible she believed she would orgasm from just that.

He was gentle as he sucked it into his mouth before he flicked his tongue over it.

"Aghh." She was going to come. She knew the feeling when she worked a vibrator in her pussy with one hand and pinched her nipples with the other. She let go of his hair that she had in a death grip and kneaded and pinched her own nipples as her hips rolled of their own accord over his mouth.

"Dante. Don't. Stop."

And he didn't. He kept on until she exploded in his mouth. Her head flung back and mouth open, she was flung into the stars, and she didn't want to come down.

But down she did come. Her body supported between the door and Dante's body. She came back to his soft kisses as he took care to avoid her sensitive clit. He kissed around it and her inner thighs. Was it over? Was he done with her?

"Madison. I want you. I want to be inside of you. If you don't want that, leave now." He stood up and moved away from her. The muscles in his chest and abs seemed chiseled from granite. His pants open and hung off lean hips. Dark hair led downward and she could see his bulge in his boxer briefs.

She should grab her clothes and go. He was giving her an out. A choice. She hadn't known him long but in her gut she trusted that if she got dressed and left, he wouldn't touch her again. But she didn't. Why didn't she move? She couldn't. This was going to be a night to remember. She walked toward him on shaky legs before she dropped down knees apart and butt hovered over the ground.

Before he could do anything she pulled his pants and boxer briefs down in one go. His cock sprang out, its eye looked at her and dripped with fluid. Before nerves could get her she took him in her hands and licked the tip. He groaned. She guessed she had done it right. It sounded like a pleasure groan and not one of pain. Not that she had heard many male groans in pleasure or in pain. Maybe you could learn how to perform sexual acts from her knowledge of romance novels she had read?

She swirled her tongue around his cockhead. The taste was salty, but what surprised her was how velvety smooth the skin was. She didn't know what she expected, but that wasn't it. She licked it one more time before she stretched her mouth as wide as she could and fed his cock in. She needed both hands to grip around his girth as she bobbed on the first quarter of his dick. She tried more, for he was what she suspected was also a good size in length, but it made her gag.

With a gentle hand in her hair, he pulled her off his cock and picked her up. He took her behind his desk and sat in the chair with her on his lap, legs draped over the sides.

"I need to get you ready to take this big cock." He slid a finger into her with one hand while the other played with her nipple. Her head fell back over his shoulder, and he kissed her exposed neck as he added another finger.

"That's it, baby. Work those hips. You're so tight, but don't worry. I will make you feel real good."

"Ahh yes, Dante."

He slid a third finger in, and she fucked herself on his hand. He stretched his fingers out inside of her and this even turned out to be different than her vibrator. She was nervous for what it would feel like to have a real cock inside of her.

He pinched her nipple and clit at the same time, and she exploded again. He pulled his fingers out and she whimpered at the loss. Which was strange. When she was done with her vibrator she was done. After an orgasm, maybe two, she would clean up and go to sleep. But this was her second one, and she was still as hot as if she hadn't had a release at all.

He brought his fingers up to her mouth. "Taste yourself."

She took a tentative lick. It was sweet and tangy. Curious, she went back for more. She licked his fingers clean as the aftershocks of her orgasm traveled through her body. Before she had come down, he spun her on his lap, so she faced him. His manhood throbbed on his stomach. With an arm around her waist, he lifted her up and aimed with his other hand and then he let her go and her folds were parted by his thick rod. Like a missile designed to seek heat, it found her entrance and he shot his hips upward as she crashed down on it.

She didn't know which one of them moaned louder. She was stretched as stretched could be. None of her vibrators had prepared her for the feeling of being completely filled. Stuffed is what it had been like. There was so much of him, it was close to being too much. She gasped in pain as he was fully seated inside of her, and he moved. She just sat there. She was no longer a twenty-six-year-old virgin.

His hands found her nipples, and the pain ebbed away with each thrust. She rolled her hips, her clit coming into contact with his pubic bone when she moved forward. She placed her hands on his shoulders and lifted and lowered herself in time to his thrusts.

"Oh Dante, I didn't know it could feel this good."

She bounced faster as she hurtled towards the edge. It was all so new and happened so fast that she knew there was something she had forgotten as it floated around in the back of her mind. There was something that she should have done or asked. But with everything that had happened it slipped away.

"Come with me. I want to feel you explode in me." She moaned.

His hands moved from her nipples to her hips. He pulled them down harder and harder to meet his thrusts and she knew he was getting close. She found her own nipples and plucked and played them as her orgasm thundered up to meet her. With a final pinch and squeeze, Dante pulled her hips down. Her vaginal muscles milked him, and he let out a guttural roar in her ear.

All she could say was, "Oh my. Yes" on repeat as he continued to release himself into her. This was different from her masturbation experience. They came down, foreheads resting together.

What had she just done? Would she regret what happened? But when she asked herself all she could think of was no. Definitely not. She didn't know if she could have imagined a better first experience, but the night was over and this was just a one-time thing. She didn't expect more and didn't want him to think she was.

"I better get home." She moved to get off. It was too late to go see Henry. The club would close soon and she hadn't gotten back down to help Zoe. She would see if Zoe needed help to clean up since she was still there.

"Why didn't you tell me you were a virgin?" He kept her in place.

She leaned back to see his face. Even though she was still naked, she didn't feel the need to cover up. Even though she would never and had never been so exposed to anyone in her life. Male or female. She was a private person. But with Dante, it was different. Maybe it was because he was her first. Or maybe she would not feel shy with her body now after she shared it with him.

"How did you know?"

"It was some of the things you said and the fact that you are so tight."

"Would you have believed me if I did?"

"No."

"See." She looked around for her clothes, which were strewn all over the office. Well, she guessed it was his office and Enzo had just been using it. The office seemed to fit him better than it ever did Enzo. The furniture, black with metal accents, was modern with an edge. Refined and rugged at the same time.

"It doesn't matter because I'm not one anymore."

"If I'd have known, I wouldn't have fucked you."

His words were like a splash of cold water on her face. She believed she had been good. He came. Why was he complaining?

"Don't worry, I won't catch feelings. It was a one-time thing." She slid off his lap and redressed herself and darted around the room. She grabbed each item of clothing in some type of quick reverse strip tease, before she snatched her bag up.

Stupid. How could she have been so stupid? But she couldn't get herself to call it a mistake. Maybe an unhappy accident. No, that wasn't it either. Even now that she knew he was an ass, it didn't make her regret what happened. She turned; he looked like a Greek god on his throne. Confusion flickered across his face. She supposed she had to be the same way. "See you around." How had they gotten here?

Chapter 4

And she was gone. She was right. With the way she danced, he believed she was more experienced, but it didn't take away from the fact that she blew his mind. And the knowledge that one time wouldn't be enough. It had been the way she moved, as if unsure of what to do and he noticed the pain in her face when he entered her.

There were so many ways he hadn't had her yet and things he wanted to try with her. And now that he knew he was her first, there was a primal need to be the one to show her everything she could know on the subject of sex and help her learn her body and what she liked and what gave her pleasure. And that wasn't a good thing. Especially when she didn't even know of his mob ties and that he didn't do relationships.

He looked down at himself. "Shit." He hadn't put on a condom. This night went from great sex to a bad finish and to an even worse ending. First he didn't even know what compelled him to tell her he didn't cheat. It was one thing he couldn't stand and didn't do, but she didn't have to know that.

He could have just said yes and left it at that. But he had to explain himself like a lovesick fool. Which he wasn't because it was just a one-time thing like she pointed out. But back to the matter at hand. No condom. He doubted she was on birth control, but she might surprise him.

Dante cleaned himself up and zipped up his fly when Enzo came in, followed by Gabe and Lucca.

"What did you do? Take a leak in the office?" Lucca slid into a chair.

"Nope." Gabe sniffed the air. "Smells like straight up sex in here."

"You were supposed to be up here to talk with Madison, not fuck some girl. Did she turn down your deal?" Enzo stood in the doorway.

"No, she didn't turn down my deal." Dante sat down behind the desk. "She told me to tell you to call her with her schedule for the next three months."

"So she left and you had some girl come up." Enzo pulled out a chair and turned the calendar around and flipped through it.

"No." Why did they care that he had sex in the office? It wasn't the first time and wouldn't be the last time. He also didn't want to say what he and Madison had done. It was private and just between the two of them.

"No way man. You fucked 'no touch' Madison?" Gabe leaned forward.

Dante's jaw tightened.

"No answer now, man?" Lucca straightened out his legs.

"Dante, man. Tell me you didn't fuck her. Please." Enzo looked up from the calendar, his eyes pleaded along with his mouth.

"Why is this a big deal?" Dante didn't understand. And why was Enzo worried? Did he like Madison? She said she wasn't seeing anyone, but he couldn't imagine anyone not wanting to date her.

Even from the little bit he knew, he wanted to know

more and if he wasn't lying to himself, which he was. He wanted to maybe see where things lead Madison and him. He could see turning this thing into a booty call until he got bored. Which was why anything more than what they had done would be a bad idea. What would she do when she found out she slept with a mobster?

"Is she open for business?" Lucca shifted in the chair.

"Yeah, let me know when you're ready to pass her around." Gabe sat down on the sofa.

"You don't get a turn with her," Dante answered, teeth clenched. Madison wasn't like the girls they would pass around when they were younger. Those women knew the deal. Madison was different. He had never had this possessiveness before, even for Monica when he dated her, and that sent alarm bells off in the back of his mind. Bells that he knew he was going to ignore.

"Damn, I knew she had to be good. The way she worked the pole." Gabe kissed his fingers.

"Wait, which Madison is this?" Lucca looked between them all.

"The one who doesn't have to follow club rules," Gabe answered.

"The ice queen?" Surprise registered in Lucca's eyes.

"That's the one." Gabe nodded and looked at the sofa. "You didn't fuck her here, did you? Don't want none of your fluids on me. Now hers, I wouldn't mind."

Before Dante knew it, he was out of his seat and had punched Gabe with a quick jab that stunned both of them. As boys, the cousins had fought, but now that they were grown, they didn't fight like they used to.

"What the fuck, man." Gabe held his jaw.

"Sorry, man, but don't comment on Madison like that." He couldn't, no he wouldn't stand by and let them disrespect Madison like that. She wasn't like the girls they would share. She was special. Which was why he should leave her alone, but he wouldn't. He knew deep down that he had to have her. She had gotten under his skin already and was in his system. All he had to do was fuck her out of it and everything would be fine. He wouldn't be thinking what if?

"You can't punch everyone who says something when they find out." Lucca stood and walked over to Gabe.

Dante turned around. "They won't find out; it's between me and Madison."

"We found out," Gabe muttered and moved his jaw around.

"By chance. It stays here."

"Fine." Gabe put up both hands, palms out. "Won't say another word."

"So what is this deal?" Enzo asked as an emotion flickered across his face that Dante couldn't quite place.

"Same one you had with her, only she is exclusive to il Signore."

"Wow, you snagged her with exclusivity. That's going to drive the numbers higher if she can only be seen here. I know some guys follow her to different clubs," Lucca said.

"Exactly." Dante clapped Gabe on the shoulder. And held his hand out.

"My man with a plan." Gabe clasped hands with Dante and let go. "We good."

"Enzo, what's Madison's address? I forgot something."

Enzo's eyes narrowed. "What did you forget? I can just tell her when I call with the schedule. What is it?"

"None ya." Why was Enzo so concerned? He acted like he was her father or something.

"Round two?" Lucca stepped back out of punching range.

"No. It's just not any of your business what it is." Dante wasn't going to tell them they had already done several rounds or that he had forgotten to use a condom.

"Here it is." Enzo pulled out his phone and sent it to him. "I hope you know what you're doing." His tone said he didn't approve. Dante wanted to know why? Was it because he wanted Madison? That had to be it. But did she want Enzo back?

"Is there something you want to tell me?" Dante sat back behind his desk and looked at Enzo. "She said she wasn't seeing anyone. Are you saying something is different?"

Enzo's jaw tightened. "No. As far as I know she is free."

The tightness in Dante's chest loosened. "But you wanted her?"

"Yes." Came out like it was said between clenched teeth.

"Then why didn't you make a move?" Dante was confused. None of them were shy around women. They had all had plenty of experience with the opposite sex.

"I was waiting. Giving her some space, and she hadn't been back to the club for a while." Enzo stood up.

"Space from what?" Dante pushed his chair back and stood too. Dante knew you could have a relationship without sex. Was that what she had with Enzo and then they broke up because Enzo wanted more? Then why did she have no problem sleeping with him?

"I don't know." Enzo sat back down and put his head in his hands. "She also doesn't know what type of business we're in. From what I remember in high school, she didn't mess with anyone doing anything bad."

"Doing anything bad like what?" Dante walked closer to Enzo.

"She was like a snitch, but not in a complete bad way."

"And you have her working for us?" Gabe sat up on the couch.

"She doesn't know," Enzo said.

"But what if she finds out?" Gabe asked.

"What does not in a bad way mean?" Dante was concerned, especially with the information he had been told.

"Like she didn't try to get people in trouble on purpose, but it might just happen."

Was Madison the informant?

"That's why I was giving her space."

"But you have her number and address. You could have called her or stopped by."

Enzo jumped up. "Like a stalker?"

"So she wasn't interested in you." Gabe stepped in between them.

"No." Enzo gritted out.

Dante knew that had to suck. To want someone who didn't want you.

"She friend-zoned you?" Lucca moved to Enzo's side.

"No."

"It sounds like you had a crush on her that she didn't return. You can't be mad that Dante hooked up with her.

He didn't take anything from you. She was a willing participant." Lucca clapped Enzo on the shoulder. "You know that right?"

"I see how it is." Enzo looked between them all. "I have some things I need to go check on. I'll catch you guys later." Enzo slipped past Gabe and Lucca and out of the office.

"Don't worry. I'm sure he'll cool off." Lucca sat down again.

Dante knew Lucca was right. Enzo just needed some time.

"What are you going to do now? Did you want to go down on the floor?" Gabe asked.

"Naw, I got something else to do. Feel free to stay, but I'll catch you later."

****

Madison finished up the newest outfit she had made when there was a knock at her door. It was late and she didn't expect anyone. The neighborhood wasn't so good, but she could afford it, and she hadn't had any problems with strangers coming to her door.

They knocked again, and the door shook. At first she thought it might be a neighbor, but why would they come over so late? And they wouldn't try to break into her place.

"Go away, or I'll call the cops."

"Madison, open up, it's me."

"Dante?" Madison was confused and tried to ignore the flutter in her heart. She looked around her place. It wasn't ready for company. She had design things out and sketches covered every flat surface.

"Yes."

Madison hustled over and opened the door and

wedge her body in the open crack. "Why are you here? I believed you were a criminal."

A look of panic passed over his face. She could understand that with as wealthy as he was, he was right to be afraid someone in the neighborhood would take his stuff. "Can I come in?" His eyes roamed over her and heated areas that didn't need to be reheated, and it was then that she realized it would have been better if she had put on more clothes than the t-shirt and panty set she had on. At least the shirt was long enough to cover her undies, but only by an inch.

"No." There wasn't going to be a repeat of earlier in the night. She was still sore, and he hadn't liked it anyway. "Why are you here? I guess Enzo gave you my information."

"I wanted to make sure you were ok."

"I'm fine."

"I also came to apologize for not putting on a condom and to let you know that I'm clean." Yeah, she had recognized what had happened when she had gotten home and cleaned up. That had been what had floated around in the back of her mind.

"I'm clean too, and I'm on birth control." There would be no little Dantes running around in her future. Which was good. She didn't even want kids.

"Can you show me your pack?"

"My pack of what?"

"Your birth control pack."

"Wow, distrust much." She slammed the door in his face, went to get her control pack, and came back. He still stood there. "Here. I guess you want to open it to make sure I'm taking all my little pills."

"Madison, I know this seems weird, but I have to

protect myself."

"Yeah, well so do I. You're not the one whose life will be ruined. I can't afford a baby."

"But you have to take them on time. You missed today."

"No I didn't." Her phone dinged. "Perfect timing, that's my alarm now. You can watch me take it." She took the pack from him, popped out the pill and dry swallowed it. "Is that better?"

"Yes."

"Great." Madison closed the door in his face.

Madison walked away from the door and surveyed her place, her mind whirled. He had gotten what he wanted and hadn't liked it, so she didn't expect to see him around and figured she would only have to deal with Enzo, which wasn't bad.

She turned off the lights and padded down the hallway and back to her bathroom. She had already showered when she came home, so she would finish up her nighttime routine with her skin care regime.

She looked at her face, she dotted moisturizer on her cheeks and chin and then smoothed it up her face and into her hairline. She didn't think she was ugly anymore, like her mother led her to believe. In fact she looked like a replica of her mother as she grew up.

Madison always believed her mom was beautiful. Even though she knew she looked like her mom now, she didn't feel beautiful. She no longer believed she was ugly, but she knew her face was just her face.

She couldn't change it. But she didn't use it to get her stuff. She wanted to be known for what was on the inside. Her mother only cared for the exterior, but Madison knew it was what was inside that mattered.

She turned off the light she walked into her bedroom and pulled back the covers and slipped in. She didn't fancy rumors around at the club that put her and Dante together.

People didn't know she knew they called her the ice queen behind her back. It hurt that people called her that. It wasn't her fault she didn't have any experience with the opposite sex thanks to her mom.

She didn't know how to act with men or what to do or say. She had no flirting skills, and so she chose to keep herself apart from those interactions and just watch instead. No one would leave her alone. Eric would be first in line if he found out. She turned out the light.

She also didn't want people to think she slept with Dante to get on the schedule. She already knew there were rumors she was using Enzo to not have to follow the club rules of thong string bikinis when on the floor for all strippers. And she didn't have to take whatever position the patrons wanted her to.

She pushed it out of her mind. She needed to get some sleep, so she could sketch ideas for her fashion week project.

****

Madison got a call a couple of days later while she sat at her kitchen table. She had her chin propped up on her knee, with her other foot curled underneath her butt and dress ideas swirled in her mind. She looked at her phone. It was Enzo.

"Hey, you got my schedule?" Madison's shoulders relaxed, but something squeezed in her chest like disappointment. She kind of hoped it would be Dante.

"Yep." Enzo's voice sounded strained. "You're to be the headliner Thursday through Sunday. Three sets and then you can bartend in between."

"Oh wow." That was better than she had expected. Headliners made more than just a regular stripping gig. "Great, see you Thursday." Madison hung up and tried not to let Dante pop up in her head. It didn't help now and didn't help last night either. She dreamed of him and what they did. She was pretty sure she had at least one orgasm in her sleep. At least with her new dance schedule, she would have more time to spend with Henry and be able to help out their father and still have enough time to focus on her fashion week design.

****

Madison walked into the hospital. Henry had been moved out of ICU and back to a regular room.

"Hey, you look good." He was hooked up to less machines, and there were fewer wires attached to his body.

"Yeah. My blood cell counts look good, and they think I should be able to go home sometime this week."

"That's awesome." She sat down in the chair that was already pulled close to the bed. "Did you have visitors?"

"Yeah, Dad and your mom came by. They left a few minutes ago to get coffee and a bite to eat."

Madison's mind shut down, and she looked at her watch. She had planned to spend a couple of hours with Henry, but if her parents were to come back, she didn't want to see her mother. She would make some ridiculous request, and Madison wouldn't be able to say no or they would gang up on her.

If her father hadn't been so old and her mother unreliable she wouldn't have had to be the sole caretaker of them and her brother. Henry's mom had passed away from breast cancer when he was young before their dad remarried her mom.

With his cancer diagnosis, he wasn't able to help with everything he needed to deal with, and before that he was too busy with his basketball career, so it left her to care for their elderly dad.

"I know what you're thinking." Henry sat up more in bed. "I don't think they will be back."

The room door opened, and in came her mother and father. Madison froze. She had nowhere to go. There was no place to hide. Madison was trapped. There was no way she could get out without them making a big deal that she was leaving. Anyway, she would have to go through them to get out.

Her dad was doing better, but the stroke had affected his whole left side and he needed to use a walker to get around. He had been proactive with rehab and had been able to avoid being wheelchair-bound.

Even her dad knew if he had to rely on his wife to get him around, she would put him in a corner and leave him while she ran off and did whatever she did.

"Oh, great. Madison is here." Her mother air kissed her from afar.

"Hi, Mom. Dad." She went to give her dad a hug and her mom side-eyed her.

"Madison." Her mom poked her on the shoulder. "Can you be a dear and go get us a bite to eat? I found some money your father had stashed away, but it's all gone now." Her mom had a smug look on her face. She knew she had drained Madison's account.

"Mom, I don't have any cash on me."

"You can give me one of your bank cards. I'll bring it back."

"I don't have one. I had to close my account and open a new one. They are mailing me a new card."

"Your father and I are quite thirsty. Milford, sit down. You must be tired and hungry." Madison helped her dad sit down on his walker, chair combo.

"Madison, are you sure you don't have any cash on you?" Madison's head snapped up. "I know you went bartending a couple of nights ago." Henry spoke up. His eyes implored Madison to help out.

Madison stood back up. "I only have a fifty and a hundred on me."

"Oh, that should be enough," her mom said, hand out.

"I'm sure Elaine will give the change back." Henry nodded at Madison.

Madison kicked herself for not telling Henry that her mom had drained her checking. Although it wouldn't have mattered. Her mom had every guy wrapped around her finger. They would do anything for her.

"Right." Madison gritted her teeth and got her wallet out. "Here's the fifty."

Her mom plucked the hundred with the fifty and left Madison with an empty wallet. She would need to stop by her bank to get some of the extra cash out to last her until Thursday.

"Thanks, sweetie. We'll be back." Her mom air kissed her goodbye. And the door closed behind her. She hadn't waited for Madison's dad, who stood and shuffled after her.

"See, that wasn't that hard." Henry adjusted his blankets.

"Henry, she took all the money in my wallet."

"You know they need the money. With Dad not

being able to work and all. And I don't have money coming in anymore, like I used to. We all need your help."

Money that he went through like water. He didn't think to try to help anyone else. But he expected her to help him out.

She believed she was guilty every time it popped up in her mind. Henry didn't deserve her resentment. It wasn't his fault he wasn't good with money or that he had breast cancer and now needed a kidney.

She pushed it down like everything else she supposed wouldn't pass the good person judgment test and went on like she always did. One step forward.

****

Madison was surprised when Sabrina called her to get together at a nearby coffee shop. She found her in the back deck section in the corner.

"Hey. We never got together after the announcement. I'm glad we could do something, and I wanted to thank you for when you subbed for me." Sabrina pointed at a chair for Madison to take a seat.

"No problem. It helped me out too." Madison leaned over to hug her, but Sabrina didn't bother to get up.

"Yeah, you got the headliner position." Sabrina was stiff and her voice icy.

Madison was confused at Sabrina's snide tone as if she had taken something from her. "Yeah, it was a surprise to me too. They said they were going to put me on the schedule, not make me a headliner. I got the news today. How did you find out?"

"When I called to get my schedule, one of the girls told me."

How had anyone else known that she got the

position?

Sabrina reached for a napkin. "I was surprised. You said you didn't like working there."

"I didn't, but they made me an offer I couldn't refuse." Madison cringed at the mafia reference.

"I bet." She crumpled the paper in her fist.

Madison didn't have anything to say to that.

"I was in the running for the headliner position. Seems I lost out to you a second time."

Madison reached out to comfort Sabrina. "Oh Brina, I didn't know." This was horrible, but she couldn't give it up. She needed the money, and she had already told her other jobs she would be out. She had to depend on this position for the next three months. She needed it to be able to survive.

"When I was at the club, I met Dante the owner, and he offered it to me. I didn't mean to take it from you." Sabrina's hand was cold under hers.

"But you're not going to give it back, are you? I guess you can't since he picked you."

"Yeah. I don't think I can, and to be honest even if I could, I wouldn't be able to."

"I know, you signed a contract." Sabrina's hand relaxed.

"Uh, right." Did she need to? She trusted Dante not to go back on his word. Enzo had called her with the schedule, so she didn't think he would take it away from her.

"Congratulations on being first in the AS competition."

"Thanks." Madison was embarrassed by Brina's praise and hurt at the undercurrent of venom. She knew she did good work, but she still found it hard to take praise, since she didn't get a lot of it as she grew up, and it was something she had been working on in therapy. She didn't understand Sabrina's animosity. They both knew it was a competition going into it.

"You made it too."

"Yeah, but by a thread."

"I don't think so. Your designs are just as good as anyone else's." And she meant it.

"Thanks." Sabrina smiled the first real smile since they sat down. "That means a lot to me."

"Anytime."

Sabrina had needed to run to meet her model after coffee so they hadn't stayed long, and Sabrina hadn't been able to give Madison a ride back home, which was ok. Madison sat down at the bus stop when her phone dinged, it was from Sabrina. But when she looked at it, it said message deleted.

****

Madison sat on her sofa and stared at the designs she had pinned up on the wall. They were all good, solid work, but was any of them special enough to walk the runway and win her a job as associate fashion designer at Anastazia Stewart's house of fashion?

No. She needed to go bigger, and she needed a secret weapon. Her signature was a hidden pocket that she put in all her work. It was for her, and she wanted it to be a trademark. Where people would try and find this hidden pocket that could be used to hold cards or keys.

Madison bit the inside of her cheek and looked at the sketches she had laid out before her on the table. None of these designs spoke to her and if she were honest and didn't lie to herself, this wasn't her best work. How could it be with so much on her mind? She decided to start fresh and decided to sketch freeform. Maybe the use of good ole pencil and paper would help her get out of the rut.

She pulled out her pencils and with it came an image of Dante. Where was he at this moment? She tamped it down. She had had more than enough of the Dante show already.

Pencil in hand, she sketched a rough outline of a female figure. She wanted to do a dress, but maybe a design with pants would be better.

What did Dante prefer? Dress or pants? It didn't matter. The design wasn't for him. Maybe she would do one of each. That settled, she grabbed a fine charcoal tipped pencil. Poised above the paper, she needed to decide her next move. Long or short dress?

Her gaze lingered outside her window and her mind drifted. Madison remembered Dante's mouth on her and it was accompanied by a heavy pull in her sex. Did he like clothes that revealed a women's body on the women he slept with? There seemed to be a pang in her chest of him with another woman or women.

She had spent too much time with thoughts of Dante. She hadn't touched herself since she had been with him and it had been three days of torture. Her body was on fire with dreams of him and what he did to her body and even imagined other things they could do to each other. She hadn't gotten any sleep.

It wasn't like she hadn't tried. But it just wasn't the same. She didn't know if it was that Dante had ruined her or what. But even thoughts to use her vibrator had turned her off. She acknowledged she was like a sex addict; it was all she could think of. Maybe she would take matters back into her own hands.

She slid off the sofa and padded back to her room. She opened the drawer in her nightstand and pulled out her thrusting rabbit vibrator and set it on the top of the nightstand. She peeled off her boy shorts and panties and pulled off her t-shirt and bralette and lay back in the bed. What would she do before Dante?

Madison would light a candle and then get herself in the mood. She didn't need help to get in the mood. She was already there. She let her hands roam over her body. Up her stomach and to her breasts before they traveled down between her legs. She was already so wet.

She moved her hands back up to cup her breasts and worked her nipples into hardened peaks. She rolled and twisted them between her fingers.

She tried to do what Dante had done to them. It had driven her crazy but she just couldn't imitate it. She went with what she knew worked and plucked them as her vaginal muscles clutched at air.

She grabbed her vibrator and inserted it. It pulled a light gasp from her throat. She liked to give it a few pumps on her own before she turned it on. It wasn't the same. Dante was thicker and longer than her vibrator. Maybe instead of pushing thoughts of him away she would embrace them.

Instead of her hand, it would be his on the vibrator. The image in her mind's eye made her muscles clench, and she sucked the vibrator in deeper. She turned it on and teased herself like she wanted Dante too. She touched her clit and moved the cockhead up and down her slit and teased herself until she had to insert it.

"Ah, Dante," she whispered, and that was the end of that. She turned the thruster on to the highest setting with the vibrator on medium vibration and allowed it to do its work. Her hands danced up her belly to her nipples and twisted and turned them as she worked her hips in a circle. That allowed the thrust to hit different spots.

It was good, but it wasn't enough. She increased the vibration and pinched and flicked her nipples. She could feel an orgasm coming, but it wasn't big and she already knew it wouldn't satisfy her. It was going to leave her wanting more. Wanting Dante. It broke over her in a small wave, like a ripple in a pond.

All she could feel was a lacking need. It hadn't satiated her. Needing the real thing. She was sure she could find some guy to fuck her, but deep down she knew only Dante would do. It was something that had to do with him. The way he commanded her body. Played it like an instrument that he was born to work.

What he had said was true. There was something between them. Something drawing them together and until that was satisfied, she wouldn't be able to move on and focus on her designs. Now if only she could convince him to fuck her again. The way things had ended, it didn't seem like it would work, but she knew she had to try.

She needed him out of her system so she could concentrate on what mattered. Winning at fashion week.

Chapter 5

Dante couldn't wait to see Madison again, which was a real problem. He didn't do relationships anymore. It was only casual, and it was rare for it to happen more than once with the same woman. No-strings-attached sex was what he was after. But he had been like a kid counting down the last days of school. He waited for Thursday to come around. He knew Enzo told her she could bartend, so if he just happened to be down there, he could get a drink from her. She needed the money, and he would tip well.

He couldn't wait to see her performance either. They had hyped it up, and the club was packed. Would Madison do something different? She gave a great show, but the idea of her doing something special, made him want to rub his hands together in anticipation.

It would be best to wait until after her set to get a drink so he would have something to say to her. It would be more than staring at her and drooling like a lovesick puppy. No, it wasn't love. Just lust, plain and simple. But after her set he would be able to speak of something that didn't have to do with sex. Then maybe he could work his way around to figure out how to get her out of his system.

Now that it was decided, he would get a drink after her set, he went back to his regular routine. He still needed to get the cousins together to discuss the call he had received. He needed to get to work on it, the sooner the better. He would do it tonight.

****

Madison found Zoe in the back of the little mom and pop diner they would go to after a shift at il Signore. "Hi." She leaned in and hugged Zoe. They had agreed to meet before work. Now that she wasn't interning and had more free time, she and Zoe were able to meet.

"I know. I miss our ninety-day fiancé watch parties." Zoe handed her a menu.

"Oh my gosh. I'm so behind." Madison took the menu and opened it. "I need to binge to catch up."

Zoe looked up from her own menu. "Girl, you do. I can't wait to talk to someone. And all the spin offs. I can't keep up."

"Where have you been watching them?" Zoe didn't have a TV so they would watch at Madison's place. Sometimes Zoe would catch them online somewhere and watch that way before Madison realized they loved the same show.

Zoe's eyes drifted away. "I have a friend."

Madison sat up in the chair. "A guy friend?" She had no idea what was going on with Zoe, and it saddened her that with everything going on she had lost touch with her friend.

"Well, yeah. I guess so, but not in the way you think. It is platonic."

"Does he agree, or is it just you?"

"He agrees. We wouldn't be right for each other."

"You never know." What did she know? She had no clue when it came to relationships or even trying to set up a friends-with-benefits situation. She didn't need to be friends with Dante. She wasn't sure if she liked him as a person. But as a booty call, she was all in.

"I know. Congrats on your headliner position."

"Thanks." Madison shrugged and looked back at her menu. "It's just for three months."

"Still." Zoe reached a hand out to cover up Madison's menu. "That's a big gig. Everyone is talking. I didn't even know you had applied."

"I didn't. Why is everyone concerned with it? I didn't think it was that big a deal." Well, maybe it was with everyone mentioning it. Had Dante just given her the position because they had slept together instead of just putting her on the schedule?

"It is a big deal. il Signore hasn't had a headliner for a while. It's been recent that they opened up the idea of having one. I was there when auditions happened. The girls tried every trick in the book. I think a couple tried to sleep with them."

"Them?"

"Dante and his cousins. They auditioned the girls for the position. You weren't there though. What happened that you got the offer?"

"They liked what I did and asked me to do it, and I took the chance." Madison shrugged.

"You mean, Dante liked what you did."

Madison's face heated at her words, and she hoped Zoe just believed it was the heat outside. Had Dante slept with the other strippers as well? She realized it was less special and the moment didn't mean as much as it had before. She knew it wasn't love, but there had been something between them that she hadn't been conscious of before. Maybe he had and it wasn't something just between the two of them.

Was it just another day for him? He had made it

seem like there was something between them. She had sensed it even if she wouldn't admit it to him. Was that a line he had thrown at her to get in her pants? She had zero experience with the opposite sex thanks to her mother.

"I'm not surprised though. You're one of the best dancers we have."

"Aw, thanks." Madison tried to smile. She hoped it didn't look as forced as it was. Her mind was still stuck on Dante having slept with the other strippers.

"It's true and the reason why the other girls are going to be even more catty with you."

"I know, but I'm so over it." Madison looked back at her menu. She wished it was as easy to ignore what the others said.

The waitress arrived and took their orders; they both got a burger and fries.

"I know you are, but I just want to make sure you keep watching your back."

Madison's head popped up. "I will, but is there another reason?" Madison wasn't sure if people had found out she had slept with Dante.

"Well, I know Sabrina is your friend and who introduced you to the club right?"

"She's my friend outside of work. We grew up together, and we both know Enzo. She worked at il Signore before me. I didn't like the rules."

"Yeah. I don't know why Dante has those rules in regards to what the girls wear. Well, I guess I do, it brings the money in. But the rumor was Sabrina had the headliner position in the bag."

"I know. We met, and she told me. I had no idea." Were Sabrina and Dante sleeping together too?

The waitress returned with their food.

Madison knew Sabrina had a thing for Enzo, but he didn't seem to return the affection.

"Yeah, I get that it brings in the money and the customers, but it's still disgusting."

"Do you have to follow the rules as headliner?" Zoe took a sip of her drink.

"No." Madison pulled a fry through the ketchup on her plate.

"I know you don't want to bring it up, but Enzo let you get out of them because he likes you, you know that right?" Zoe pointed her drink at Madison.

Madison set the fry down. "I suspected it, but I also bring in a lot of money for the club."

"True. So, you're not interested in Enzo?" Zoe picked up her burger.

"Nope. With everything I have going on, I don't have time." There was no time with her thoughts filled with Dante instead of dress designs.

"If you wanted to, you could make time." Zoe dabbed at her mouth with a napkin.

Zoe had her there. Madison stirred the straw in her drink. She would make time for Dante, but that was different. That was just for sex, not a relationship.

"Wait. You met someone? Spill." Zoe leaned forward, elbows on the table.

"No, it's not that." Even though it was. Madison took a quick sip of her drink. "I'm not interested in Enzo like that."

"Yeah, and I know you're not looking to getting caught up in the type of life he lives." Zoe laid her napkin on the tabletop.

Madison paused and put her drink down. "What type

of life? Having so much money so young?"

Zoe rested her chin on her hand. "Yeah, I guess that, but they are also part of the underworld."

"What underworld?" Madison's glass landed with a thunk.

"Girl you didn't know they're Bianchis?"

Madison shook her head. "I didn't remember Enzo's last name. What does being a Bianchi mean?"

"They're part of the mafioso."

"What?" Madison lowered her voice. She had kind of caught whispers the rumor going around, but decided it was just that, a rumor. Dante told her he owned the club, not the mob. But with what Zoe said, Dante was the mob.

Zoe leaned forward. "Yes. Why do you think they have heavy security?"

"I figured it was because of the girls and the clients."

"Nope." Zoe sat back.

Madison's stomach dropped. She didn't want to be a part of that. Had she slept with a mobster? Why did that turn her on even more? And why did she still want to?

"You don't need to worry; they won't make you do anything related to that."

"Well, that's good to know, I guess." What did that mean for her and Dante?

"Dante was interested in you."

It was now Madison's turn to look away. "Yeah, but like I said. I don't have the time. Also can you imagine me dating a mobster?"

"No. But you could be Dante's girl."

Madison's body tingled at the mention of being Dante's girl. "We better go or we will be late for setup."

****

68

Dante checked his email. He had another email from the head of HR at Stanley and Richards. They wanted to know if he was still interested in the position and to narrow down his start date. They were still interested in him and were willing to wait until he was available, but the offer wouldn't last forever.

"Hey, man, you coming down? Madison told me she was doing something extra special for the first set." Enzo stood inside the doorway.

"Yeah, let me come down. I wondered what she was would do." Dante followed Enzo down the back stairs and over to their VIP table that was only for the owners. It had a prime view of the stage but was somewhat hidden. Lucca and Gabe were already there. Dante was surprised Enzo had come to get him. He had kept his distance since he found out he had slept with Madison. Maybe he had gotten over it.

"Let's get this party started." Lucca raised a glass of clear liquid.

Dante sat down, and the hype man who announced the girls came up.

"Tonight, we have a real show for you. Madison is now exclusively at il Signore. So that means if you want to see her, you gotta be here. It also means you need to show her some love, because she is going to do something special just for tonight." He stepped down.

The lights went low, and then the spotlight was turned on and Dante was blinded at first. Madison was nude except for a fishnet bodysuit. She had pasties and maybe a thong on, but that was it. The whole bar went quiet except for the music Madison danced too. Everyone, him included, was mesmerized.

She took control of the stage and demanded their

attention, which they all were willing to give it to her. Her eyes caught his at an intense sexual move, and he swore she winked at him. It had to be the lights. Couldn't it? The way she had slammed the door in his face at her place, he didn't think she wanted to see him again.

Again at the floor portion, it appeared like she was crawling straight to him and looking deep into his eyes. But it couldn't be. He wanted to see if someone was behind him, but he knew no one was. Then there was the fact that their position was somewhat hidden, but it was like she knew where he was. When she did a fan with her legs into a front split and then a pull-through into a backbend, she ran her hands from her neck to between her legs. He swore she mouthed along to the suggestive song while she looked straight at him.

He shook his head. His mind invented all sorts of things. There was no way she wanted more. Could she? There was also the fact that she would run in the other direction if she knew who he was.

Then there was the fact that he had seen her nude before, it shouldn't turn him on as much as it did. But it didn't feel right. It was like her body, but not quite it. It could be the fishnets making it look different. It wasn't like he was an expert on her body after one night.

It wasn't until she hooked her leg high up on the pole that he could see that he couldn't see. She wasn't naked. She had on a flesh-colored bodysuit under the fishnets with what looked like pasties and a thong sewn onto it so it seemed like one piece. He had been right. She had fooled them all. She finished up and left the stage.

Able to take his eyes away from her, now that she was gone, he could see that the floor was stacked high with the money that had been thrown out for her. It was sure to net them both a nice sum of money at the end of the night.

****

Madison finished her set and went up to change. In a normal performance, she did a good job at looking around the room to make each customer feel like she danced for them. But each of her sets, her eyes had found Dante's. It had been magnetic. No matter how many times she tore her gaze away to work the room, her gaze was dragged back to his. When he was watching her, she could tell it was his eyes on her. Her nipples had gotten hard, and she got wet during her sets.

Something that never happened.

Dancing wasn't sexual for her even though the moves might be considered that and that the patrons found it stimulating. For her, it was moving her body to the music. Her body was the machine, and she would test its limits with her strength and flexibility. For her, it was the power and control she had over her body and somewhat the audience. The way she used her body could cause a desired reaction from the crowd.

She headed to the bar to help Zoe out.

"Hey, that was a pretty awesome fake-out. You looked like you were naked." Zoe wiped down the bar during a lull.

"Thanks. I wanted my first night to be good so I said to go big."

"You did."

Madison looked over the bar top, and there was a horde rushing towards her and Zoe. They got busy serving drinks. Madison tucked her tips into her jeans. Lots of the patrons were eager to get a drink from her and were willing to tip well. Most of them were

71

harmless.

"I didn't expect you to come out naked on the first night, but it was worth the high admission." Eric leaned on the bar.

"Well, you didn't see me naked. What can I get you?"

"You know what I want."

"Well, we both know that's not on offer, so do you want a drink?"

"No, I—"

"Then move aside, some of us want to get a drink," said a man down at the corner of the bar.

Madison moved down the bar to the older gentleman who looked like he could be everyone's grandfather.

"What can I get you?"

The night wore on and after they closed, she helped to clean up behind the bar and get it ready for the next night.

"You want to walk out together?" Zoe picked up her bag.

"No, that's ok. I still need to get the money from my sets before I leave."

"All right, I'll see you tomorrow night."

"I'll be there with bells on."

"I wouldn't put it past you after tonight. Oh no, I've given you an idea."

"You have. I'll see if I can work some musical instruments in."

Zoe walked away shaking her head and laughing to herself.

Madison went up the back steps and hoped that Dante wasn't there at all or if he was, that Enzo was up there too. She knocked on the half-opened door.

"Come in."

Crap, it was Dante. She pushed open the door. He was sitting at his desk flipping through papers. Did the mob do paperwork? What Zoe said couldn't be true, it had to be a rumor.

His blue suit looked good. What did he look like when he wasn't wearing a suit? Not naked, her face heated at the memory of his body. She would never see him in jeans and a shirt.

He had taken off the jacket he had worn on the floor, and it was draped over the back of his chair. She had seen him on the floor both during her sets and while she was bartending.

But besides some heavy eye contact, there had been no sign of him coming near her, which was good. At least that was what she told herself. She pushed the door open wider. "Hey, I wanted come to get my money from my sets. Zoe told me besides tips, that we get a check every two weeks for tending the bar."

"Yeah, that's right." He reached under his desk. "I have your money right here for your sets on stage." He held it over his desktop.

She hadn't expected it to be that easy. Or maybe she hoped it would be that easy. Her dreams had been fire, and after having the real thing her vibrator still wasn't enough.

"Great. Thank you." She didn't want to seem like she expected a repeat performance, even though she kind of did. There was no point standing there like an awkward girl. She should turn and go.

"It looks like the sets went well." She shifted side to side next to his desk.

"Yeah, I think this was the most we've made in a

night." Dante angled his chair towards her.

Her face heated at the memory of what they had done in that chair. "Well, that's good, right?" Her eyes darted to his face. Was he thinking the same thing? Or had he forgotten it.

"Yep. It's good for both of us."

"Yeah, uh, right." She remembered what was good for her, and maybe it had been good for him too.

Dante's head tilted to the side. She guessed he wanted to know why she was still standing there.

"I forgot to ask if I needed to sign a contract or something."

"Oh yeah, right. I forgot to get you to sign it for some reason." He shuffled some papers.

Some reason? They had had sex in this office, and he called it some reason.

"Here you can look it over and sign it."

Their hands brushed as she took the papers and her eyes jumped to his to see if he detected it too, but he didn't even look at her. She was sitting over here pinning for him and he couldn't care less. "You want me to do it now? Do you have the paperwork for independent contractors? I want to make sure I save the right amount for taxes. Don't want to be on the wrong side of the law, you know."

Something like surprise and confusion flickered over his face. "Sure, you can also fill out these forms." He pulled some papers from the file cabinet near his desk and handed them over to her.

She was going to make sure to avoid touching his hands, but he kind of shoved them at her and let go so she didn't have to worry. He didn't want her to touch him for a different reason. It was clear he was done with her and had moved onto the next woman.

Madison looked them over and signed the contract papers and the W2 forms. "Ok, here you go. Do you send out your 1099s at the end of the year?"

"You can leave them there. I'll get them later. Yes. I can help you calculate based on an estimate so you can pay the taxes early."

"Great. That would be helpful. I don't want to do it wrong and get in trouble." She figured he would show her at some later point. "Ok, I guess I'll go now." She went to walk away. There was no way he would want to sleep with her again. she shouldn't have even bothered. That's why she was just as surprised by what came out of her mouth as Dante had to be.

"I want to sleep with you again."

Dante just stared at her, and she believed the sun was climbing up her face.

"That's cool if you're not interested. I wanted to ask."

"Ok." Dante nodded his head.

Ok, what did that mean? Ok yes or ok I'm not interested. Before she could get clarification Enzo walked in.

"Am I interrupting something?" Enzo's voice was roughened.

"Yeah, you are. We were ready to discuss the headliner shows. What did you need?"

"It's family-related."

Madison could feel the animosity roll off of Enzo like a tsunami. What was family-related? Didn't the mafia consider itself a family? Was that it?

"That's ok. We can discuss it later." Madison stood.

"No. We'll finish it now." Dante stood up. "Give me

a second." He strode outside the room to the corridor. She could tell Enzo was supposed to follow, but he stood rooted to the spot. There was a power play happening, and she didn't think it had to do with "family" but was over her.

It was kind of made her hot, to think that Dante was laying claim to her. If that's what he was doing. He could just not want anyone else to touch her and he was still done with her. She wasn't going to be passed around if that's what either of them believed.

Enzo stood still, but then walked out to talk to Dante. She couldn't hear what was said, but Dante walked away from Enzo. Enzo's gaze pierced through her before he turned and stomped away. Dante went back to sit behind his desk.

"Something has come up so we'll have to discuss your show ideas later."

"Ok. Great, well I'll go now."

"I'll drop you off. I shouldn't have lost control with you when you were here last time."

"Right, yeah. Someone could walk in."

Dante stood up and walked around the desk. This was her first time she focused on him. His olive-tinted skin glowed in the light and his piercing slate-gray eyes were dark with something that should have scared her, but instead turned her on more.

Why was it that Dante made her so hot and wet? Was it because he was her first? Was it always like this? Was this only him? Dante put his hand on her back, and her skin was seared through her clothes. He guided her out of the room.

"Ed, lock up for me and if anyone asks, I'm out. Ok. Alone."

"Gotcha, boss."

Madison followed Dante out to his car and was shocked when he opened the door for her. She didn't know most guys who would do that. But she didn't know Dante at all, so she wouldn't know if he did this for all the girls he drove in his car, or if it was just for her.

Her stomach squeezed at the reality that he might do this for other girls. It was clear he was experienced in the sex department, but a crazy thought flitted through her mind that she wanted to be special to him. But she didn't believe that he would do these things only for her. Because of what pulled them together. At least what she recognized drew them together. He might have experienced this before.

They drove to her place in silence. It wasn't weird, and there was no need to talk anyway since he knew where he was going and if Madison had read the situation right, she would be getting fucked again soon.

She squeezed her legs together. She was so hot she would come fast once he got inside her. But she couldn't help it. She wasn't ashamed either that she had tidied up before she left for the night in hopes that she would bring him back to her place.

Madison had taken care to tuck her latest designs away and hid her sewing machine and other tools. She opened the door and let them in. He stopped in the doorway. Was he just giving her a ride home and she misunderstood what was happening?

"Before I come in I want you to be sure that you want to do this. Last time, you said it was a one-time thing."

"Last time, you said you wouldn't have fucked me if you had known I was a virgin. I'm not anymore, so I figured it could be a more than one-time-thing. That is if you're interested."

"Spell it out for me, Madison."

She didn't know why she didn't come out and say it. But this was going to be only her first time propositioning a man. "I was thinking that I didn't get you out of my system and so we could be a booty call for each other."

Chapter 6

Dante had been stunned when she had said she wanted to sleep with him again. He didn't want to appear too eager, but inside he was jumping up and down. Now she had proposed her own deal that would benefit them both. He was a businessman through and through.

Why wouldn't he take it? One time wouldn't be enough, but she was willing to be available to him whenever he wanted. It was something he could get behind. The only problem was her mention of not getting in trouble with the law. She didn't know the club was run by the mob, the Bianchi family in particular, and that he was a Bianchi. Well, it didn't matter. This wasn't a forever thing.

"Ok, I'm in. I accept the terms of your deal."

"Great. My bedroom is back this way." She turned and walked down the hall, like she expected him to follow. And he didn't. Madison looked over her shoulder. "Aren't you coming?"

"We both will be soon." That he could promise. He didn't know what he wanted to do to her first.

"All right, then let's begin." She turned, and he touched her arm. Trailed his hand down her forearm to entwine their fingers together and rub the soft spot on her wrist with his thumb. Her hand relaxed in his, and he followed her to the bedroom. He had no idea why he wanted to do that, at this moment but it had been right, and, all the stars had aligned, and he had gotten what he wished for. Access to Madison whenever the mood hit him. Try her a couple of other ways that had come to him in his dreams and be rid of her.

In her bedroom, there was a pole and a chair set up. He looked at her.

"I wanted to give you a private dance."

Dante cocked his head to the side. "How'd you know I would come?"

"You did the last time."

He chuckled. She was something else. That was the second time she made him laugh and out loud too. "You know that's not what I meant." He brushed a soft lock of hair from her face and tucked it behind her ear. He turned her around to face him and laced fingers with her other hand, before he pulled her close then he brought their lips together.

The kiss was as explosive as the last time, if not more so. But he determined it was better now that he knew this wasn't the last time. He deepened the kiss and she moaned into his mouth, and he cupped her face. When they came up to breathe, she said, "Let me dance for you." And she pushed him into the chair.

The music wasn't something that he was familiar with. The routine that she was doing wasn't like any she had done at il Signore. He knew because he had looked back at the footage from when she had danced at the club. They had the club under surveillance that was monitored by Enzo.

It had been easy enough to find her sets as Enzo was in charge of security. Everything had been saved. It made his gut tighten when he realized his cousin had watched her videos over and over again. He knew other people watched her sets, and it didn't make sense to feel this way, but that was different.

It was a one-time thing. But the fact that Enzo watched them whenever he wanted and could pause, slow down or speed up the performance bothered him.

"I'm honored."

Madison brought her hands from her hips to the back of her neck and released her hair. "Oh?"

"That you made this routine just for me." Dante reached for her waist, but she sidestepped him and moved behind the chair.

She wrapped her arms around his chest, she whispered in his ear, "And what makes you think this was made just for you?"

Dante stiffened. Had she done this routine at another club?

Madison nipped his ear and gave a throaty laugh. "Who knows, maybe I did make this just for you." She pulled down his zipper. And then moved to the front to grind on his lap. "Or maybe I didn't."

Then his mind went blank when the lap dance portion began. She did everything to her body in his lap that he wanted to do to her with his own hands.

When she finished, she ended up on her knees in front of him. He was hard as a rock, but she still managed to get him out without the zipper scraping him.

"I think this was the first thing you wanted from me."

And she gave him an amazing blow job, she had learned some technique from the last time that he would have to ask her later. His chest squeezed at the image of her practicing on someone else. He had considered sex with someone else after Madison, but he couldn't bring himself to do it.

The one time he tried, he just couldn't get hard and the fact that the woman wasn't Madison flashed in his mind.

He couldn't think in the moment. He didn't want to come too soon and they had never discussed if she wanted to taste his semen, so he pulled out. Dante would be sure to find out for the next time though. He pulled her up into his lap and undressed her of her standard uniform of skintight dark-blue near-to-black jeans and a racer-back tank. Her legs were draped over his.

"I think I need to punish you for keeping me away from this pussy." He turned her in his lap so that she was face down and her ass was on his lap. The golden globes of her ass cheeks bare before his eyes. He was gentle when he rubbed them and it caused Madison to squirm over his unclothed erection.

"Hold still. This will only hurt a little, but I'll make it feel better soon enough." That was the only warning he gave her before his hand came down on her ass, just shy of gentle. Then he rubbed the sting out. He waited for her to tell him to stop, but she didn't so he smacked her bottom harder.

"Oh."

"Spread your legs, I want to look at my pussy while I spank that ass." He put a hand between her legs to find her wet with her own hand furiously worked her clit. Already from the one night they had been together, He could tell she was close to coming.

"No, no, no." He moved her hands away and gave her a smack that let his fingers land on her wet folds. He picked up on the shiver that ran through her. It would be something he would want to explore with her later, but now he couldn't wait.

Dante stood up and took her over to the bed. "Climb on."

She went to roll over on her back.

"No. Stay on all fours." He parted her slick folds with his fingers and then pulled his hand back.

"Show me how you play with yourself." He expected her to hesitate but instead she lay her head down on the bed and kept her ass high in that air and plunged two fingers into her wet tunnel. They both groaned.

She pushed and pulled her fingers in and out of her slick hole. Madison alternated with circling her clit before she dove back in. His pants had fallen around his ankles and he stepped out of them and his briefs to take hold of his manhood. Dante stroked it in time to her plunges.

"That's enough." His voice sounded hard and gruff to his ears. She was so far gone that he had to pull her hand away before she stopped. And even then she whimpered and tried to get back to her wet folds. He rubbed his cockhead up and down her pussy lips and that seemed to calm her at least.

"I have a condom, but I want to fuck you raw. Are you ok with that?"

She answered by pushing her hips back, but he stopped her. He should have asked earlier. She was too far gone and would have said yes to anything if it would get her closer to coming.

"Madison, I'll make sure you come, but I need you to focus and tell me what you want."

"Aghh, I want you inside of me. Nothing. In. Between. If you're fine with me just taking birth control, then—"

He didn't need for her to finish. He was fine and with her only taking birth control. She came when he entered her and he held still while her muscles spasmed around his cock and squeezed it with all of its might. He kissed her exposed back. He was gentle as he rubbed her hips as she came back down. He ran his hands up and caressed her ribs before he moved his hands to her breasts. He kneaded her breasts and pinched her nipples as her body finished shuddering.

"Dante. I wanted you to come with me."

"We have all night. But I will have to punish you for coming before I was ready." He launched into long, slow, deep pumps into her slick hole. And moved his hands down to her hips and pulled her hips back harder and harder. She pushed back to meet each thrust and he used his hand on her low back to push it down. It caused her to arch her back and allow him to get deeper.

"Oh Dante. Right there, don't stop."

"I wouldn't think of it."

She kept her back arched on her own so he slid the hand up to her head. He ran his fingers through her hair. He took a light hold of her hair and pulled, which caused her back to arch more. She shivered and ripples like a wave went through her body.

"Whose pussy is this?"

"Yours."

"Whose?"

"Yours."

"Whose?"

"Dante, ahh. I'm coming. Please come with me. This pussy belongs to you."

Between her vagina clenching his dick and her

words, he shot his load into her. He could feel each pulse shoot another thick stream of semen into her. As he slowed his pumps, he hoped maybe one of those jets of cum would beat the odds.

****

Madison collapsed on the bed. She didn't know she would like spanking and hair pulling, but her body was sure she did with the way she responded. She couldn't hold herself up anymore and lay motionless on the bed. Dante's weight pressed into her and his cock still pulsed in between her thighs.

She could feel him oozing out of her. "I guess I better get cleaned up."

"Yeah." He rolled off of her, and she moaned at the loss. Not wanting to examine that, she padded nude to the bathroom. Strange that she was still unashamed of being nude in front of him, but she had still changed in the changing room at the club for each of her sets. She turned on the shower and while the water heated, she wiped her inner thighs with toilet paper.

What it would be like to have his cum in her mouth? She threw the paper in the toilet and flushed. Next she climbed into the shower and let the hot water sluice over her body. It wasn't a second before the shower door open and Dante step in.

"What are you doing?"

"I need to clean up too, and there's no point waiting until you're done, so I figured I would join you." He grabbed the body poof she had just put vanilla and honey body wash on. "Here, let me clean you up since I got you dirty."

Madison didn't want him to clean her up, but instead get her dirty again.

"I can do it."

"No, let me, I insist." He guided her to the wall and placed her hands high up. Then he used the poof he took from her hand. He was gentle but still teased her as he rubbed the poof over her breasts and nipples and then down her stomach to the special place between her legs. The smells tickled her nose as the scent grew heavy in the air. Her face heated at the memory that she told him her pussy was his.

It wasn't one of her finer moments. In high school, they had called her a goody-two-shoes in addition to ice queen. But in the moment it had been right, and even after, it didn't feel as wrong as it should.

She was all for women's empowerment and owning your own body. But she believed that her pussy belonged to him and would only answer to him. And that was all she could think before her brain short circuited as his hands traced the path of the poof. She went to move her hands and legs to stop his exploration.

"Ah, ah, ah. Keep the position until I'm done. You don't want to get dirty again."

Madison stayed still as Dante worked her body into a frenzy before he rinsed her body off. It was over, and she hadn't gotten to come again. Not that it could be possible after what they had done in her bedroom.

"Aw, don't worry. I won't leave you like this." His hands cupped her boobs and pinched the peaks before he lined his cock up with her entrance and plunged home. And that was what it was like when he was inside her. Like she had come home to a place where she belonged and was wanted for herself and not what she could do for others.

He took his time and made love to her. He refused

to speed up no matter how much she pushed back and begged. Something trembled inside of her as he continued to stroke her until she exploded in white hot light. With Dante following behind her. He growled in her ear, before he turned her head to kiss her as his lower body continued to pump in and out of her.

Sex was amazing. No wonder so many of her friends had done it and they wrote tons of books that had people doing it.

****

Madison woke up to being wrapped up in a warm and heavy cocoon. She had been meaning to get a weighted blanket. She tried to wrap herself up in it more. It was warm and inviting and she wanted to just snuggle in longer before she had to face the day. Wait. She didn't have a weighted blanket because she couldn't afford one. Did they have them come in scents? One that smelled clean and citrusy with a hint of musk. So what was on her?

She opened her eyes to see a muscular forearm thrown over her stomach, a hand with a possessive grip, that cupped her breast. A breast that had a nipple that had chosen that moment to get super hard. Dante was in bed with her. Still. She stopped moving because she didn't want to wake him and did a mental scan of her body.

She was naked and as far as she could tell he was too. He was spooning her, but besides his arm, he had a leg draped over hers. As if keeping her there. In place. Up against him. She could feel his manhood heavy against the crack of her ass. She couldn't help that her center pulsed, but she could have stopped herself from pushing back into him.

He chose that moment to wake up, or at least let her

know he was awake. She wasn't sure which it was. But his dick came to attention and his thumb flicked over her straining nipple. Madison bit down on her lip to stop the moan, and heat pooled in her center.

"Aw, don't be like that." He pinched her nipple. "Let me hear how I make you feel."

"I think you can already tell." Her voice came out breathy and not bored as she was hoping it would. She didn't want him to know how he affected her. But, she needn't have worried. He already knew.

"I don't want you to get a big head."

He pushed into her rear and nipped her shoulder. "You like my big head. Couldn't get enough of it last night."

Madison's face flushed. It was true and if she wasn't trying to keep herself in check, she would be begging for it right now. She figured this thing between them would have lessened by now. Or at least not feel like a desperate need that was clawing at her insides.

"How's my pussy this morning?" He didn't wait for her answer and his hand slipped down her stomach and in between her legs. Of course he found her wet. Dante dipped a finger inside her tunnel and her inner muscles sucked him in deeper.

"She's a greedy thing, isn't she?" he asked and then added another finger, and Madison was shameless as she rode his fingers.

She was sore. But that didn't stop her from wanting more. She was burning up inside with a need that seemed like it would never be satisfied. Maybe it was just an intense beginning phase of sleeping with someone. Like the honeymoon period in a relationship, and this need would die down and then disappear. This couldn't last forever.

Dante kissed up her neck and pulled his fingers out. He brought them up to her mouth.

"Lick it like a lollipop."

Madison flicked her tongue out and tasted herself on his fingers. It was a perfect mix of her sweetness and spice mixed with Dante's saltiness. He fed his fingers into her mouth, while at the same time he took his time and slid his cock into her wet core. She moaned around his fingers and he finger fucked her face while his penis pumped her from below.

Somehow his other hand found her nipple and he played her body, which caused all kinds of sounds to come out. He pulled his fingers out of her mouth and replaced it with his mouth and tongue. Being fucked so slow on her side was like heaven. He moved his top leg off of her and threw hers over his hip. It opened her up more.

He might have known her body, but she wasn't in the dark with regards to his. She could tell he was close and she pushed back into him and arched her back so her breast pushed into his hand.

"Madison." She liked the way he groaned her name. She wasn't the only one being affected.

"Dante, come with me."

And he did. He shot jets inside of her as he continued to pump inside her body. He triggered another orgasm in her, a soft but no less powerful one that wiped her out. She didn't think she could move after that.

Dante pulled out and picked her up off the bed and carried her into the bathroom. He cleaned her and himself off and then dried them off. She was still wrapped in a fluffy towel when he kissed her on the lips.

"I have to go." He wrapped his arms around her, pulled her close to him. "I'll see you tonight."

"See you tonight." She walked him out to the front door and watched him leave. It was later than she would wake up. She would have had breakfast by now and be ready to go visit Henry. She would get dressed and grab something on the way.

****

Dante left Madison's place. Why hadn't he been able to leave without kissing her goodbye? Lucky for him, she didn't live that far away from the club, so he wasn't going to be too late for the meeting with his cousins. He hadn't bothered to check his phone when he was with Madison and there was no point in checking it now. Whatever they had sent him, he would see when he got there.

Inside the office he found Enzo, Lucca, and Gabe. Lucca was a coffee snob so he had brought coffee from his favorite place for everyone. Dante grabbed a cup and sat down behind the desk.

"What was this important early morning meeting that you called and are late for?" Gabe asked, taking a sip from his drink.

"Yeah, where were you?" Enzo eyed him with suspicion from the wall. "Ed said you left early. That's not like you. I dropped by your place, and you weren't there."

"I had something to do."

"Something or someone?" Gabe gave him a knowing look.

Dante trusted Ed with his life, so he knew he didn't say anything. Gabe was fishing around. But, what worried him was Enzo. He didn't want anyone finding out that he was seeing Madison. No. He wasn't seeing her. They were just sleeping together. Nothing more than that and it was good to remind himself.

Dante leaned forward. "I got a call."

"Wait, you were out last night so you didn't hear Lucca's news." Gabe slapped Lucca on the back. "Tell Dante there will be a wedding."

"What wedding?" Dante looked between Gabe and Lucca and tried to avoid Enzo's eyes.

"I won a man's daughter in a bet. And Dad said she's to be my wife." Lucca sank into his chair.

"Isn't that some crazy shit?" Gabe let out a laugh and sat on the corner of the desk.

"What? Are you serious?" Dante stared at Lucca.

"Yeah, her pops bet the business and her. I had collected her, but when I bought her to the all hands meeting last night, Dad decided I needed a wife." Lucca rubbed the back of his neck.

"Is she on board?"

Lucca shook his head and pinched the bridge of his nose. "I don't think so. Her dad hadn't even told her yet. I'm supposed to pick her up and move her into my place to get to know each other for our engagement period."

"How long is that?"

"Three months and then we tie the knot." Lucca's hand moved to his temple.

"Is this what you want?" Dante leaned back and brought his hand to his chin.

"You know I can't refuse Dad." Lucca's hands came down on his thighs with a sense of finality.

"Right." Dante nodded. This was some serious shit.

"Anyway, besides my news, what's yours? I hope it's better than mine." Lucca stretched out his legs.

Dante would process what Lucca had said later. He hoped the Don didn't plan on matching them all up. He had missed an all-hands meeting. That wasn't good. A picture of Madison flashed in his mind. He wasn't ready to give her up.

"It's not. You know my contact in the FBI's financial unit gave me a tip that they are in the last three months of a sting operation against the Bianchis. They are planning to bring us down on money laundering."

"Shit. So what is the plan? I'm too young to go to jail." Gabe set his cup down. "But I'm serious, remember when Tata went in? The Mertuccis carved his face like a pumpkin. When he got out he couldn't see out of his left eye after that run in. You know they run that prison."

Dante ignored Gabe's too young to go to jail comment. But what he said was true. The Mertuccis were the Bianchis' rivals, and if they went in they would come out in a body bag.

"I'm not planning on going down for this. I don't know what you guys think." Dante took a sip from his own cup. He had to admit, Lucca's coffee place was good. He trusted his cousins, but not enough to tell them he was cleaning up his mob-tied business and that he had a job offer on the table.

"Nope," said Gabe.

Enzo and Lucca echoed his sentiment.

"So what are we going to do?" Lucca asked.

"Here is my plan." They all leaned forward as Dante explained to them what they could do to clean up the business' books and the best way to divide them up so that they each had what they wanted. "So the one thing we need to do is figure out who's helping on the inside, take care of them, and use our contacts to make our side look lily white."

Something flickered over Enzo's face at the mention of a rat, but it was could have been because he was in charge of security and the fact that someone had either gotten in or turned traitor under his watch.

"We need to find out who it is as soon as we can," Dante said. If they were still there, they could give up their new plan to the Feds.

"I'm going to have to tell Dad that someone's been turned," Lucca said.

"They had to have planned this for a while. They could have come in months ago with the new recruits," Gabe said.

The room got quiet with the heaviness of the situation and the possible outcomes.

Dante's voice broke through the thickness in the air. "I think everyone knows their roles. I have a meeting with Ed. I'll see you guys tonight?"

"Yeah, I'll be here." Gabe threw his drink in the trash.

"I'll let you know. Wifey situation and all." Lucca gave a small tilt of his head.

Dante looked at Enzo.

"Yeah. I have a few things to take care of, but I should be here sometime before the night is over."

Ed walked in as the guys left.

"What did you find out?"

"Looks like she has someone sick with cancer."

"Who?"

"My guy hasn't found out yet, but he will get back to me. He's chatting up a nurse on the inside. So far he has found out that she is a regular when he is in the hospital and they've seen them holding hands, but for the most part she sits by him while he sleeps. He's older than her, not like ancient, but not fresh out of college."

A stab pierced his chest. Had she lied to him and was seeing someone else? There was also the better blow job that she had given. Had she practiced on this guy after she slept with him?

The band around his chest tightened, and he struggled to take in a breath. She had cheated on or with him. He remembered Madison saying she didn't know it could be like that. Maybe the guy only took care of his needs when he was with Madison, so she had never climaxed during sex.

They weren't exclusive or even dating, but he would add that to what they were doing that they wouldn't see anyone else until they were finished with each other. He planned to keep her so busy she wouldn't have time to find someone else.

"But your sidepiece is smart and talented. Getting her Masters in Fashion Design and she is getting a chance for her work to be shown at fashion week for a chance to win a job at one of the top fashion houses."

Dante was disgusted at Ed's words and his stomach turned when he mentioned her as his sidepiece. It didn't make sense because all they were going to do was fuck. It was just some itch they were scratching. But she made thoughts he believed had died with Monica come back again. But it couldn't be. She didn't know what he was a part of. They weren't meant to be more.

He was jealous Lucca was getting married. Dante had wanted the wife and kids with the picket fence and dog too, but what did he have to offer? He was good with numbers. Numbers didn't lie, well, maybe they did, but he could spot it. He was more than just a numbers guy, but no one had taken the time to look past the mafia name.

Madison made him feel things that had died before, which was strange. They had only had sex twice, so none of what he was feeling made sense.

Besides, what did he have to offer Madison? Nothing right now when they would need to work hard to avoid jail. He shouldn't see her again so he could focus on the task at hand, but he wouldn't. If he had to stay up all the nights that he wasn't with her to be with her he would. She was like a drug for him. Which was dangerous. Because he couldn't let her go.

****

The next night, Dante was torn. He wanted Madison again, but he didn't want to seem too eager. There was also the fact that she might be seeing someone else between the week when they had first had sex and last night.

He was too old to play the game of don't see her until next week to make her think he could take it or leave it. He couldn't leave it. But he knew one way to clear things up. He would propose his own deal so no one needed to be waiting by the phone.

They would be exclusive so if she was seeing someone else, she would need to break it off and they would see each other Thursday through Sunday after the bar closed. They would have this arrangement for the time she was headliner. Or at least until he stopped craving her body. It would be four days a week until he got tired of her. It might take a couple of weeks, but he knew it wouldn't take three months let alone one.

They had exchanged numbers, so he shot her a quick text to come to his office after she got in. Then he tried to act as if was a normal day.

****

Madison entered the club and headed to the changing rooms to put her things in a locker. In the room were Amber and Brittney.

"Hey, how are you guys doing?"

They looked at each other and giggled.

"We're good." Brittney spoke for the both of them like normal. "We should be asking how you are. You should get checked." Then they turned and walked away.

Madison was confused. It wasn't like she was friends with any of the girls. She tried to be, but they all didn't get why she got out of club rules and it set her apart from the others. She was like an outsider looking in. Even though Madison and Sabrina were friends outside of the club, Sabrina didn't talk to her at the club.

She stored her bag and locked it up and then headed to Dante's office. She knocked on the door.

"Come in." His voice didn't sound inviting. Had he moved on already and wanted to tell her it was over before it had even started.

She pushed open the door and stepped inside. "You wanted to see me?"

He looked up from his desk. "Yeah, shut the door and lock it."

Madison's sex tingled. Was he going to fuck her again in his office? It would have to be quick, because she was needed downstairs. The image of a quickie made her squeeze her legs together. To go on stage with Dante's cum inside her sounded hot. Would he get turned on knowing he had fucked her and could fuck her whenever he wanted?

"Uh, sure." She locked the door and turned back

96

around.

"I had some concerns with regards to our arrangement."

"The headliner shows?" She walked over to the chair in front of the desk.

He shook his head. "No, our other deal."

"Oh ok." She sank down to the floor; lucky that there was the chair to catch her. Did he want to stop it already?

"I wanted to make sure that we were exclusive. I won't be sleeping with anyone else, and I expect you to not do the same." He leaned forward over the desk.

What? "Ok." Did he think she was sleeping with someone else when she had been a virgin only a week ago? She dry swallowed.

"Also I think we should have a schedule; we fuck Thursday to Sunday after you leave the club. For the three months that you headline for us. I mean we both feel this thing, and I think we just need to work it out of our systems. I could meet you at your place for the three months or less, to work it out."

Madison was taken aback by the word fuck. She knew that's what they were doing, but it didn't sound pretty. "What happens if one of us has it out of our system before the other?"

"Then we go our separate ways. No hard feelings, business as usual."

"Ok." This hadn't been what she had expected at all. It was like a present with dog poop inside. It looked good on the outside but was not so great when you had time to consider it.

He wanted to work out this "thing" as he called it between them. It wasn't like she believed they would turn what they had into a relationship, but it was weird to put a deadline on it. Was he only sleeping with her because she was the headliner and after her time was done he would move on to someone else? Maybe even Sabrina? That was if they hadn't had sex already.

"Ok, you can go."

And just like that he dismissed her. She unlocked the door and walked out feeling low.

Everywhere she went in the club that night the other women giggled and laughed at her and the patrons side eyed her. She got half in tips than she had the previous night.

Zoe hadn't said anything and now it was time to go to her place and wait for Dante. Zoe would have told her if there was a rumor that had to do with her wouldn't she?

"You want to walk out together or do you need to collect your money? I wanted to talk to you."

"Sure, I can get it later. What's up?"

"Let's get out of here first." Zoe looked around.

Madison went to the room to grab her stuff. All the girls were in there talking, but stopped when she came in. "See you guys tomorrow."

"Maybe," Gina said.

"Not if we have anything to say," Brittney said and sashayed past Madison and bumped into her and pushed her into the wall. The other girls followed, until it was just her and Sabrina who gave her a smug smile and walked out. Sabrina didn't bother to say anything. Madison was hurt. This seemed beyond them being upset that there were different rules for her and them. But she didn't understand where it was coming from. It was like everyone knew something Madison didn't. She wanted to hide away and cry.

Madison headed out to find Zoe. "So, what's up?" Her voice was shaky, and she kept bringing up what had happened in her mind.

"There's been a rumor going around for a couple of days now that you've been playing innocent, but you haven't just been on the stage but are sleeping around with others and with Dante and that you have an infection. The rumor and the infection have spread to the customers. That's why there were not a lot tonight and only a few went to you."

"Oh." Fear and panic clawed at her throat. Each fought to get out.

"Yeah, the thing is some of the girls got tested and they have crabs and so do some of the clients. Enzo came around while you were on stage and said everyone needed to get tested and that they would have someone come."

"Oh." This was bad. If it affected the business and that meant she wouldn't be making the money she needed and if she wasn't bringing in money, would Dante let her keep the headliner position for the three months she needed to get her finances back on track?

"I know it's not true. But I did want to tell you what's going on, before you hear it another way."

"Thanks. I appreciate it."

"I can give you a ride."

"That's ok. I guess I need to be alone to process this." Madison was going to head to the bus stop when one of the bouncers, Ed, called her name.

He walked over to her. "Boss wants to see you in the office." His tone was gruff, but it always sounded like that. His face was as blank as a mannequin. Madison followed him into the building and up to Dante's office.

As they reached the top of the steps, Gina, Amber and Brittney were leaving.

"I hope he fires her," Gina said.

"I know, giving everyone crabs." Brittney glared at her as the girls walked past.

"Go on in," Ed said.

Madison's head was on the chopping block. She hadn't done anything wrong, and now she was going to lose her only source of income. As headliner, she had made way more than she had expected.

It was a consistent thousand dollars extra which made her wonder if she was getting special treatment and it wasn't because she was the headliner. The girls worked at other clubs so the rumor would spread and no one would want her to work for them.

Inside the office was a man in a white coat sat on the couch. Dante stood in the corner, hidden in the shadows so she couldn't make out his face.

"Madison, we're doing mandatory STD testing on everyone. It seems someone had something and passed it around. Dr. Emory here will take your blood and give you an exam."

Madison's eyes widened. She had never been seen by a male doctor. She made sure all her doctors were female and even then getting her yearly pap exam was an embarrassing experience.

"Can't I have my own doctor do it?"

"I would prefer it to be done now." His tone said he wouldn't take no for an answer. Did he believe she had something? Did he have something and pass it on to her? She looked at where she guessed his face was, her voice pleaded. "I've never been seen by a man before."

"No problem," spoke Dr. Emory, "I have a female assistant who is just finishing up."

A back door opened, and out came Sabrina with a female nurse.

"She'll be clean because she's had it treated."

"We'll be able to tell."

Sabrina's smug smile slipped, and it looked like she was going to be sick. She hurried out of the room.

"Miss, if you'll come with me," the female nurse said.

Madison chanced a look at Dante, he had moved out of the shadows, but his face wasn't unreadable. It was pissed. She turned and went with the woman.

"Sorry, I know this can be uncomfortable. If you can just undress and put this paper top on and you can use the blanket to go over your legs. I'll be right back." The door made a soft click in the room.

Madison was glad to be alone, but she didn't know for how long and was quick to undress and put on the paper top and lap cover. There was a portable exam table set up and she sat down on it and waited.

The woman came back a short time after Madison had sat down.

"This shouldn't take long. I'll do your pelvic exam first and then the blood work. Slide down to the end of the table."

Madison did as she said and gripped the blanket for dear life.

"It's ok. I promise I'll be gentle. Slide all the way down to the end."

Madison did as she was told.

"Relax and let your knees flop open."

Madison tried, but she knew she was stiff. She

couldn't relax. She had a routine with her doctor, where she would tell her what she was doing before she did it. It helped Madison to relax a bit.

"It's ok, I promise not to hurt you."

"I know, it's just hard for me. My regular doctor talks me through it each time."

"That's easy enough for me to do."

The rest went as expected, except for the part where the nurse combed her pubic hair.

"Ok, you're all set. You can get dressed and come out when you're ready."

Madison came out to find the room empty except for Dante. She went to walk past the desk when he stopped her.

"Madison."

"Yes."

"I'm sorry, but with the rumors, this was the only way to clear it up. It's affected the club as well with patrons coming to us with their medical bills requesting reimbursement. I can't have rumors that il Signore's headliner has crabs and has spread it to everyone."

"Right." This was the part where she got fired for something she hadn't even done.

"I'm going to clear your name and find the real culprit, who will be dealt with for the rumor and the crab infestation."

"So, I'm not fired?"

"No."

Madison sank into the chair like she had been cut out of a too-tight outfit. She could breathe again. But what did that mean for whatever was happening between them.

"I won't be able to come over tonight. I have some

things I need to take care of, but I'll see you tomorrow night. Come over here please."

Madison walked over to him and he pulled her into his lap for a kiss that soothed her nerves and washed over her like a soft cashmere robe.

He broke the kiss. "Our deal still stands. We don't fuck anyone else, and we meet Thursday through Sunday." He placed a soft kiss on her lips. "Ok."

"Ok." Madison assumed it was good that he still wanted to continue their quasi relationship, but why had he stressed exclusivity again. Did he still think she was sleeping around?

Madison walked out feeling confused. Dante called Ed into the office and then the door was shut and she was left alone. She took the bus to see Henry. He was at his own place. He had been released from the hospital.

****

Dante waited to speak until Ed had sat down in front of his desk. "Have her tailed. I want to know where she goes and who she sees."

"You got it, boss."

"Have you found out anything more as far as the guy she'd been seeing?"

"No, not yet, but we're still working on it. The financials have come back. I can leave them here for you to review."

There was a knock at the door. "Come in."

Gabe, Lucca, and Enzo stood in the doorway.

"Ed, I think we're done here." Ed set the folder on the desk and got up and left.

"So did you clear it up?" Lucca asked.

"Yeah. It's done. The test results will confirm it."

"Who was it?" Gabe asked.

"Sabrina. She got crabs and spread it to others before she found out, and she decided to make up the rumor that had to do with Madison."

"So she's not seeing some other guy?" Enzo moved off the wall.

"Who?"

"Madison."

"No." Well, at least she wouldn't be now with their deal, but he would make sure someone kept tabs on her.

"So where are we with covering our tracks?" Gabe leaned forward.

Dante was ready to get down to business too. This was what kept him away from Madison tonight. He knew they would finish late. Too late for him to go to her.

Chapter 7

Madison kept waiting for something to go wrong. It had been three weeks since the mandatory testing and things had picked back up.

Madison and Dante had fallen into a routine. She would come up to his office after the night was out and collect her money and then she would leave and go home and wait for Dante to show up. They would have amazing sex that just kept getting better. Sometimes she would cook breakfast for them before he had to leave for the day. Sometimes he would get up early and surprise her by having breakfast prepared and brought in. It was a nice routine.

Maybe too nice. She kept waiting for them to get caught. Dante only ever came to her place as that was what was part of their deal.

One thing that didn't feel nice was her friendship with Sabrina. They hadn't spoken to each other since the night of testing. Sabrina hadn't even bothered to apologize for what she had done. The old Madison, the Madison before Dante, would have tried to reach out to her to see what made her do it and try to rekindle the friendship, but she wasn't going to say anything until Sabrina said she was sorry.

The one thing the rumor helped was that Sabrina had said Madison pretended to be a virgin. Since the other things she said had been false. People assumed Madison was still a virgin, and it drew more clients to see the virgin headliner.

She didn't want anyone to know that she and Dante had slept together, as the tips had been outrageous ever since. But her and Sabrina's time apart had let her observe that maybe their friendship was dying and couldn't make the test of time. Sabrina had been put on probation for the crab infestation and starting the rumor, which she believed factored into why Sabrina hadn't talked to Madison.

****

Madison walked into the club and set her bag down in the back. She didn't feel like doing anything tonight. Her period was here, and she would have to have the conversation with Dante that they wouldn't have sex this week. Her period lasted five days, maybe six. But that would put them into the next week.

They didn't get together outside of Thursday through Sunday. That was the deal, and they stuck to the plan. Who cared if early in the week she wanted to share something with him. She held herself back. She didn't even know why she wanted to share personal things with him. That wasn't the nature of their relationship. She just had to remind herself of the fact.

She might as well go and tell him now before she got to work so he could make other arrangements for the night. Madison didn't know why thinking of him with someone else made her stomach dip. Though they had said that they were exclusive, he had a healthy appetite, she couldn't expect him to not do anything while she was out of commission.

She knocked on the door.

"Come in."

"Hey." She shut the door behind her and flipped the lock. The only thing worse than being caught fooling around with your boss was getting caught telling him you were on your period. That was a definite not need-to-know, and you couldn't pretend you passed out and he was just giving you mouth to mouth.

She didn't know how to say it. He had turned his chair as expected her to come and sit in his lap like it was custom for her to do. They hadn't hooked up in his office since the first time. They kissed and did some heavy petting, but nothing besides that.

She walked over to him and sat down in his lap with her back to his chest. She didn't want to have to look at him face to face and explain she was having her menstrual cycle.

Dante pinched her chin in a gentle hold. "What's up?" He peered at her face from the side.

With the things they had done together, she shouldn't be nervous to tell him, but she didn't know how he would take it. Would he push her out of the lap? She didn't think he would still come to hang out since their deal was more sex only, but she didn't want him to treat her like a leper. She had no idea how a grown man would take it. She bet it was more embarrassing for her than for him.

"I just wanted to tell you, you don't need to come by this week. I'm on my period. So no Dante Jrs." She tried to be funny and lighten the mood, but a look flickered across Dante's face so fast that if she didn't know better she would have seen it as disappointment.

It was disappointment she reminded herself. Disappointment that they couldn't have sex. Not disappointment because she wasn't pregnant. That was silly. And she definitely didn't feel her own twinge of sadness at not being pregnant with Dante's baby. That was even crazier.

"So?" He wrapped his arms around her waist. "What's up?"

"Oh nothing. I'm just saying I only want to be home, and rest and catch some shows, eat in, relax. You know, just chill."

"Sounds good. I bet you need some rest too." He kept her chin between his fingers and leaned his head down to bring their lips together. Dante applied gentle pressure with his lips until she responded to his kiss, but then he deepened the kiss and she found her body responded to him.

He ran his hand from her chin, around her neck and down her back to her hips and held them on his erection, before he moved them up to cup her breasts that were now heavy with need. Dante played with her nipples and her hips rolled on his cloth covered cock. He kissed down her neck and across her collarbone, all the while, his hands never stopped playing with her nipples.

"Dante." She moaned. She wasn't sure if she was telling him to stop or to keep going. Lucky for her, Dante knew what she wanted even if she didn't. He didn't stop, but moved his mouth back to hers and he thrust upward. His hands dipped under her shirt and freed breasts. He pushed her boobs together and used his thumbs to work her nipples like joysticks. Joysticks that were giving her pleasure.

She turned in his arms and he knew right away what she wanted and his mouth let go of hers and dropped to the tips of her breasts and he sucked on them and teased them with his tongue. Her hips moved faster and there was no doubt. They were dry humping each other. She ran her fingers through his hair and grabbed on tight as she held his head in place and moved her hips for all she was worth.

Madison had of course never had sex during her period. Sometimes if she had bad cramps, she would use her shower head to give herself an orgasm and that could lessen the cramps. Who knew cramps from pleasure canceled out cramps from pain. Maybe Dante knew that too.

His cock hit the seam of her jeans at the right angle and she came, her hips jerked in his lap and she would have screamed his name out loud for everyone to hear if he hadn't covered her mouth in a kiss.

She came down to him rubbing her back. He put her boobs back in her bra and fixed her shirt, then gave her another kiss. This one softer, tender, close to loving.

"You better go down before they come looking for you."

"Right. But you didn't."

"That's ok." He gave her a double pat on the butt and then lifted her off his lap and set her down on the floor. "See you downstairs." He lifted his hand to her face and pushed the loose strands behind her ear and down to her chin.

"You better go before I can't control myself."

Madison took the hint and unlocked the door and left. In the hallway, she ran into Enzo.

"What were you doing in there?"

Madison was taken aback by the hostility in his tone. He had never been rude to her before. She had suspected that he might have liked her, and that's why he didn't make her follow club rules, but he never said anything one way or the other until now.

"Nothing." She looked back over her shoulder. She had left Dante's door open. She turned back around.

"You were in there for a long time with the door locked. I tried it. I guess you guys didn't hear while you were doing nothing." He spit the last word out.

Madison didn't think she owed him an explanation. She and Dante hadn't said anything outright, but she didn't think they were telling people what their side deal was. Maybe she should have specified that. Well, it was too late now. Somehow Enzo had found out. She hoped he didn't tell anyone else. She didn't want rumors to spread again.

Madison just stood there. Enzo approached her and backed her into the wall. "You know…Nope. Never mind." And he walked away.

Madison didn't want to get between the cousins, so she didn't bother to let Dante know that Enzo knew. Enzo would get over it.

****

Dante got up to shut the door Madison had left open. He had several phone calls he needed to make, that he didn't want overheard. But he stopped at Enzo's voice. He stayed behind the door to listen in. He'd have to speak to Enzo. He didn't like his tone, and he definitely didn't like what came next.

It wasn't any of Enzo's business what Madison and he were doing in there. He would have stayed where he was if he hadn't seen Enzo back her into the wall. Dante came around the door so Enzo could see him, but Madison couldn't.

That stopped Enzo in his tracks.

Dante sat back down at his desk. He didn't know

what to expect when Madison came in to talk to him. He worried she was going to tell him she had him out of her system. He was so relieved when he found out it was only her period. That wasn't a big deal.

He knew he should have left her alone, But he couldn't. They had a routine when she would come up to the office to get her money. Some days he was better at keeping his hands to himself than others, and today wasn't one of those days.

But she had seemed so down, he had wanted to do something to cheer her up and he didn't have a lot of time to do it in, so he went with what he knew would work. But after that exchange he'd have to talk Enzo later.

He didn't know what he was going to tell Madison before he noticed him in the doorway. But he wouldn't let Enzo ruin what he had going on with her. It wasn't like it would last forever. But he didn't want it over before he was ready.

Dante did his usual nightly routine at the club. Well, the new one that he had since Madison and him had struck their deal. He didn't miss any of her sets. He would get a drink from her before he went up for the night.

Once Ed told him what her mom had done and the financial pressure she was under while she tried to prepare her design for fashion week he had added a grand extra to her cut. He didn't know if she would take it from him, even as a loan, so he gave her a gift every night she worked.

The only problem was he wanted more from Madison. But her mentions of not wanting to be on the wrong side of the law gave him pause. Would she care if he was getting clean or think once dirty, always dirty?

His stomach churned that he might not have her for long.

Dante was still at his desk when Enzo came back in.

"Is there a problem?" Dante stood up.

Enzo moved into Dante's personal space. "You were going to leave Madison alone."

"Why?" Dante moved forward.

"That's what we agreed." Enzo jabbed Dante in the chest with his finger.

Dante didn't bother to smack his hand away but just pushed forward into Enzo's face. "No, that's what you suggested. I didn't agree to anything. I said it's between Madison and me."

"What is going on between the two of you?" Enzo raised his voice.

Dante kept his voice even, but his tone hardened. "I don't know why it matters to you. I still don't think it's any of your business."

"What business?" Lucca came into the room.

"Whoa. What's going on here?" Gabe looked between Dante and Enzo.

Dante was still in Enzo's face. He wasn't above a fight, but he didn't need to fight over Madison, because she had made her choice and she was his and nothing would stop him from seeing her.

"Nothing. I'm just finishing up and then I'm going down."

"You going to her again? You have to be there for all her sets?"

"Who?" Both Lucca and Gabe spoke.

"Madison. I caught them in here together with the door locked."

"Then how did you get in?" Lucca looked around. "Where is Madison?"

"And if you knew they were in here together, why did you try and get in?" Gabe stepped in between Dante and Enzo, moving Enzo back.

"I just tried the door. It was locked. I waited until she came out. That's how I know they were in there with the door locked." Enzo stepped around Gabe.

Dante moved back and sat down. He needed to finish up the cash slips, and Ed would drop them off at the bank so that he could get to Madison sooner. If he didn't know that he was Madison's first in every way, he would have believed something had happened between her and Enzo.

Even the thought of the two of them together made him want to claim Madison again so that everyone knew she was his. She. Was. His.

Lucca held up his hands. "What's the deal, Enzo? What Dante and Madison do is between them."

"She was mine, and he took her. Why do you think she didn't have to follow club rules so no one would touch her?"

"Did you ask her if she wanted to be yours?" asked Lucca

Enzo turned toward Lucca. "That's rich coming from you, Lucca. Does Ainsley want to be yours?"

"Ainsley and I are different, and we are getting to know each other."

"Dante didn't even know Madison, and the first day he comes in she drops her panties like a whore." Spit came out of Enzo's mouth.

Dante was up before anyone could blink and had slung Enzo up against the wall, with his forearm on Enzo's throat. "For him. When I was here giving her space."

"Don't. You. Ever. Ever. Speak those words and Madison's name together."

"Let's all calm down and take a step back." Lucca and Gabe pulled Dante off of Enzo, who dropped to his knees before he stumbled to his feet.

"What's going on?" Lucca asked again.

"Nothing," Dante repeated. "I need to go."

"Oh, I was hoping we could all do something together." Gabe looked around.

"Sorry, G. I've got plans." Dante stopped by Enzo who still gasped for air. He wanted to say something and paused, but he had made himself clear. And he strode out.

He trusted Enzo not to say anything else. Even if Enzo was pissed. It was family first. Yeah, but Dante hadn't cared when he found out Enzo wanted Madison. He wouldn't give her up for anything. But that shit with Enzo had made him miss her sets. He headed back to the office to wait for her so he could pay her before she left.

His chest tightened at Madison moving on and dating Enzo instead of him.

****

Madison had looked around for Dante during her sets, but he didn't show up, and he didn't come to get a drink either. He didn't need to come down and see her, she bet he was making other plans for the night and the rest of the week.

She still had to go up and get her money from her sets. That was going to be awkward. She trudged up the back steps to get to his office. Dante sat at his desk with his head in his hands.

"Dante?" His head popped up. "Is something wrong?"

"No. It's nothing. Remembered some deals I made."

Madison's heart dropped. The deal where they were supposed to be exclusive, was he going to cancel their deal? He had a healthy appetite, and she doubted he could go eight days before they would be able to have sex again.

He sat up straight and cracked his neck. "Here's your money."

Madison reached to get it, but he wasn't even looking at her. She figured this would happen. She didn't know why she acted like she hadn't expected this coldness towards her.

"Great, thanks." She turned. She didn't even bother to say bye. He wasn't listening to her anyway. She left and closed the door behind her.

****

Madison was sitting at her table as she sketched some designs when there was a knock on her door. She had ordered take out, but that was fast. Maybe she had sketched longer than she thought. She had thrown on lounge pants and an oversized t-shirt that hung off one shoulder when she came home.

She didn't want to see anything tight until late tomorrow night. She opened the door and expected to see the delivery guy. She was friendly with Brian, and he would bring it in while she got his tip because she always forgot to have her cash ready.

"Brian, that was fast—Dante? What are you doing here?" Madison was startled to see him at her place.

"I came to spend time with you. I brought you this card."

"Oh, thanks." She took the card from him. She would open it later.

"Who is Brian?"

"The delivery guy. I go to this place a lot so we've become friendly."

"Oh. Ok. That makes sense." He walked around her apartment. She had nothing out when he came over, so today he would get to see some of her designs and sketches and what her place looked like on a typical day when he wasn't coming over.

How would he see it? To her it was homey. She had a bunch of sewing things out. There were dress sketches tacked up to the walls. What would he think? From what she knew, which wasn't a lot, would he think they looked like good designs? There was a negligee she had drawn out, that looked like it was just made of see-through lace and maybe some ribbon. Would he want to see that on her?

"Come on in. Let me clean up. I didn't expect you."

"Why not?"

"I told you, in your office."

"Yeah, well, I believed it would be a good time for us to talk. There are a few things about our agreement that I wanted to straighten out."

"Oh. Like what?" She put things in a tote bag and put it in a corner of the room.

He tugged her hand until she sat down in his lap on the sofa. "I wanted to ask where you were on spitting or swallowing or even allowing any of my cum in your mouth."

"Oh. I guess I don't know." She bit her bottom lip. "I do want to taste you."

Dante got hard at her words. "I think you liked the light spanking and hair pulling. I would never do more than that."

She wiggled on his lap. "Yeah. I did like that. I didn't think I would."

"What else do or did you like?"

"I liked the dirty talking." She turned around in his lap so her knees were outside his thighs.

He palmed her bottom and then moved his hand to cup her mound. Could he feel the heat coming through her thin pants?

"You like when I fuck my pussy?"

"Aghh, Dante. Yes. I like everything you do to your pussy."

"Take your top off."

She whipped it over her head leaving a lace covering for her boobs. It wasn't a bra. There was no clasp. She liked to wear bralettes when she was at home. He pulled the scrap of fabric down below her breasts and worshiped at her nipples. He was kneading her boobs when there was a knock at the door.

"Oh. That's Brian."

"Don't worry. I'll get it for you."

"He's never seen anyone but me. I've got it." She covered her breasts and threw the shirt back on. And opened the door.

"Hey, I have your tip ready this time. How is your girlfriend and baby doing?"

"Good, thank you so much for the things you had sent over. Susie and the baby liked it."

"No worries. Here you go. Have a nice night."

"Thanks, you too."

She closed the door and turned around to find Dante stood behind the counter. He would have been visible. If she didn't know better she would think he was jealous and wanted to make sure everyone knew she was taken.

And that made Madison feel good. That he wanted her enough to make sure other guys knew to keep their hands off.

"What did you order?"

"My usual. I'm not adventurous with my food sometimes."

"What's your usual?"

"Chicken lo mein. I have extra, if you're hungry. I was planning on just staying in this weekend. Besides my time at the club."

"Do you drink wine?"

"I only know the names of drinks because Zoe has told me. I'm not a big drinker and if I do drink, I don't want to taste the alcohol, so I do a mixed drink or a Moscato."

"Good to know. I would like to get you something one of these nights, maybe we eat in. Have picnic in your living room."

"Oh, that would be nice. Come, I'll make you a plate. You must be hungry."

They sat down at her table and talked into the night. She shared with him that she made the final round in her master's final and showed him some of the designs she was working on for the club. She told him she hadn't picked a final design yet, but when she did she would show it to him.

He told her of his time in college and some of the things he, Enzo, Lucca, and Gabe used to get up to.

Could she trust him enough to tell him that Enzo had confronted her outside the office.

"I forgot to ask, but no one knows our deal right?"

"No. Why?"

"Because Enzo was outside your office when I left

after our…talk."

"What did he say?"

"Nothing, just asked me what we had been doing with the door locked and I said nothing. He made some remark that he tried to get in, but that we didn't hear him while we were doing nothing."

"Yeah, he knows. Only my cousins. They found out when they came up to the office after you had left."

"How?" She knew the color had drained from her face.

"They came in after you left and I was cleaning up. Gabe smelled the sex in the air," he rushed to say as if he wanted to reassure her.

Madison was confused, and it must have shown on her face.

"There is a distinct smell when people have sex that comes from the body fluids."

Now her face heated, and she was sure it darkened in color. Could he tell she was blushing?

"But it will go no further. It was only by chance they found out, and I trust them to not tell." Concern flashed across his face.

"What's the matter? You look upset."

"Oh, nothing. It's some business stuff I have to do."

"I wanted to ask you, aren't you guys young to own il Signore?

"It's a family business."

"Your mom is ok with the club rules?"

Dante choked on a piece of chicken.

Madison got up to pat him on the back. "Are you ok?"

"Yeah, it just went down the wrong pipe. I think." He patted his chest with his fist. "I know you mentioned things concerning the law. Have you had a run in with some criminals?'

"No. I've never met someone who doesn't follow the law, at least not that I know of. I would never associate with someone like that. Why?" Was he going to tell her he was in the mob?

"I was just curious I guess."

She couldn't interpret the look that crossed his face. Maybe he wasn't in the mob, but they paid protection money to them and that's why it was said to be owned by the mob. She had read things like this in books. She hadn't slept with a mobster. Only someone who paid them to keep his business running.

"What things do you like to do?"

****

Dante should have been grateful for the change in topics. But the acid in his stomach roiled for two reasons. There was no way he could have a future with Madison, unless he got out of the business before she found out.

Dante shouldn't have been surprised that Madison wanted to know what he did. She was like every other woman. Interested in the man's job and not in the man. "I have several business and investment properties. I also invest for myself and others."

"Oh, that's nice. But I meant what you like to do besides work. Like for fun?"

He couldn't believe it. He had misjudged her. She wanted to get to know him. The man behind the numbers. Most of the time when they got together any conversation they had was fast and turned into sex. He couldn't keep his hands off of her, and she was so responsive to his touch. With her on her period, things had slowed down and they were able to get to know each other outside the bedroom.

"And don't tell me work. I want to know besides work. Even if you're not doing it, what else do you like doing?"

"You know that's a tricky question. No one's ever asked me that since I was a kid. I've always been known as the numbers guy and nothing else."

"But there is more to you than that." She stated it like fact.

"True. I like basketball, to watch and to play. I would play pickup games with my cousins, but we haven't done that in a while."

"My brother was a pro basketball player, so I understand the rules and such."

Was that the guy she was seeing? Her brother? Dante was impressed and relieved. Maybe they could see a game together. He had season tickets he hadn't been using.

"What else? Who else is Dante?"

"I like to fix things and work with my hands. I'm pretty handy around the house and renovated my place on my own." He would have to bring her to his place. He didn't know where that had come from. He had never brought a girl to his place. Monica had been to his old place, but his renovated place was for him only.

He hadn't planned to share it with someone, but he wanted to share it with Madison and see what she thought of the things he had done.

"Wow. That is pretty cool. I know enough renovation stuff to get by. I'd love to see it."

"And I'd love to show it to you." And he did, it wasn't a lie.

"What else makes Dante tick?"

"I'm a movie man. I like to watch the Oscar picks ahead of the Oscars."

"That's interesting. I'm not a movie girl."

"Maybe you haven't found the right movies yet."

She shrugged her shoulders. "Maybe you're right."

"I like to read history and autobiographies of people."

"What's your favorite time period?"

"I love it all, but I guess I gravitate to the Renaissance period. I'm also a pretty decent cook and enjoy food. I guess you could call me a foodie."

"Oh my gosh. Me too. When I have time, I love going to the farmer's market to get fresh ingredients and try my hand at something new. My goal after fashion week is over is to take a cookbook and cook everything in it and document it on a blog or something."

"That sounds interesting. I would join you."

Madison elbowed him. "Sounds like a plan. Anything else I should know?"

"I like a neat space, tailored clothes, and even though I'm a businessman, I still feel like I'm playing dress up when I wear a suit."

"You look good in a suit." Her phone dinged. "Oh wow, it's late. That's my birth control alarm. Be right back."

Madison got up and padded to her bedroom. Dante helped clean up the table while she was away. He stored the leftover food and put the dishes in the sink. He had the water on when she came back out.

"Oh you don't have to do that."

"I don't mind." He wanted to stay over. It had been a great time, and the truth was he enjoyed Madison's company. He also loved waking up to her. The days they were apart, he missed her. And that was dangerous. He should go.

"Do you want to stay? I know it's late. Not sure if you had other plans."

"I'd love to stay. Nothing else I'd want to be doing." He dried his hands and reached for hers. They walked hand in hand to the bedroom and it was right. She went into the bathroom to change clothes, she slept in a scrap of lace and fabric masquerading as a night dress when they were together. He got undressed and left his boxer briefs on.

When he stayed the night, he slept naked. Hell, he pulled them off and got into bed. Madison wouldn't mind. He just wanted to be close to her. As close as he could be. She came out in her signature lingerie, this one emerald green. It highlighted the brown in her eyes.

"Ready for bed?" She looked at him already under the covers. He had been at home in her place in the short few weeks they had been together.

"Waiting for you." What would she do when she saw he was nude like usual? He would cover up if she wanted. He never wanted to make her uncomfortable.

She climbed in, glanced down and then laid down in the bed with her back to him. She moved back until her hips were in the cradle of his thighs and he laid his arm over her. This was the normal way they slept together. He pushed his leg between hers, for the final movement that made up their sleep routine. It kept them interlocked together.

"Good night, Dante."

"Good night, Madison." He kissed her shoulder and closed his eyes, comforted by their routine. They had moved past just sex and into a friend relationship. It had been nice sharing together and learning more of what made Madison tick and even himself. It had been a good night, and he couldn't wait to see what else was in store for them. He fell asleep thinking that he wanted this to be a real relationship, and that was dangerous. He didn't do relationships.

Chapter 8

Madison awoke to being blanketed by Dante. It was a nice warm feeling and something she missed during the week when they were apart. She found herself wishing he could sleep over every night, but she wouldn't be able to handle sex every day and multiple times a day, because she knew they wouldn't stop at just once.

They never did, and it seemed like they wanted each other more than they had the first time. It had to be lust, but after last night, she wasn't so sure. Dante had come over even though they couldn't have sex and had brought her a card, which had been sweet of him. They had fooled around and talked over dinner.

Then they went to bed, and he just held her. His hardness had pressed against her, but he didn't ask her for any help with it. He was content to just lay there with her and that made her heart do funny things, to feel funny things, and to think funny things.

Like maybe this was a real relationship, and maybe they could make it work. That they didn't just have an agreement, and he wouldn't grow tired of her. That this wouldn't be over because all they shared were bodily fluids. This was the first real relationship she'd ever had, and it was fake. In another two months or less, it would be done. She had fallen in love with the first person to treat her like a decent human being.

And she couldn't help remembering the connection

they shared when they talked. It seemed like a real friendship and like the getting-to-know-you stage. She was surprised that they had things in common. And her heart had jumped when they talked of catching a game and cooking together.

But that had to be just something he said in the moment. Just like him saying he wanted to show her his place. She would have loved to see what he did with the place and how he decorated it. It would give her more insight into the man Dante was and what he liked and didn't like.

She didn't know why it mattered. It wouldn't happen. But it had given her an idea. This four-day-a-week thing didn't work. She would propose that they meet every day for a month to get each other out of their systems. That way they could get past this honeymoon phase.

The anticipation for Thursday to come around kept them in this lacking stage that made them desire each other even more. But if they had access to each other every day, then they were sure to get their fill and work each other out. Because she couldn't be in love with him. It had to be just puppy love.

Now to get Dante to agree. It might be too much for him and feel like a full-blown relationship, and then he would get tired of her sooner. But it would still give her more days with him before this thing between them was over.

"I can feel you plotting something." Dante's voice was rough with sleep and sent shivers down her spine.

"I'm not plotting per se. Just thinking."

"Oh yeah. Of?"

She rolled over in his arms, and his hand dropped to

her rear. He was propped up in bed on the other arm. "Well, I wanted to talk to you."

"Oh, this sounds serious." Something like fear flickered across his face before it disappeared. She had to have imagined it. Because why would Dante be afraid of her need to have a talk with him? Unless he believed she was going to try and make their relationship more serious, which she was kind of, but within the limits of their original deal. He had made some amendments like the exclusivity clause, so she decided that she should be able to at least propose an addendum.

"It's not serious. Just kind of a change to our agreement, I guess. I want to suggest a change to it I guess."

"What kind of change? You want to end it?"

"No. Never. Not that." She sounded desperate to her own ears, and she cringed inside.

This time what she was sure passed as relief washed over his face. It made her feel good that he still wanted to be with her and wasn't ready for the relationship to end yet.

"Then what?"

She looked down at his chest. A sudden feeling of insecurity overcame her, and she was afraid to look him in the eyes and see what they might show.

"Look at me, Madison. Don't get all shy on me now. Where is my Madison who tells it like it is?"

Her heart fluttered at the words "my Madison." But there wasn't time to dwell so she just pushed through.

"I still haven't gotten you out of my system yet, and we only have two months of our deal left, so I was thinking for this upcoming month we see each other every day. That way, we don't have this anticipation build up that keeps us craving each other."

"You crave me?" he said with a huge grin

"Yes. I can't get enough of you." And that should be a warning to end this. Because deep down, she knew she wouldn't be the one to end it. Deep down, she knew she wanted it to go on forever. He couldn't feel the same way, but as long as he did she was willing to do so until he got bored.

His hand caressed her face, and she looked back into his eyes.

"I crave you too. And I think you're right. Us not seeing each other every day drives up the lust."

Lust. Not love. Not friendship. But lust. It hurt even though she knew it to be true. And she didn't love him either. How could she? It wasn't a real relationship. It was like she had made a friend. A friend that she slept with, friends with benefits was the natural next progression.

The final progression. Because even with her inexperience, she knew you couldn't turn a FWB situation into a real relationship. It was for the faint one percent. Maybe even less than one percent. And she didn't want a relationship anyway, especially one that led to marriage. She had no idea what a healthy relationship looked like between a man and woman. Or, if it was even possible. How was it any different from what they were doing now? This thing they had going worked for her. She would stay in it as long as he wanted to.

But maybe they could remain friends. She had enjoyed what she learned about him last night. So much so, that she wanted to learn more. Learn more of what made him tick.

"So what do you think?" She looked into his eyes, and they darkened like storm clouds.

"I think it's a great idea." His lips came down on hers, and she kissed him back for all she was worth. She poured all her feelings into it. To let him know her feelings, since she couldn't say it. Couldn't even name it. But with this kiss she could represent it with her passion.

Dante rolled her over onto her back and freed her nipples from the nightie. He supported his weight on one elbow. He used his other hand to toy with her nipple. She arched up into him. His length pressed into her. The way he was positioned the thick stalk of it was settled over her clit, and she humped up. Already in search of the release only Dante could provide.

He ground back at her and released her mouth to find her other nipple to suckle it. His hands on her nipples always got her wet. Too bad she was on her period. Because she wanted him inside her in that moment. He humped her back and then rolled them over so she was on top.

She leaned forward to give him access back to her boobs as she rolled her hips on him for all she was worth. An orgasm on her period was explosive for her, and she couldn't wait for Dante to give it to her.

"Oh Dante. Yes."

Her hips moved faster and faster as her toes and head tingled and worked their way to the middle. Her movements became jerky as she rushed faster to a release she didn't know she needed until now.

Dante's hands moved to her waist and then hips. He grabbed hold and helped her move faster while he thrusted upwards.

"Oh Dante. Oh." It poured over her and drenched her like a monsoon rain. Her nails dug into his shoulders as she held on for dear life. Her whole body was on fire and cold at the same time. This orgasm was it all rolled into one.

She came down to their foreheads connected, and his hands were gentle and he kneaded her breasts and moved his thumbs over her nipples with a light flicking motion. As she came back to, she realized he hadn't come again.

Madison slid down his body, happy there were no clothes left to take off of him. She reached for his manhood and pulled it up towards her mouth. She swirled her tongue around the cockhead and then flicked her tongue over it. It caused a deep groan from Dante.

She fed his cock into her mouth and bobbed up and down, using her hands for the part she couldn't squeeze in. She pulled her mouth off with a plop and looked into Dante's eyes which were focused on her. And she remembered why he had looked deadly when she had first met him. He was like a predator with his prey.

"I'm going to lick and suck you until you come, and I want it all in my mouth." With that, she went back to work, but she kept her eyes focused on him. He threaded his hands through her hair and helped guide her up and down his cock.

"Madison, baby, that feels so good. Your mouth is so hot and wet. I don't think I'm going to last long."

She lifted her head up and took a broad lick of his shaft. "Don't worry. That's what I want." She circled her tongue around the tip before she sucked in as much as she could. Dante did a slow pump of his hips but increased his pace. She tried to keep up, but even with his hand guiding her she couldn't.

Moisture pooled between her legs. Seeing Dante close to release and looking in his eyes while it happened had her ready to climax again. If not for her period she would have her fingers buried inside her at that moment.

Dante added another hand to her head, but this time instead of using it to push her head down, he held it in place while he fucked her face. She could see the strain on his face and knew it was only by his willpower that he didn't thrust as deep as he wanted to so as not to gag her, and she appreciated it.

"Madison."

His body tensed, and his shaft pulsed as it shot jet after jet of cum into her mouth. She pushed her head down, taking him in deeper and relaxing her throat until her nose was buried in his pubes.

"Oh."

If she didn't know better, she would believe that that had made him come again. When he stopped squirting she lifted her head. She closed her mouth, so nothing escaped. The silky texture and salty taste on her tongue. Then still looking him in the eyes, she swallowed it and licked her lips.

Dante pulled her up his body and kissed her. She kissed him back and then laid on her side next to him again.

"That was fun." Madison nuzzled his chest.

"Yeah. It was fun." Dante ran a hand down her back.

"I'm hungry, not sure if you are. I'm going to clean up and then go make us breakfast."

"Ok. I'll be out in a minute to help." He gave her a double pat on the butt.

****

Dante laid on the bed and stared at the ceiling. Things had changed. A lot. He should be mad. If he didn't care for Madison like he did, he would think she had tried to trap him into a relationship. A relationship that he didn't want. And there was the problem.

He cared for Madison, and he wanted a relationship with her. That wasn't what she offered. Just an increase in the frequency that they met. His heart had stopped when she had said she wanted to talk. Had she wanted to end things because she had gotten tired of him?

His heart had soared when she suggested that they see each other every day. It was more than he could hope for. When they had talked last night, something between them had shifted.

Their relationship had gone from surface level to a connection outside of sex. And then this morning during their kiss, it was different. His mind couldn't process it, but his heart did, and it did crazy things to his heart. It made him want things that he shouldn't. It reminded him of dreams he never assumed he could achieve. But after he met Madison everything had changed.

He hadn't been able to touch another girl since the first night he met her. Now it wasn't that he couldn't admire a good-looking woman, but they didn't hold a candle to Madison. She was all that he wanted. The only thing he wanted. Being with her was nothing like being with Monica. It was uncomplicated and easy. Something he didn't think could happen in a relationship, and something that he wanted more of. When he was with her, he was able to block the world out for a time.

He had been jealous of Lucca's engagement. It had seemed so far away for him and something he might have to give up on. But as he had gotten to know Madison, he wanted more. But with her beliefs on criminals and people on the wrong side of the law, how would she take it if she learned he was in the mob? It seemed impossible for them to be together long term. But if she fell in love with him, maybe she would overlook it.

With their new arrangement he would be able to do the things they said last night. He could see if there was a game he could take her to. But what he was most excited for was to take her to his place. That would be the real test. If she looked at it and asked for money, then he would have his answer. He knew she needed money due to her family situation and the fact that she funded her design herself.

Madison had left the room ten minutes ago, so he got up and cleaned up, then went to find her in the kitchen. They had slept in, and he would be late to a meeting if he didn't leave now. But he couldn't. She looked so cute in the kitchen. Her hair atop her head in a messy bun. She was wearing another loose shirt that hung off her shoulder and showed a navy blue bra strap and leggings.

"Oh, there you are. I was worried you fell back asleep and were going to let me make the breakfast alone." She elbowed him and gave him a shy smile.

"No, of course not. Someone wore me out this morning with a special treat. So I moved a bit slower." He lifted her chin when she dipped her head down.

"I forgot to give you a good morning kiss." He didn't know why he said that out loud, but as she raised her face for his kiss, he knew he would make this part of their routine. He wanted as many kisses and as many memories with her in case things didn't work out the way he wanted.

He hoped to use this time to show her what it could be like for them to be together in a more formal situation. Dante could see him and Madison having a future together, and there was another bump of excitement at being able to see Madison pregnant with his child.

They moved around the kitchen like they did this all the time together, even though this was their first time cooking together. He let Madison take the lead as it was her place and she knew where things were.

"Direct me. I'll be your sous chef."

"Ooo, I get to boss you around? That might be nice." She winked at him. "Let's do an omelet because that's quick. I have all the veggies out. If you want to start chopping them, I'll crack the eggs."

She had already set out a cutting board and a knife, Dante got to work. At the same time, he thought of what it would be like to have Madison boss him around. He liked to see her when she took control on the stage. In the bedroom she was unsure and didn't trust her instincts, but he knew she would learn in time.

Her eyes were on him and he knew when she stopped cracking eggs, that he had impressed her with his knife skills. That had been his goal when he offered to help. He wanted her to see that what he said was true. He knew his way around the kitchen. It was important to him for her to trust him.

To protect her, he wouldn't be able to tell her a lot of things, but he didn't want her to feel like he kept secrets from her on purpose. It was typical in mafia relationships that the women were kept out of the business side. It kept them safe from danger and rivals, and also they couldn't be used against their partner.

He didn't have a lot of time to build up trust with her

while he cleaned up the financial and real estate portions of the business, so he would need to make his time with her last and work in his favor. Dante finished chopping and looked up from the cutting board to find Madison with an egg hovering over the side of the bowl, waiting to be cracked.

"Chef, with the way you're looking at me, I think you could get in trouble for sexual harassment in the workplace." He gave her a teasing smile, then walked over to her, positioning her in front of him, he helped her crack the remaining eggs.

By the time they were done, they both panted for breath. He wanted to tease her until she came again and again and again. He never would get tired of her moans during her climaxes or the way she dug her nails into his shoulders, arms, or ass, depending on where her hands were.

"Yeah, that might be true, but I think you are holding your own in the workplace harassment domain." She pushed back into his erection, which he could never hide when he was around her. He seemed to have no problem staying hard for her and was in a constant state of arousal when they were together or of anticipation when they were apart. Even now, while with her he was thinking of his day and how to get back to Madison. The most important thing was to get back before Enzo cornered her again.

With the last egg in the bowl, he monster walked her over to the sink, and they washed hands together. As soon as his were dry, he exposed her nipples to the air.

"Dante."

He loved his name on her lips. Her head rolled back on his shoulder, and she exposed the length of her neck to his lips and let them roam. He found her sweet spot and gave it nip before he traced a path with his tongue.

If she wasn't on her period, he would have had her panties and leggings down and have bent her over a table or chair. But he couldn't. He would have to save it for another time. Maybe she could wear an apron and heels and cook at his place.

He would ask to get on her social schedule before she had too many plans. During this intense month with each other, he wanted to embrace the change that they had made to their agreement and hope she could see as much potential for them to be happy together as he did.

Dante wanted to tease her, but he didn't have time. She was efficient as she whipped up the omelet and the delicious smell of bacon wafted into the room. He knew it was her doing, to have everything ready at the same time.

"Sorry it took so long."

"No worries. I had fun." He kissed her nose.

She looked up at him and smiled. "I did too."

He picked up his fork. "Let's eat before it gets cold. I hate eating cold—"

"Food. No way, you too? I like mine piping hot, like burn your mouth hot."

"Same." He ate fast. He still needed to get out of there and get to his appointment. His being late would cause more questions and bring up more speculation in regards to the nature of his relationship with Madison. He couldn't define it, let alone tell anyone what it was.

The current words didn't fit. She was more than a friend or a lay to him. She was interesting, had a good sense of humor, and helped bring out his playful side. He would do anything to be with her for as long as she would allow him.

He slowed down his eating pace so they were closer to being finished around the same time. He didn't want her to think he was trying to leave. If he didn't have this appointment, then he would have loved to have stayed with her for the day.

Once they were both done, he helped her clean the dishes. "I better go. I have something."

"Oh, I'm sorry. I didn't think to ask if you had somewhere you needed to be." She looked sad. "No need to help clean up. You get to where you need to go." She stood by the sink.

He should take her at her word and leave, but he couldn't leave her looking down. "I'm right where I want to be. What if for tonight you pack a bag and we go to my place for the weekend? There is a farmers' market nearby, and we could go there Saturday morning. What do you think?

"Sounds good." She leaned into him and gave him a kiss.

"Pack enough stuff until Monday. I know you have to get back to your place to work on your designs." He stood in the doorway

"Ok. You better go."

"Ok. Come here for your good morning kiss."

"No, you need to go."

"I won't leave until you come over here."

"Fine." She walked over and gave him a quick peck on the lips, then pushed his chest. He didn't move.

"No. no. no. Like this." Before she could dart away, he lowered his head and caught her mouth. He should have just done a short kiss, but he couldn't stop himself from deepening it. He walked her backward until they hit the counter and he lifted her up and sat her down on top. Her legs wrapped around him and he pushed himself into her. She whimpered and thrust her hips forward, before she broke the kiss.

"Dante, you better go."

He rested his forehead on hers and took a deep inhale of her sweet and spicy scent and then made himself walk away. If not, he wasn't going to leave her anytime soon.

Chapter 9

Madison watched Dante walk away from her. She wanted to call him back but knew she shouldn't. She had settled on a design and should work on that instead of pine over Dante. Besides, she would see him soon.

Madison was stunned when Dante had told her to pack a bag. She couldn't believe he had meant it when he said he would have her over to his place. It made her heart speed up and showed her that he was someone she could trust.

He hadn't said an exact time, but she assumed he would come back sometime before tonight to pick her up and bring to his place. Or maybe they would just leave together from the club. She was excited to see his place and to spend more time with him.

Things were feeling different. Different in a good way. She didn't have any personal dating experience to go off of, but it had been like they were more than just friends who slept together. She was falling harder when she needed to be focused on other things like her designs and Henry. And there was the fact that she didn't want a relationship that led to marriage. She wasn't getting married or having kids. Which was why what her and Dante had was perfect.

She felt terrible, she hadn't seen Henry in two days. They had talked on the phone, but she had been busy with making and cutting out her pattern. She knew he understood and she would go see him today since she would be at Dante's for the weekend.

Madison hadn't visited Henry on the weekends as she reserved that time for Dante. She was unsure of what she would do now that they were going to be together every day.

But, with only two months left before fashion week, she would need to focus.

****

Madison knocked on Henry's door.

"Hey. I didn't know it was you. I thought you were a guest. Why didn't you use your key?" Henry stepped back to let Madison pass

"I know we have each other's keys for emergencies. I don't want you to think I would come in your home whenever, because I have a key." Madison walked into the living room.

"It's no problem, that's what I gave it to you for. To be able to let yourself in when you come to visit me." Henry shut the front door and followed Madison.

"Oh." Madison hadn't interpreted it like that, and she hoped Henry wouldn't just come into her apartment whenever he wanted. "Well, you might be doing something and might not want someone to walk in on you." Madison sat down on the couch

Henry sat in the wingback chair across from Madison. "Is that the case with you? You haven't been around to see me as of late." He looked at her with quiet directness.

"Yeah, and I'm sorry. I decided on a design for the competition and have been focused on that. You know I want to win."

"Of course I do, and if you do, your salary will help

all of us out." He leaned back in the chair and stretched his legs out.

Madison frowned. She was confused and hurt. Did he only care for the money that she gave him and didn't care if she won the competition because she was good at what she did, it all concerned what it would allow her to do for him?

"Yeah, that's true, but aren't you going to look for a job after the surgery since you're in remission?"

"Well, I don't know." He shifted in his seat. "There is nothing that I could do to make the same amount I made playing ball."

"True, but every little bit helps." Madison sat forward.

"That's what I'm saying. Your sign-on bonus for winning will help out."

"You or me?"

"Both of us and Dad too."

"I planned on saving that."

"How could you do that when we need it? I'm starting to think you don't care that Dad and me need your help." Henry leaned forward into her space.

"No, no. That wasn't what I was saying. I just need to have a cash cushion in case something comes up."

"I don't think you need the whole ten thousand." Henry didn't back down.

"Well, I hoped to get a car—" Madison shrank back.

"Why get a car when public transportation is so much cheaper." Henry leaned back.

"You have a car."

"Yeah, but I'm used to driving myself around, I wouldn't be able to wait on anyone else's schedule. But you're used to it. Why change? It would help you save more money."

"Right." Madison picked up her phone at the notification ding. "I have to get going to catch the bus back to my place to meet my model." Madison stood.

"Ok, well, I'll see you tomorrow." Henry continued to stay seated.

"Oh, I'll be busy this weekend and won't be able to come over." Madison picked up her bag.

"No problem, I can stop by your place."

"I won't be there. I'm going to be staying with a friend."

Henry cocked his head. "Sabrina?"

"No. Another friend. One you don't know."

"Is this friend a guy?"

"Why?"

Henry stood and placed a hand on her shoulder. "I know you don't have a lot of dating experience. I don't want you to end up hurt, by some guy who takes advantage of you."

"Right, well, I gotta go or I'll miss the bus and be late." She leaned over to give Henry a hug and then turned to leave."

"Madison, before you go, do you have some cash you can spare?"

"I only have some hundreds I was going to put in the bank."

"Great. I'll take two." Henry held his hand out.

"Sure. Here you go." Madison closed her wallet and walked out and softly closed the door behind her. To him, she was a wallet to get money from. Did he even care? To her, they had become close, but now she it seemed as if he was only close with her wallet. She shouldn't have given him the money, but that would be selfish to keep it for herself.

She knew Henry was used to so much more based on the money he earned playing ball. Of course he would miss things like eating out and going to shows. What right did she have to stop him?

****

Madison went to meet her model Becky. They had talked and texted to set up a meeting time, but it was the first time they would meet in person. They would meet at Madison's place. Since Madison didn't have a car and was doing everything out of her apartment, it was easier and more convenient to meet there instead of carting everything to the fashion house and back.

Madison went to answer the knock at the door. "Hi."

"Hi, it's nice to meet you." Becky held out her hand.

"You too. Come in. Thanks for being willing to come to me." Madison shook it and opened the door wider.

"Yeah, no problem, I don't mind." Becky walked inside.

"Well, I would like to get started with the latest measurements. I got them from your agency, but I like to do my own." Madison closed the front door and locked it.

"No, problem. Where would you like to do it?" Becky looked around.

"I do my designing at my kitchen table, so let's go there."

"Ok." Becky followed Madison into the dining room.

"Let me pull the blinds, and then if you can take your shirt and pants off, I'll get the measurements. I do have part of it cut out so I'm going to pin it on you too if that is ok?"

"Sure." Becky set her things on the countertop

"I like to leave a large border so I can take it out if I need to and still have fabric without needing to insert a panel."

"I've never worked with a designer that has done that before." Becky removed her top and bottom

Madison was light and bubbly at being called a designer and hung her tape around her neck.

"What's that smile for?"

"No one has ever called me a designer before. It feels nice." Madison grabbed her notepad.

"Not even your family?" Becky held her arms out to make a T with her body.

Madison remembered her conversation with Henry and measured Becky's arms.

"Oh, you guys don't get along?"

"No, we do. They, well, my mother doesn't see it as a good career." Madison measured Becky's neck.

"My parents at first weren't too crazy that I wanted to be a model, but they've become more supportive. I don't know how I would have done this competition without them being there for me." Becky turned to the side.

"Yeah, it is hard." Madison's mind turned to Dante and how he supported her last night when she told him her dreams.

"You don't have anyone?"

"No, I do." Dante believed her designs were good.

"Is it a guy?"

"Yeah, it's not serious though." Madison wrote the latest numbers down next to the ones the agency had given her.

"But you want it to be?"

"I wish it could be, but it's not our deal." Madison hung up the muslin she had cut out and placed pins in to hold the design together.

"Oh." Becky made a face.

"Oh no, did I poke you?" Madison pulled the pin out.

"No. It's just I was in a relationship like that and it ended."

"Not well?" Madison poked herself on the next pin.

"Well for me. I wanted more, but he didn't. But my family has been great, and my girlfriend reminded me that you can never turn a booty call or friends with benefits into more than what it was, but you can ruin the friendship."

"Oh." Madison rubbed her finger where the needle had pricked her skin.

"That's kind of where we were at. I can't be happy for him when I see him with another girl, so our friendship suffered. I don't know if it will come back, and it sucks because he was a great friend."

"Yeah." Madison looked down at the ground.

"So enjoy it while it lasts, but know that it will end. That's the one thing I wish someone would have told me. Maybe then we would still be friends."

Becky had given Madison tons to ponder. Madison pulled another pin out of her pin cushion.

"What else do you like to do for fun?"

Madison finished up, and they talked shows they had watched and things they wanted to do after the competition was over. It had been nice, and she believed she could call Becky a friend at the end of it.

For some of the projects they had worked on for the

fashion house, the models had been super hard to work with.

Some of them had lived up to the high maintenance stereotype, so it was refreshing for the final project to get a model who didn't think she had to be demanding as a requirement.

Madison got into the flow and time slipped away from her and she and her sewing machine became one. She was startled by her alarm. She had skipped lunch and was close to missing dinner. She had a meet up with Sabrina and Zoe before work for dinner and to catch up with them.

Sabrina still hadn't apologized for spreading the rumors and had been standoffish and didn't come near Madison. She left the room if Madison came in. Zoe had been busy with something or someone. She wasn't sure if it was the friend she had mentioned earlier. Madison didn't want to press her. She got wanting to keep some things private and to herself. She was the same way with what was going on between her and Dante. It wasn't going to last forever, so why mention it.

But even if she wanted to share what was happening, she and Dante had agreed not to share. Maybe it was something like that with Zoe and whoever her friend was. Madison was quick to get dressed, happy she had packed her bag before she had started sewing.

Sabrina was going to pick her up. She hoped the tension between them had lessened, and she suspected Sabrina wanted to say she was sorry when they were alone. She knew Sabrina might still be upset she got the headliner position. Sabrina must have been over it since she had offered to pick Madison up.

Madison had just set her dance duffle next to her

overnight bag when her doorbell rang. She opened it up to see Enzo. He had also avoided her, and she was wary after their last interaction to see him.

Even though he had her address, he had never come to her place before.

"Enzo? What's up? I'm getting ready to leave."

He looked over her shoulder and though she knew Dante wasn't there, she pulled the door tighter to her body.

"I just wanted to talk to you without a whole bunch of people around to overhear."

"Oh ok." Madison was confused. He had made himself quite clear what he believed she had been doing and how that made him feel.

"I know you slept with Dante, but I'm willing to forgive you."

Madison's head moved back as if she had been slapped. "I'm sorry?"

"We, Lucca, Gabe, and I, came in after you had left."

"Ok." Madison had no idea where he was going with this conversation, but she was ready for it to be over. "I'm not sure what the point of this conversation is."

"I should have told you earlier, but I'm interested in you. I didn't expect you to sleep with Dante right after you met him." He moved forward.

"Right." Madison didn't want to acknowledge the fact that she and Dante hadn't only slept together once. Dante, true to his word, hadn't told anyone and she wasn't going to tell Enzo. "I'm sorry I didn't know you were interested in me. I suspected, but I wasn't sure." Madison shifted side to side and touched her hair.

"That's ok. It was my fault I did not make it clear. I

just didn't expect you to sleep with Dante." He looked at her as if he expected her to apologize for that.

"Enzo, I—" Madison looked over his shoulder to see if anyone else was coming.

"It's ok, you already said sorry. I'll overlook the fact. I know Dante is done with you." He put his hand on the door jamb.

That was news to her, and she just stood there.

"I don't mean to be so blunt, but he would never be interested in a real relationship with you like I am."

"Right." Madison wanted to end this conversation, and she didn't know whether to be happy Sabrina was late or not. She didn't want her to overhear this conversation. She knew Sabrina liked Enzo, and she didn't want her to know she had slept with Dante either.

"So like I said. I will overlook your mistake of sleeping with Dante the first time you laid eyes on him and take you back."

Madison screamed inside her head, what the fuck? "Enzo. I think you might be confused, but I wasn't apologizing for what happened between Dante and me. I'm not interested in dating you even if, as you were so gracious to put it, you were willing to 'take me back.' You never had me, and I'm not looking for a relationship with you besides what we have at the club."

"Dante will never date you." He got in her face.

"And that's fine. I'm not looking for that." Even though now in her heart she was. Which was strange as before Dante it wasn't something she had considered. "I think this conversation is over, and I would appreciate it if you don't bring it up again."

She gripped the door handle. "Like I said I'm getting ready to leave. I guess I'll see you around the club, and please don't come to my place again." She moved back and closed the door in his face. There was nothing else for her to say, and she didn't want to hear anything else that came out of his mouth.

Enzo stopped the door from being closed and pushed his way inside her place.

"What do you think you're doing?" Madison backed up into her place.

"Dante shares his girls after he is done with them, so it's my turn." He grabbed her and tried to kiss her.

Madison slapped him across the face, but that didn't stop him, and he reached for her shirt, so she kneed him in the groin and shoved him out the door and locked it.

She hoped he took the hint and left, and she would prefer if he stayed away from her at the club as well. She hoped from now on he would keep his distance. Madison's phone dinged. A text from Sabrina.

—*Sorry I'm running late. Be there in five*—

—*No worries. See you then*—

Madison sat down to process what Enzo had said. Dante and the others used to share girls. Maybe still did, if what Enzo said was to be believable. And she didn't think he was as trustworthy as she had first presumed. She didn't care if Dante was done with her. She ignored the stab in her heart. She wouldn't be passed around.

Madison's doorbell rang twenty minutes later.

"Sorry, I got caught up in my design."

"No problem." Madison ran her hands up and down her arms. She was cold and shaky. "I, uh, understand. How is it going?"

"Good. Are you ok?"

"Uh, yeah, I'm fine." Madison shook herself and tried to block out what happened with Enzo. It wasn't something she wanted to share with Sabrina.

"Are you ready to go?"

"Uh, yeah. Let me grab my stuff and lock up."

Madison caught Sabrina looking at her sketches.

"Is that your design for fashion week?"

"Nope. Just some ideas I had."

"They look nice."

"Thanks. I'm ready."

Sabrina walked out in front of her and she grabbed her bags.

"Whoa, you have a lot of stuff."

Madison looked down. "I don't think so, it's my usual stuff. I just have an extra bag of clothes."

"Oh, to drop off for Henry. How is he?"

She didn't know why she assumed the clothes were for Henry, and she wasn't going to tell her what they were for. "He's good. Doing much better." She locked the door behind her and followed Sabrina to her car.

"Thanks for being able to pick me up. We haven't had much time to talk."

"Yeah, that's been my fault. I was still upset that you got the headliner position. It was mine, everyone knew that, and then you came and took it."

"Yeah, I'm sorry. It just happened." She climbed into the car. She hoped the whole ride wouldn't be this topic. And where was Sabrina's apology for the rumor she spread?

"It's just I needed the money, and I doubt I'm going to win fashion week. I mean let's be honest. I'm in last place.

"You never know. Besides, other fashion houses will be there, so it's not like you can't get in with another fashion house."

"Yeah, I guess that could be a possibility." Sabrina parked outside the restaurant. "There is something I need to say to you, and something I need to ask you." She turned around and looked at Madison.

"That sounds serious. Yeah, sure." Madison turned her body towards Sabrina and expected her to apologize.

"I know we have known each other since we were kids, but I have to know something."

"Ok, sure. Ask?" Madison had no idea what Sabrina was going to ask.

"Did you sleep with Dante to get the headliner position?"

"What? No." Which wasn't a lie. She had slept with Dante after he had agreed to put her on the schedule. True she didn't know it was going to be as a headliner. Did he do that because she gave him her virginity?

"I didn't think so, but I had to ask."

"Why would you think that?"

"I don't know. It was the only thing that kind of made sense as to why you just happened to sub for me and then you all of a sudden you were exclusive there."

"That was the first night I met Dante."

"But there is also the fact that you don't have to follow club rules."

"Dante had nothing to do with that. That was a deal between Enzo and me."

"You know why he made that deal right?"

"Yes." Madison shivered at the memory.

"Do you like him?"

"No." And her feelings wouldn't change now that she knew how he was deep down. "I know you've had a crush on him, and I would never date someone I know you like. I'm not that kind of person."

"I know." Sabrina gave a chuckle. "Goody-two-shoes, perfect Madison would never be that kind of person."

"Hey, wait. I never said I was perfect, nor do I think I'm a goody two shoes. I have my own problems, just like anyone else. I'm not perfect, and I don't pretend to be. What does this have to do with the headliner position?"

"I guess I'm tired of coming in second or more behind you." Sabrina slapped her hand down on the wheel.

"Wow. Ok. I didn't know that's how I made you feel. I never meant to make you think you were second to me or that I was better than you."

"I guess deep down I know that, and that is what makes it worse. You're not a bad person. You're my friend."

"I am your friend, and I would never do something intentional to harm you. Like you did to me with the rumor that said I was a ho and had a STI."

"I know, I was just upset. We better get in. Zoe could think we aren't coming."

****

Dante sat in his office as he tried to clear things off his desk. He didn't want to be focused on business or the progress he made toward turning his businesses clean. He wanted to be able to focus on Madison for the weekend.

He and his cousins were having a status report meeting. It would be his first-time seeing Enzo since the incident when he had slammed him against the wall. They had both kept their distance. Dante, more so, because he was spending time with Madison.

It hadn't been long, only last night. But they were all close and spent a lot of time if not being in the same room together, then they exchanged texts or phone calls. Hell, even emails. But it had been radio silent.

He figured Enzo just needed time to cool down and realize that Madison was off limits. He hoped, this time had gotten that into his head. Lucca was the first to show up.

"Hey man. How's it going? Have you talked to Enzo since last night?" Lucca sat down.

"Things are moving. I'll give an update when everyone is here. I haven't talked to Enzo since last night. What did he say?"

"I don't know man. I tried to message him and he never responded. I could see that he read them, but no response."

That concerned. Dante didn't know why, but he had a bad feeling. He was going to text Madison when Gabe walked in.

"Gabe, have you talked to Enzo?"

"Nope, I haven't seen him since he left last night. When I contacted him last night, he ignored my messages and sent my calls to voicemail."

"Do you think he will show up today?"

"No idea."

Dante reached for his phone to see if he had any messages from Madison or Enzo.

"I wanted to tell you guys that Dad is having an engagement party for Ainsley and me, so you guys can talk to her, since the last time you met her everything was kind of rushed."

"That's great I guess. Do we have to come?" Dante had nothing from either Madison or Enzo, and he shot off a quick text to Madison

—D: Wanted to make sure you're ok. I was thinking about you. I'm looking forward to spending the weekend with you. "— He waited for a response.

"Mom is making it a big deal, so I think you will have to come." Lucca shifted in the chair

"My mom already said to me there would be nice girls there to settle down with." Gabe checked his watch.

Dante looked up from his phone. "This isn't some type of matchmaker thing is it?"

"I'm not going to lie. I think so. Aunt Sharon and Linda are upset they aren't any closer to planning a wedding and want to help things along."

"Damn, so we have to show up? I might try to bring someone to keep mom off my back," Gabe said.

"Is that an option? If it is, you can put me down for a plus one." Dante knew who he wanted to bring. If only she was willing to make what they had official in front of his family and friends. But first he would have to tell her that he was part of a crime family. He couldn't bring her without telling her first.

"You have someone you want to bring?" Lucca looked at him.

—M: I'm ok and me too.—

Dante smiled. He had been worried Enzo might confront Madison again because he had gone off the radar, but she was fine. Dante also knew Madison would tell him if Enzo had come by or done anything so that was good.

"I guess let's start since Enzo isn't here. I can at least give the update."

"Sounds good."

"So things have moved according to plan. I've

transferred some holdings over into different names in case we get caught so they can't seize them."

"Make sense."

"Did you talk to the lawyer, Tony?"

"Yeah. I let him know what's happening and he has the funds for bail if it's necessary."

The office door opened, and Enzo came in with a bag of ice held up to his face. He came in and slumped down in a chair.

"What happened to you?" Gabe asked.

"Bitch smacked me." He stared at Dante and put the ice in his lap.

"Did she get your balls too, man?" Lucca leaned forward.

"Yeah."

"What happened?" Dante was curious. None of them manhandled women as far as he knew. He sensed Enzo hinted it was Madison, but he had checked on her and she was fine and hadn't said Enzo was there or had been by.

"I got my signals crossed. She acted like she was interested, but it turns out she was only a tease. I know better now."

Dante looked down at his phone again, but there was no new message from Madison. He knew she was out with Sabrina and Zoe before work, so he would see her when she came in. She always came up to his office as part of their routine after she got in.

"I was just giving an update. Things are moving as planned and we should reach our target date, which is a week before the sting date. Tony has access to the funds to bail us out when they come to pick us up. I'm pretty confident that once they get their hands on documents, that they won't find anything."

"That's good." Enzo moved the ice pack back to his face.

"Enzo, Dad is throwing a party for Ainsley and me to celebrate our engagement."

"Yeah, I know. Mom told me when she asked why I hadn't brought anyone home. She had expected me to bring someone that I had mentioned."

Dante took the hint and ignored it. "Any word on the mole?"

Enzo had a shifty look cross his face, and it made Dante concerned.

"We're just finding out who it is. No need to take care of him."

"I won't. Ok good. I think that's it for now. I need to get down on the floor." Dante stood up and everyone else followed. He wanted to talk to Enzo in private, but he didn't think it was the right time. Maybe later tonight. He didn't want Enzo in the office when Madison came up.

****

He sent a quick text to the guys he still had tailing Madison.

—D: *Did Enzo show up at Madison's?*—

—A: *Yeah, he wasn't there long.*—

—D: *Ok, next time stop him and let me know.*—

—A: *Will do boss*—

Dante looked up from his desk to see Madison come in the door. She held her dance duffel and another bag. She locked the door behind her. She came over and dropped her bags at his feet before she climbed into his lap and rested her head on his shoulder.

Something was wrong. She was shaking and curled

up in his lap and nuzzled his neck.

"What's wrong?" He stroked her back.

"Nothing."

He didn't trust her. And it made his gut tighten. Was she going to lie to him? She wouldn't look at him. He leaned back so he could see part of her face and lifted her chin so he could look into her eyes.

The hairs on the back of his neck stood up. Something had happened. And he suspected it had to do with Enzo. Thinking of Enzo touching Madison and her having to try to defend herself made his blood boil and he kicked himself for not being there.

Madison wasn't violent, and the knowledge of what Enzo could have done to make her not only slap him in the face but to kick him in the balls. Dante had an idea and if Madison didn't need him he would have gone after Enzo. Now he just needed Madison to tell him everything that happened.

"I don't believe you."

"Sabrina asked me if I slept with you to get the headliner position. She wanted it and rumor was that it was hers." She turned to face him. "Did you give it to me because we slept together? I believed you were just going to put me on the schedule for the three months."

This hadn't been what he expected. "What? No. It had nothing to do with us sleeping together. That is separate and had no bearing on what happened at il Signore. What brought that on?"

"She asked me when she came to pick me up for dinner. She said a bunch of things that kind of hurt me and made me feel like a bad person."

"Like what?" He rubbed her back.

"Just stuff like she feels like she is second best to me

and that I think I'm perfect and too good. As if I think she is beneath me. Henry had told me she was jealous of me earlier, but I hadn't believed him." She leaned into his chest.

"When she confronted me, it let me know how much it was true. To me, we were good friends, but I feel like all this time she has been hating me in secret. She didn't even say sorry for the rumors she spread."

"How long have you been friends for? Sometimes work-friend relationships don't last long."

Madison sat up. "We've been friends since we were kids. At least I believed we were."

"Aww, baby, it's ok. She might be having a hard time right now and doesn't mean it." He gave her a hug.

"I think that might be true. I think she wants me to give up this headliner position for her, but I can't. My mom went through my savings that I had built up for use during my unpaid internship, so I need the money. I can't give it up."

"I know and I don't expect you to, and I don't think she means or wants that from you. I think she is just hurt now."

"Maybe, it's just some things that upset her, I have no control over." She snuggled closer.

"Like what?"

"The fact that there are special rules for me."

"Yeah, how did those come to be?"

"It was part of the original deal I had with Enzo when he asked me to work here."

"He knew you danced?"

Fear flickered across her face and then disappeared. Alarm bells rang in the back of his head. It confirmed for him that Enzo didn't run into another woman, but that it was Madison who had hit Enzo.

"He came to some of the clubs I had been at and asked why I didn't work at il Signore. I told him it was the rules, and he said he could make a no touch rule with me if I would come and work there."

"And he did."

"Yep, so I came to work here twice a month."

"Did anything else happen?"

"No." It came out quick, like a lie. But he didn't press her. He wanted her to trust him enough to tell him. He also hadn't told her he was having her followed so he couldn't tell her how he knew for a fact Enzo had been there without giving everything away.

He didn't know why he kept the tail in place. She wasn't cheating on him and the only people she visited were her parents, her brother, and Zoe.

Dante cupped her face. She had still brought her overnight bag so that meant she would spend the weekend with him.

He still wanted to use the time they had together to convince her that they could be good together in permanent relationship. In five weeks' time, he planned to take her to Lucca's engagement party and let everyone know he had found the special someone.

This way they could date without having to sneak around. For as long as they would be together, he wanted to be out in the open. Deep down he wanted a forever life with Madison, but he doubted it was possible.

She didn't seem like the type to be a mafia wife and even though he was cleaning his businesses up, and wanted to leave the family, that would still always be a part of him. And there was the fact that he could go to jail. He didn't doubt that Tony would get him out. But he didn't know how long he would spend in.

Would Madison want to stay and wait for him to get out? Would she want to be with someone who had been to jail and had a possible prison sentence looming? No. He would need to wait until after everything was settled before he approached Madison for something more.

"I better go. I just came here first. Zoe will look for me." She kissed him and then got up. "Can I leave my overnight bag here? I wasn't sure if we were leaving from here or from my place."

"Yeah, you can leave it with me. We'll leave from here. You can come up after you're done getting the bar ready for tomorrow. I'll have a few things left to finish up, but it shouldn't take too long and then we can leave."

"Ok. I'll see you downstairs." She picked up her dance duffel and left. Leaving the door open behind her.

He listened to see if Enzo was waiting outside or if anyone else lurked around, but it seemed like the coast was clear. Madison was a good girl. Hell, it had been very recent that she had been a virgin. He didn't want rumors to upset her or ruin her reputation.

Dante would choose to have people know they were dating and had kept it quiet, than that they were in a casual relationship and think that she had slept with him to get favors. Then he could wait until he had cleaned up everything and didn't have jail over his head, and then he would tell her how he had feelings for her.

Dante headed downstairs to be ready for Madison's sets.

Chapter 10

It was the end of the night, and Madison and Zoe cleaned up. Things had been different in the back room. No one talked to her, although they hadn't been tried to befriend her before, so it shouldn't have been a big difference.

But it was different. She had a feeling that people were going to find out soon that she was sleeping with Dante. How could they not? She would leave with him tonight and he would be bringing her over the weekend to work. It didn't make sense for them to try and come on their own when they would spend the whole weekend together.

"Feels like something is going on right?" Zoe said.

"Yeah, I was feeling the same thing."

"It's the good old rumor mill at work. I figure we will find out soon enough."

"Yeah."

"Do you want a ride?"

"No, I'm going to go later. I need to go get my money too. Besides, it's in the complete opposite direction for you."

"No worries, I don't mind, but I understand. I'll see you tomorrow."

Madison climbed the stairs to Dante's office. The door was ajar, so she knocked on it in case he was meeting with someone. She didn't know where she would wait if he was busy. She had planned on waiting in his office, but now she knew that that would for sure get the rumor mill going.

Maybe she should go back to her place and wait for him to pick her up.

"Come in."

Madison pushed open that door and went inside. She was relieved not to see Enzo. She wasn't sure if she wanted to see Gabe or Lucca. Her face still heated when she remembered that they knew she had slept with Dante at least once.

She was grateful when she got there that Dante was alone. He looked up when she entered and he gave her a huge smile. It caused tingles to travel inside her body. She was positive, that if she wasn't on her period, Dante would have bent her over the desk or fucked her on the desk. Imagining it made her nipples bead against the lace of her bra. Maybe another time.

"I was just thinking that it might make more sense for me to go back to my place and wait for you there."

"Why?"

"I don't know how it will look with me sitting here when the other girls come up to get their money."

"No worries. I gave their money to Ed to take down and hand out."

"Oh, but I better go down for mine. If I'm not there, that will cause suspicions and rumors.

"No worries. They will think you are still cleaning up the bar and when you're not there, they will either assume you came up to get it or you left for the night."

"Ok."

"Come. Sit on my lap."

"Dante. We better not." She wanted to sit on his lap

and kiss him without a care in the world. Not having to wonder if people were going to come in and catch them together and what their coworkers were going to think or say.

She longed for it to be real which was weird. She knew Dante was as anti-relationship as her. Why else would he have agreed to her deal? But she was tired of sneaking around like she was a bad person doing something she shouldn't be doing. They were two consenting adults and it shouldn't matter, but it was the whole workplace romance that was the issue.

"Come on." He held out a hand for her.

She couldn't deny him or herself so she moved closer and took his hand. She let him pull her down into his lap, with her legs draped to one side. He lowered his head and kissed her.

"Dante, wait." She tried to stop him. The door wasn't closed or locked, but it was quick to disappear when he deepened the kiss. Her hands slid up his chest and around his neck. Her fingers tunneled a path through his thick hair. She moaned into his mouth and he used the entrance to slip his tongue inside her mouth.

His hands dropped down to her rear and he helped guide her hips over his cock. He held them still while he ground up on her and she ground on him.

Madison was panting for breath. Dante used that time to kiss down the side of her neck.

"Dante."

"I know, baby. I just can't get enough of you. Go sit on the couch as far away from me as possible. I hope then I won't be as tempted."

Madison climbed out of his lap and went over to the couch. She needed something to distract herself so she pulled out her sketch pad to work on some new designs. She was happy with what she had picked out of her designs for fashion week, but she always had new ideas.

She looked up to see Dante back at work and with no longer the threat of them losing control. She lost herself in her designs. That wasn't to say she blocked him out in a complete way. She still was giddy that not only did she sit in his lap with the door open where they could get caught, but she was excited to go to his place.

Madison was sure they would have a great time and it would be another great memory to add to her growing pile to reflect on and remember after they broke up.

It seemed like only a short time later that Dante came over and tapped her on the shoulder. He sat down next to her on the sofa.

"Hey, are you all right?" He looked into her lap at her designs. "Oh I see, you were lost in your designs. They look nice."

Madison looked up at the clock over his head. It was on the verge of time for her to take her birth control pill. They had spent another hour and half in Dante's office while he finished with what he had to do.

"Yeah, sorry. Were you calling me?"

"Yes."

"It's normal when I'm designing or working I get in the flow, and everything else gets pushed to the side. Are you ready to go?"

"Yeah, let me pack up a few things. I like to clean my desk before I leave. Gives me a fresh start each day."

Dante finished packing up and Madison packed up her stuff as well. They were done around the same time. He picked up her overnight bag and then slung her dance duffel over his shoulder before he reached for her hand.

They walked out hand in hand together. Dante opened the door for Madison and got her settled into the car before he put her stuff in the back of his car before he climbed in the driver's seat and then took her to his place.

When they got there, Dante helped her out. "Let me let you in and then I'll come back and grab the bags."

Madison followed Dante into his place and was impressed with what it looked like. She couldn't believe he had done most of it on his own.

"Wow, this looks amazing. This must have cost a lot of money." She told him when he came back to the house. "How much did you spend on everything? I'd love to know what things you did. Do you have before and after pictures?"

"I do. Let me give you the tour." He set her bags near the front door and then took her hand as they walked around the place.

Dante showed her where he replaced the tile and took off the wallpaper. The light fixtures that he had changed out. There was so much to look at, she didn't know where to look first.

The kitchen wasn't state of the art, but it was functional with stainless steel appliances. He kept the same aesthetic as he had in his office, with minimal clutter and sleek black furniture with metal accents. They ended up back at the front door.

"Let me get your bag and we can look at the bedroom. There I did a ton of work."

"I can't wait to see."

Dante bent down to get her overnight bag and then led her to his bedroom. To say it was impressive was an understatement. She didn't know what to look at first.

The focal point of the room was a huge king-size bed.

It was also black, and the nightstands carried the theme of black in color with the metal accents. The sheets and comforter were black and looked like satin from what she could see. The bed was neat, as was the rest of the room.

She turned around and found in the other wall across from the bed was a tiled fireplace. It looked warm and inviting and like something you could enjoy when it was cold outside, but nothing she wanted on this hot August day.

"Come, I want to show you the master bath."

Madison walked in, and it looked like something out of a magazine. It looked like it was done in black marble or granite with silver flecks in it. There was a huge soaking tub and on the other side was a freestanding shower that looked big enough to hold at least three adults.

"Here I know you've had a hard and long day. Let me run a bath for you." Dante drew her over to the bath and sat on the edge. He turned on the chrome faucets to get the right temperature and then plugged the tub and let the water run to fill it.

"Here you go. I'll leave you alone to soak in the tub. Take as long as you want, and I'll have something special for you when you get out."

"Thank you." Madison appreciated that he left her alone to undress. On the edge of the tub she found some bath salts. They smelled like Dante's cologne. Did he enjoy taking baths too?

She was a water girl. She loved baths and long hot showers. As the tub filled, she adjusted the temperature hotter and closer to her liking and then threw in a handful of bath salts.

The salts hit the water and sent their fragrance into the room. It smelled like Dante was surrounding her, and she couldn't wait to get into the water and have it wash all over her.

She was appreciative of Dante taking the time to set a bath for her. She was tired and sore, not only from work at the club, but the work she had done on her design and then just the fact that she was on her period.

She finished undressing and slipped into the warm and inviting water. From the water the scent was even stronger. The scent of musk and wood tickled her nose and filled her lungs with each deep breath that she took.

Madison was curious as to what the surprise was. She knew Dante still remembered that she was on her period so they wouldn't be having sex. Did he plan on teasing her and giving her an orgasm without penetration? She guessed she would find out soon enough.

She didn't want to get out of the tub. The water was still warm, and there must have been some type of moisturizer or something in the bath salts because the water was velvety smooth, as if she was surrounded by warm cashmere that was drenched in Dante's scent.

She would have stayed in there until the water got cold but decided to get out and get dressed. That wouldn't make her a good guest if she hid in the bathroom forever. She climbed out and grabbed a towel from the rack, which turned out to be heated.

Madison could stay at Dante's place forever, so she dried herself off and then picked up her overnight bag to search for her night clothes. She couldn't wait to get out of the bathroom and see what Dante had in store for her.

When she left the bathroom, it was as if she stepped into a romance novel. The lights were dim and there were candles placed in strategic places throughout the room. And there were red rose petals on the bed.

She couldn't believe that he had done all that for her; it was like something out of a dream. There was even something that looked like maybe it was some type of oil or something on the nightstand.

Dante had changed his clothes and wore some casual sweats or lounge pants, she couldn't tell in the light, but it was easy to see that they hung low on his hips and drew her eye to the shadow between his legs, but she knew what it held.

She liked to think that it grew before her eyes as she stared at it. She scanned her eyes up over his chest, covered with a tight white t-shirt that was stretched over his muscles and left little up to her imagination. Although her imagination was running wild with ideas of what would happen.

"Did you enjoy your bath?"

"Yes, thank you. It was like heaven. A girl could get used to things like this." She winced inside at her words. She didn't want him to think that she expected him to do it every time she came to his place. This might be the first and last weekend she spent at his place. There was no guarantee that he wouldn't get bored of her this weekend with all the time they had spent together and decide that he had gotten her out of his system.

"What's all this you have here?" She looked around the room again taking in a small towel and larger towel next to what looked like oil. She hoped he didn't have that because he planned for them to have sex. She had learned that she was adventurous in the bedroom, but she didn't know if she was ready to try that or even if she wanted to try it.

"I want to give you a massage. Do you want to take your top off? I don't want the massage oil to stain it. You can leave your panties on."

"Ok, thanks." Madison took off her nightie and lay face down on the bed. She made a pillow with her arms and turned her head to the side so that she could breathe. Her skin tingled with anticipation and it wasn't long before the bed dipped as Dante climbed on the bed and moved closer to her body.

She trembled with need. She didn't think she would ever stop wanting him. She didn't want to think of the day when he would no longer want her and instead wanted to focus on soaking everything up in the moment.

The oil was warm as he dripped some onto her low back and she shivered in suspense. Then came his hands. Big and strong and rough they slid up and down her back. The strokes going further and further until he reached her shoulders. He kneaded them and Madison couldn't stop the sigh of contentment that came out.

"That's it, Madison. Relax. Let me make you feel good."

And that was exact thing that Dante did. His hands massaged her back, neck, and shoulders before he moved down to her legs. He massaged her inner thighs. His hands were slow and deliberate as they brushed her panty-covered mound. It sent tiny shockwaves through her body. His hands traveled down to her calves and then to her feet where he massaged her insteps of both feet and even rubbed her toes.

Her body was like Jello on the bed. She was complete boneless puddle, like an unattractive blob, but she couldn't get herself to move.

"I was going to do your front too, but I'll save that for another day. I think you're ready to go to sleep now. Do you want me to help you put your top back on?"

"Yes, that would be awesome. I don't think I can move a muscle right now."

Dante was careful as he redressed her and he took care not to touch her too much but his hand brushed Madison's nipples by accident and they hardened even more.

There was an extra warm glow at Dante's words. There would be another time of this. She hoped one that ended with him inside her when the time was right. There was the rustle of fabric as he took off his clothes and then slipped into bed and held her in his arms.

Madison was warm and comforted and snuggled back into him until the thick length of his manhood pressed against her rear. This was how they always slept together. Dante nude and her in her nightie, they spooned as they fell asleep.

Dante kissed her shoulder. "Good night."

She turned in his arms and kissed him back. "Good night. This was wonderful. I appreciate it and am having a lot of fun."

He kissed her back and deepened the kiss and then he broke apart. "We better get to bed. I have lots more fun things planned for us for tomorrow." He kissed the top of her head, and Madison's eyes drifted closed and she knew she had a smile on her face. This had been a night to remember and she was sure it would keep her warm on those cold nights when they were no longer together.

Chapter 11

Madison woke to the smell of hot coffee and something delicious she couldn't quite figure out. She stretched in bed and then went to do her morning routine. She threw on some shorts and a t-shirt and headed to the kitchen area.

There she found Dante at the stove. He wore an apron, pajama pants, and nothing else. There was a tingle in her center. Her period wouldn't finish before this weekend, so they wouldn't be able to have sex and that was ok.

If Madison had marriage in the cards, Dante was the kind of man she would choose.

But she wasn't going to get married or bring kids into the world.

Deep down, she could feel she might like Dante more than she would let on, but it wasn't something she was willing to examine at the moment.

She just wanted to enjoy the time they did have together. "What smells delicious?"

She stood in the doorway.

"French toast."

"Ooo, French toast. I haven't had that in ages."

"Well, then I am happy to be able to make it for you."

He turned around from the oven and took her in. His gaze smoldered as his eyes traveled up and down her body before landing back at her eyes. His eyes darkened and they beckoned to her.

"Come over here, please."

Madison's legs seemed to listen to Dante and she moved over to him. She tilted her face up for the kiss she knew he was going to give, and he didn't disappoint. Her insides melted as he wrapped his arms around her, spatula and all.

"We better stop." She came up for a breath. "Don't want to burn the food."

"True." He placed another peck on her nose and then turned back to the stove and flipped the French toast and placed it on a plate next to the stove. "I hope you are hungry."

"I am." At that moment she was starved for something other than food, but she would take the French toast. "Let me help you set the table."

"No need. I've already done it. I just need for you, beautiful, to sit down and let me take care of you."

She was quick to sit down. She didn't have a lot of people who took care of her so she was going to soak it all up. Dante treated her so well it was like a fairy tale she didn't want to leave.

Dante placed the plate before her and then sat his own plate down before he took a seat. On the center of the table there was a fruit salad. They both dived into the food.

"This is delicious." Madison popped a strawberry into her mouth. Seductively, she hoped. "Thank you for making food for me." She meant it. And couldn't think of the last time somebody had.

Her mom hadn't been into cooking and preferred for Madison's grandma to feed her or to hire help that as an adult, Madison knew they couldn't have afforded.

"No problem. I love cooking. Happy to be able to whip something up for you. You deserve it." Dante finished off his last bite of French toast. She wanted him to use that mouth on her next.

They ate the rest of the meal in comfortable silence. Both snuck peeks at each other. It seemed like they were more than friends with benefits, and she was excited for it. Her first real relationship. But was this what she wanted, a long-term relationship with a possible criminal?

Madison hid all her doubts and set her fork down. "It was delicious. Let me help clear the dishes."

"Sounds good. I'll take any help I can get." He gave her a wink. "Let's do your suggestion of going to the farmer's market and get some fresh food to make for the weekend."

"That sounds like a great idea. Let me go change."

****

Dante looked forward to spending the day with Madison. There was so much to learn, and little by little he was peeling back the layers as they spent more time together. Madison went to the bedroom to change clothes, and he followed to grab a shirt for himself.

He decided to change into jeans and dropped his pants before he put on boxer briefs and then pulled up his pants. When he turned around, Madison's eyes on him and they were heated with desire. It made him feel good that she wanted him, but he wanted to share some things with her as they built up more trust between each other.

"Come, let's go." He held out a hand out for her, and there was no hesitation, she placed her hand in his. He curled his fingers around hers, careful not to hold too tight.

"It's down the street. Let me grab some bags to put our finds in."

Hyped as they left and went to the farmer's market, he could feel her excitement as they moved through the stalls and looked at various produce, as well as some people's stalls that displayed their crafts."

"Oh wow, isn't this painting pretty?"

Dante nodded. Not as pretty as her.

"I'm a sucker for a sunset or sunrise picture. I just love them."

He decided to come back and get it for her. Maybe see if the guy could make a special one for her. He had noticed the sunset and sunrise pictures tacked to the walls at her place in between her designs, it looked like she had taken them herself.

They walked hand in hand through the market and stopped to chat at various interesting finds in crafts and food items. They filled their bags as they went.

"We better get home," Madison said.

"Why?" He had a warm feeling in his chest that she called his place home.

"The bags are getting heavy; we won't able to carry them soon."

She smiled the most beautiful smile at him, and he wished this wouldn't end, and could go on forever.

"Let's stop at a couple more stalls. I want to check out the cheese and honey vendors."

Holding hands still they traipsed back and forth from one end of the market to the other and added to their finds. Dante knew he had to find a way to make this relationship work.

He had started to care for Madison. Even still he wasn't willing to put a name on what he was feeling or allow his plans for the future to take hold. He didn't want his dreams to be shattered. And he could see a future with Madison.

And that scared him. He hadn't considered the possibility of marriage since Monica, and even then the feeling hadn't been as intense as it was with Madison.

"Ok, I think we stopped at every stall and you almost bought something from everyone. This was an expensive trip." Madison smiled up at him.

"I guess, I did, didn't I? But I like to support local businesses and some of it was your fault."

"My fault? How?" She brought her hand that wasn't holding his hand to her chest.

"You liked something at every stall, so I had to buy it. I couldn't resist giving you what you want." And that was true. He would move mountains to give her what she wanted, and he hoped one day she would realize she wanted him. But this was the second time she mentioned something being expensive. Was she enjoying his money more than him?

She rose up on her toes and pressed a kiss to his mouth. He knew she meant it to be quick, but he couldn't resist and deepened it and even with all the packages he held. He still wrapped his arms around her and drew her closer to him.

When they came up for air, her eyes were dazed and glassy and he couldn't wait to get her home. He knew she was still on her period and would be for the entire weekend visit, but that didn't mean he couldn't kiss her.

And kiss her he would.

"Come, let's take our purchases back to my place."

Something like a frown passed over her face and disappeared. "Sounds like a plan."

Dante was curious if something had changed? It seemed like they had both enjoyed their time out. They walked hand in hand toward his car. He carried all the packages in one hand. They were cutting off circulation in his fingers as they twisted up around his fingers with movement.

But he wouldn't let her carry any. He wanted to hold her hand and keep this idyllic experience going for as long as he could.

****

Madison watched Dante unload all the bags. He wouldn't let her help. "I feel like I'm just sitting here like a bump on a log."

"A pretty bump." He smiled at her and her heart melted. He thought she was pretty. She looked down at the table. She wasn't used to getting compliments and didn't know how to take it. Was he was feeling the same tugs and yearnings for a longer arrangement?

She couldn't believe she was thinking that. She needed to snap herself out of it. What they had going was fine. She didn't even know how much longer these intense emotions would last. Besides, they only had two months left to their deal. Who knew what would happen after their time together was up.

"What can I help with?"

"Well, now that I have all the ingredients out, shall we look them over to find out what we can make with them?"

"Sure." Madison got off the stool and walked over to the counter where he had displayed everything.

"What are you thinking?" Madison looked at the

spread.

"I don't know. We have that garlic bread, spinach, peppers, and tomatoes. We could do salad with homemade croutons and maybe that thick-cut bacon on the side. What do you think?"

"That sounds delicious. I was thinking that for dinner we do the free-range chicken with the kale and potatoes and maybe an orange or lemon sauce." Madison set the ingredients to one side.

"That sounds good. Are you going to make it?"

"Yep. What if you make lunch and I'll be your sous chef and then we make dinner together?"

"Ok, let's get eat. I'm getting hungry."

They worked in companionable silence. It was seamless as they moved around the kitchen together as if they had been doing this for years. It was nice to be able to work together in such a smooth way, and they had the meal prepared fast and sat down to eat.

"So what was it like for you growing up? Did you have any other siblings? I know you mentioned your brother that played pro ball. Is that right?" Dante picked up his silverware.

"Yeah." Madison didn't want to discuss her family life. She never said anything to anyone else, but this time she wanted to share. She wanted Dante to know more, and she wanted to unburden herself and find more out about Dante as well. You couldn't ask questions if you weren't willing to give up some information yourself.

"Well, I grew up with my parents and older half-brother. I was a later-in-life baby for my dad since my older brother's mom passed away due to breast cancer that hadn't been caught in time. My dad met my mom, and she didn't think she would get pregnant and didn't plan to have a kid, but here I am. I'm the oops baby."

What had gotten into her? She had never shared with anyone. That knowledge didn't stop her from continuing.

"As I got older, my mom got more jealous of the time my dad spent with me, so to make her happy he spent less time with me."

"Your mom was worried you would like your dad more."

"No, she was worried she would get less attention. So I spent a lot of time with my granny who was still young for her age since my mom wasn't even in her thirties."

"That must have been nice. None of my grandparents were alive when we were born."

"It was nice. She taught me everything that I know. I know how to sew because of her and she inspired me to not just be a seamstress but to design my own clothes. It's what pushed me to where I am now."

"That is cool. It's nice to have someone in your corner."

"Yeah it was. She passed away from a sudden heart attack."

"Oh no. I'm sorry." He reached for her hand.

"It's ok. It was a long time ago."

"I'm sure she is watching over you."

"I like to think that too." She stared off to the side thinking how much she missed her granny.

"And you? Any siblings?"

"No. But Lucca, Enzo, and Gabe and I grew up together and were kind of raised like brothers."

"Oh, that must be nice, and you guys are all the same age or close to it." She didn't even know how old he was. "My brother and I are ten years apart. So we haven't been close up until his cancer diagnosis."

"Yeah. Breast cancer, that must be hard."

"Wait, how did you know?" She didn't remember telling him, it was something she kept private because that's what Henry wanted. Breast cancer was still considered a woman's disease. She wished Henry wasn't embarrassed by it and was an activist for it, using his platform of former pro baller to help other men get tested.

Dante's face looked like a deer in the headlights. "Didn't you tell me?"

"No."

"I guess I just assumed because of his mother's diagnosis."

Madison didn't believe him. Not that she didn't think Dante was progressive, but many people didn't know men could get breast cancer too. She didn't know why he would have come to that conclusion unless he knew more than what she was telling him. He hadn't seemed shocked with regards to anything that she had said.

"Did you have me investigated?"

The confirmation was on his face.

"I can't believe you." She pushed back from the table. "Why would you do that? What did you find out?"

"I wanted to know more."

She stood up. "You could've asked."

"This was right after we slept together. Enzo had told me you needed money bad, and I wanted to make sure that you weren't going to scam me to get money if you were pregnant."

That kind of made sense. She remembered when he came to her place, he had said he needed to protect himself, but she still had the air of being violated. How much did he know?

"I'm sorry, I know it was wrong and I should have told you once we were sleeping together on a more regular basis."

"Is that why you made the exclusivity clause?"

"Yeah."

"Did you think I was sleeping with someone else? I was a virgin when we slept together." Madison walked away from the table. She couldn't decide if she wanted to hit him, cry, leave, or do all three.

"I know, but I didn't know you, and I had to be sure I knew what I was up against."

What had he found out? But she didn't want to discuss it anymore. It was already ruining what had been a pleasant day.

She knew they wouldn't be together for much longer, so there was no point making a bigger deal out of it than they already had.

Dante stood and reached for her hand. "Can we start over?" He looked like he was repentant, and she was willing to move past it.

"You're right, breast cancer is hard. He needs a kidney, and I'm a match so I'm going to give it to him once he is stable enough to go through the surgery."

"Are you sure you want to do that? It's a big deal to give an organ."

"Of course I'm sure. I looked at all the options, and it's what is best."

"He must be lucky to have you."

Madison didn't think so. She could always be doing more than what she was doing. She agonized over never doing enough.

What about you and your cousins, are you all close in age?"

"Enzo is the oldest at thirty and then me and Lucca are twenty-eight and last is Gabe who is twenty-six."

"Oh, that's nice that you all are so close." She didn't want to think of Enzo and what had happened when he came to her place. She wasn't sure if she should tell Dante, but she was worried he might not believe her, or worse it would cause a rift between the cousins, and she didn't want that. Besides, she didn't want anything else to ruin the fun they were having.

"Does everyone work as a family?" Madison knew he mentioned il Signore was a family business.

"Yeah, I guess you could say yes, but I want to branch out. Do things in a different way than what we have been doing."

"Oh wow. Change is hard. Is everyone taking it ok?"

"There is a snag in that I need to fix with some of my clients and the people we pay money to."

Madison figured he was trying to get out of the protection money racket.

"And I guess some are harder to let go of than others."

"Yeah, you could say that. I've changed a lot of things up. I have close to a month and a half left to finish cleaning up, and then I hope to move onto something else. I have something lined up."

"That will be nice I guess. Is that what you want?"

"Yeah. I've looked to move in another direction since I hit college. It's just taken me a while to execute it."

"So what was the other direction you wanted to take? Where did you think you would be by now?"

"To be honest, married and with a few kids and working for my own company. You?"

Wow, Madison didn't think Dante would see himself being married. He seemed afraid of commitment so to think he could see himself married was not expected at all.

Any hope of them maybe continuing on as they were was dashed. Had there been someone special that he had wanted to settle down with? Was that why he wasn't married? Madison's stomach was queasy.

"I think I'm where I want to be. Now in a year or five years that's different. I hope to have won the competition and be working at Anastazia Stewart's house of fashion and moving my way up the ranks and in five years My big hairy goal is to open my own fashion house."

"Big hairy goal?"

"Like that thing that seems impossible, but you want it. Kind of like your biggest dream that is just shy of achievement. You have to push yourself to get it."

"I like that idea. Then my big hairy goal would be to leave the, uh, family and do something above board on my own. And in five years I will open my own brokerage firm."

"Sounds like we are both entrepreneurs and have pretty similar goals."

"Yeah, you didn't mention marriage." Dante's face looked hopeful.

"I hadn't planned on getting married or having kids. Because of what it did to my mom and dad and to me, and I wouldn't want that. My dad lost himself to whatever my mom wants to the point that he spent less time with me to please her."

"From what I know, I don't think that would happen." Regret showed on his face.

"Maybe not. But I guess you could say at this moment I am unsure when it comes to marriage." She wanted something permanent with Dante. Something she hadn't wanted before, but every minute that they spent together held more appeal. Did they have to get married? Couldn't things continue on how they were?

"I didn't think you wanted to get married?"

"Why?"

"I don't know, with our arrangement and everything, I didn't think you would be interested in anything serious."

"I would for the right person. You? Would you get married for the right person?"

"I don't think so. I mean, is there even a right person? It's not something I have focused on." This whole conversation made Madison feel uncomfortable. Dante would settle down for the right person, which it was clear it wasn't her. So even if there was a chance they continued as they were, there would always be the fear that he would meet someone else and end the arrangement.

She also didn't believe Dante wouldn't be able to handle it if they went full-on relationship. She knew it wasn't what he wanted. At least not with her which made her heart squeeze.

"You don't believe in soulmates?"

"No. I think a game is on. Do you want to go watch it?" Madison suggested.

Dante cocked his head to the side with a confused look on his face. "Sure." He pushed back from the table. "Let's clean up real quick, and then we can go catch the game."

They worked side by side and then went into the living room.

Chapter 12

Dante sat next to Madison on the couch. They touched from hip to thigh. It was like as if neither wanted to be far apart from the other. He held her hand in his lap and rested it on his thigh. He didn't want her to feel how hard he was, although he guessed she could tell.

She kept side eyeing him. If he didn't know better he would think she wanted to fool around instead of watch the game. But he knew she wasn't looking to have penetrative sex while she was on her period, which was fine by him. He never wanted to do anything to make her uncomfortable.

He wasn't watching the game, but instead processing what had happened over breakfast. He had opened up to her, and he had been comfortable talking to her, and he knew deep in his heart that she would never reveal what he said or throw it back in his face like Monica did when he told her he wanted to do something different.

But he also couldn't believe that Madison didn't believe in soulmates and didn't want to get married. It wasn't something he had expected at all. He didn't know where that left them.

"Aw, come on. That was a bad call," Madison said to the television screen.

Her voice brought him back, and he focused his eyes to catch the instant replay. She had been right. She knew her stuff when it came to basketball, and they spent the rest of the day enjoying the game.

They were quick to prepare an easy and light dinner for themselves, and Madison went to the bedroom to change and get her dance bag that he had set down inside of his bedroom.

She came out in her standard club uniform and looked at him, then down at the floor.

"What's up?"

"What are we going to do about my arrival? I don't feel comfortable with people knowing we're together."

That hit Dante like a punch in the gut. Was she ashamed of him? So much so that she didn't want people she knew to know. He knew she didn't have a problem going out with him in public where there was no one that they knew.

But if there was a high probability of a friend or co-worker seeing them, she didn't want to chance it.

"I don't want any more rumors to start at the club or for people to think this is proof I slept with you and am sleeping with you to get the headliner position."

Dante relaxed. It was more her reputation but still again, did that mean she assumed he would ruin her reputation? He got not wanting rumors. Because some people would take it to mean that she could be bought with money. Which he wasn't sure if she could. There was the fact that she had slept with him after learning he was the owner of il Signore. And she had mentioned money and how expensive things were.

Madison was strong willed and loyal to a fault. He couldn't believe she was still thinking of giving her brother a kidney when she was still in the running for the fashion competition and he knew she needed to spend all of her time there and not at his place with him.

She had still brought some sketch pads and pencils to work on at his place. He had gotten her a sewing machine so that they could spend more time together, but he had decided against giving it to her and had left it in the closet.

He didn't want her to feel like he was trying to make her stay at his place when that wasn't his intention. He wanted her to feel comfortable in his place and able to work on her designs when they were together, so she didn't lose time on her project.

But would this be the first and last weekend she would spend with him at his place?

If she didn't want to ride with him to the club or risk anyone seeing them that wouldn't be good for him.

His place was much further away than hers from the club and he knew she didn't have a car. Her trying to take public transportation would take her hours to get there when it wouldn't if she was at her place or was comfortable going with him in the car.

"Maybe you can drop me off at the bus stop on the way in and then I can walk from there to the club?"

Dante didn't want to say yes and that scared him. But he wanted to be able to show everyone that she was his. That Madison belonged with him and no one could tear them apart.

"Ok." Dante shrugged his shoulders and whispered. He didn't mean it or agree with it, but he understood it was her choice.

"Ok, great. I'm ready when you are."

"Sure, let's go." He wanted to reach for her hand but worried she would reject him. He was feeling vulnerable in a way he didn't like.

"Wait." She grabbed his arm and turned him back around to face her. "What's wrong?"

"Nothing."

"Aren't we past lies? Tell me what's wrong. Please."

"Are you embarrassed to be seen with me?" He was like a gawky teenager as he asked the question, but when he voiced it, he knew he needed to know the answer. It would determine if they had a future together.

It wasn't until now, that he realized how important it was to him to have some type of long-term future with Madison. He leaned towards wanting to marry her, but if she wasn't interested in marriage, as long as they were exclusive, he would be happy.

"Oh Dante." She turned into his body and she wrapped his arms around her. Then she cupped his face.

"I could never be embarrassed to be seen with you. You are an awesome guy. I love being with you. It's just my own hang-ups I have with people talking behind my back, but most of all thinking I got something not because I earned it but that I gave up something, sex, to get it. I'll be judged. No one will say anything to you. It will all be directed at me."

That made sense to him. He didn't want people to talk or to think poor of her. Which was his own reason for telling his cousins that the knowledge that he and Madison had had sex stayed in the room. She was just trying to protect herself the same way.

"Ok. I get what you're saying."

She rose up on her toes and kissed him. It was a peck, but he wanted more. He kept her in place and deepened the kiss. His hands slid up her sides to her ribcage and then up to her breasts.

He found her nipples already hard, and he rubbed his thumbs over them.

"Dante." She moaned. "We have to go or you'll be late.

He knew she was right, but he couldn't help himself. He gave her nipples a pinch and then released her.

"Dante." She begged this time.

He knew what she wanted, and he would give it to her. He picked her up and turned her around so her back was against the wall. He used the wall and his body to help support her. He lifted her up and she wrapped her legs around his waist. He could feel the heat that came from her mound, and he rubbed his suit-covered cock against it.

His mouth captured hers, and he used one hand to play with her nipple. He slid his hand under her shirt and pulled the cup of her bra down to expose the hardened peak. Dante kissed down her chin to the side of her neck and down her collarbone until he reached the tip, which he took his time with as he sucked into his mouth.

He flicked his tongue over the nipple and was gentle when he bit it as they rubbed their lower bodies together, he could tell Madison was close to coming and he moved one hand to her bottom to keep her from sliding down and then used his other hand to pinch the twin nipple and sent Madison out of control.

Her hips jerked against his, and her nails dug into his shoulders. He loved feeling the bite of her nails; it drove him wild. He slowed down as she came down. He hadn't come, but he didn't need to. Seeing Madison orgasm was pleasurable to him.

He let her down slow and allowed her to slide down his body.

"What about you?" And she dropped down to her knees, but he lifted her up.

"Seeing you come is enough for me. I don't need to come every time we're together. Come, let's go." He tugged on her arm. "We don't want to be late."

****

Madison walked in from the bus stop. She felt silly, as she looked around her to make sure no one had seen Dante drop her off at the bus stop. She was earlier than was normal for her usual start time because Dante needed to be in early.

She only had her dance duffle as her overnight bag was still at Dante's. She was halfway between the bus stop and the club when she turned back around. It would be more suspicious for her to show up early than at her regular time. She would walk home, if she had time, maybe work on something.

No, she couldn't do that. She would get lost in what she was doing and not show up for work. She would just walk back, maybe grab a glass of water if she had time and then head back either walking or catch the bus like her normal routine.

That was a better plan. She would walk home and catch the bus at her usual time. When she got to her place, Sabrina was there.

"Hey, what's the matter?"

"Nothing. I was looking for you. I called and texted but you never responded."

Madison looked at her phone. "Oh sorry, I was focused on something else and I didn't check my phone after. Is something wrong?"

"No, I guess not." Sabrina looked around at their surroundings.

"Do you want to come in and talk? We have time before we have to be at the club." Madison looked around too, wondering what Sabrina was looking for.

"Sure that sounds good. I need to get something off my chest."

"Oh, ok, sounds kind ominous," Madison joked.

"It isn't just some rumors going around."

"Rumors?" Again? What else could they say? Or was Sabrina now ready to apologize for the rumor she created.

"Nothing bad I guess, it's only started. I tried to tell them it wasn't true, but you know how people get a hold of something and don't want to let it go."

Madison let them in and put her dance duffle near the door before she walked further into her place. Sabrina followed.

"So, what is the rumor?" Madison didn't bother to offer Sabrina a seat.

"That you had been sleeping with Enzo, and then you dumped him for Dante, and that was how you got the headliner position."

"What? That's a complete lie. I never slept with Enzo or dropped him for Dante. That's not even how we made the decision for me to be the big act." Madison pushed off the wall she had leaned against.

"I didn't believe that, and I told them. I also know you haven't sex with anyone because you're still a virgin."

"Yeah…"

"Wait, did you have sex?"

Madison's face heated. She didn't want to discuss this with Sabrina. Or anyone for that matter. What had happened and was happening between her and Dante was private.

"That's why you've looked happier and why we haven't seen each other as much."

"We both have been busy with our fashion week projects. I don't know how you've been feeling, but for me the pressure has been intense."

"That's true, but you haven't been home the last couple of times I'd come by."

"I do visit Henry." Why had Sabrina been coming to her place so often? They were friends, but she didn't and it hadn't been typical for her to come by as much as she was seeming to suggest she had.

"How is he? I went to visit him a couple of times when I was looking for you. He seems to be improving."

"He is. Treatment is going well and knock on wood, he hasn't had any illness so we are going to find out when they will schedule the transplant." This was weird. Why had she looked for her at Henry's and he hadn't told her? Was something going on between them?

"Are you and Henry…?"

"Oh no. I only went because I figured you were there. I told him it was no worry to tell you and that I'd catch up with you later."

"Oh ok." Madison had been calling Henry because she hadn't had time with Dante and her fashion project. She had felt guilty and had told him so, but he had assured her that he was fine and to work on her project.

Of course she hadn't mentioned that she was spending time with Dante. That was a private experience that would soon turn into memories that she would cherish. She doubted they would be together much longer. Dante wanted a wife and kids.

That was something she knew she didn't want. At

least she believed it was a definite deal breaker for her, but now she wasn't so sure.

Madison looked at her watch. "Oh crap. I missed the bus. I'm going to be late."

"No worries. I can drive us both. We'll get there on time."

"Thanks." Madison meant it kind of. She wasn't sure if she wanted to spend more time while Sabrina probed into her life. It made Madison uneasy.

****

Madison had just put down her dance duffle when out of nowhere Dante appeared.

"Can I see you in my office?" He sounded pissed.

The other women in the back snickered at her and whispered behind their hands. She couldn't make out what they had said because she was focused on Dante's retreating back. He didn't even bother to wait to see if she could come. He left and expected her to follow.

She didn't like how he was treating her. Madison decided she would go up to see him when it would be her normal time.

She dropped off her music with the DJ and let Zoe know she would be right back. She went up the stairs to Dante's office. The door was cracked open and she knocked on it.

"Come in." His voice sounded strained.

She pushed the door open and found him seated behind his desk.

"Close the door."

She didn't know why he told her that. She always closed and locked the door behind her when she came in for one of their "talks." She did as he said and locked the door like usual.

"Come here." His hands were in fists on the desk.

That was the final straw. She didn't like his tone. It was an order or a harsh command. Not a statement or invitation.

"What's wrong?"

"Come here."

"No. I'm not a dog. Why are you talking to me like this?"

"Where the fuck were you?" His knuckles were white with how hard he was squeezing.

"First, I don't like your tone and second, don't cuss at me. I was at my place, why?"

"Why didn't you answer your phone?"

"I didn't hear it ring." She looked down at her phone to see all the missed calls and texts from Dante along with the ones from Sabrina.

"Why did you go home? You were supposed to walk here from the bus stop."

"Because I'm an adult."

"What is that supposed to mean?"

"I can do what I want. You're not my father."

"I know I'm not, but I'm your man." He slapped his hand down on his desk

"But you're not, and you're also being a dick."

"I'm sorry, I was worried."

"Why?"

"When you didn't get here, I worried that something had happened to you."

"Oh."

"Come here, please."

She walked over to him and he moved his chair from behind the desk to turn it to the side so that she could stand in the cradle of his thighs. He tugged her down onto his lap and wrapped one arm around her.

Madison was stiff in his arms. He cupped her face and looked into her eyes.

"I'm sorry. I was worried when you didn't come and then you didn't answer your phone. It drove me crazy. I was worried Enzo had confronted you again."

A chill ran down her spine at the mention of Enzo, but she melted in his lap. He had been worried for her. That had to mean he cared, and that made her heart swell.

He moved to cup both sides of her face and rested his forehead on hers before he pulled her in for a tight hug.

"I know you need to go. We'll do the same thing tonight. You leave with me at the end. You can come up here and wait. I'll keep my door closed."

"Ok." She kissed him, and he deepened the kiss until she pulled away for air. "I'm sorry too. I didn't mean to make you worry. I'll see you tonight."

Chapter 13

Madison went back downstairs to help Zoe out.

"Hey." Zoe's face was drawn and her lips were pressed together into a thin line.

"What's wrong?"

"I found out what the rumor is."

"It's that bad?"

"It has to do with you."

Madison turned from the bar top to look at Zoe. "What?"

"That you're sleeping with Dante."

"Sabrina told me. Why would they think that?"

"Because you go into his office every day after you get here. I told them as the main act you have to discuss things, but there is no getting through to them."

"Ah, yeah." Madison drew the words out. That was a good reason for her to be going into his office. She hadn't believed they would draw attention, but now she knew better. She would have to warn him before it got back to him, not that she believed he would or even could stop them from gossiping behind her back.

"That's right and every one of the dancers goes up at night to collect their money, just like you do. You just do it at the end of the night after you finish helping clean up the bar."

"Right." Madison realized that she and Dante should have come up with a plan together before they had

196

agreed to dating. Well no, they weren't dating. They were just sleeping together. It was different. There was no real relationship between them. Maybe a small friendship, but even then it was more like an acquaintance.

They were still getting to know each other. For what, she didn't know. It had to be for something else to do since they had now made the everyday deal.

"Well, it's whatever. People are going to think what they want to think. Besides, if we were sleeping together, why would we do it here where we would be easy to get caught?"

"I don't know why they didn't think that either because it makes total sense."

"I'm just going to ignore it."

Zoe took a deep breath.

"What?"

"There's more."

"Oh my what else?"

"That you had slept with Enzo to get out of the club rules."

"Ok, this is getting ridiculous now. Why would I be shifting between the cousins? Do they think I'm going to be with Lucca and Gabe too?"

"I don't know. That's just what they are saying."

"Well, I'm not going to let that bother me." Even though all the gossip and rumors was getting to her.

Madison turned around to pick up a crate of beer, she was done with the conversation and wanted time alone to process it. She wouldn't get time alone, until later while she waited for Dante to wrap up, if she decided to stay.

She might just go back to her place and wait for him

to come get her if it would help the rumors to die down. Anyway, by the time they had broken up, or went their separate ways, the rumors should have ended.

Madison shook her head. She always got sad thinking of the end of their relationship. But that was their whole arrangement. It wasn't meant to last no matter how much she wanted it to, and she needed to remind herself of this. It was not permanent. It was a temporary arrangement; they only had less than two months left.

Madison pushed through everything and did her sets and helped out behind the bar, but she couldn't shake away the gloom that sat on her weighing her down like a ton of fabric.

By the time the night was over, she just wanted to go home alone and eat ice cream and hide under the covers and cry.

She trudged up the stairs to Dante's office and found it looked smaller than normal. It was filled with Enzo, Lucca, Gabe and Dante. "I'll just come back later for my money, or I can get it tomorrow night."

"No need. They were just leaving." Dante gave a pointed stare.

"Give her the money. We'll wait. We need to finish this discussion." Enzo spoke as he stared at Madison.

She didn't know which was better, Enzo who ignored her or this nasty look. It would be him ignoring her. It was like he was undressing her while hating her at the same time. It made her skin crawl and she wanted to go and take a shower.

There was some kind of standoff here and it was as if she had walked into a hurricane of tension. It was swirling around ready to destroy anything in its path.

And now she had been sucked up into it.

Now she couldn't leave. There was a power play happening between Enzo and Dante, and she was stuck in the middle. She knew if she left, Enzo would win, and she didn't want that to happen so she stood there rooted to the spot.

"Fine," Dante said. "Madison, come here please."

She walked over thinking he had decided to send her away and he was going to give her the money and ask her to leave. She took a wide path around Enzo, her legs heavy.

Dante opened the drawer and added a stack of bills to another stack and handed it to her. She put it in her pocket and went to leave when Dante pulled her down onto his lap. She gasped and forgot the extra roll of money that was added.

"Dante."

"I'm bringing Madison. We're together. This discussion is over for me. Feel free to stay in the office and continue to talk, but I'm out." Dante set Madison down off his lap and stood up. She tucked the money in her pants, and Dante reached for her hand. She took it and they walked out hand in hand and walked to his car.

Madison had not expected that to happen at all. It made her feel good that Dante wanted his cousins to know she was his and that they were together. She couldn't keep the little skip out of her steps as she walked out the door with Dante.

She was in a relationship. She had never dreamed this day would come. But instead of putting her off, she was happy. In truth, she was ecstatic. It was as if fireworks were going off in her chest, and she was part of a big parade. She couldn't keep the smile off of her face.

She was glad she and Dante held hands. If not she might float away.

****

Dante had been pissed when Enzo had tried to pull rank on him. Who did he think he was? And to use the family to do it. Lucca had come to warn him, but it had been too late. He had sat at the desk and read the edict from the Don.

He wasn't to fool around with Madison anymore. If he wasn't serious enough to bring her to Lucca's engagement party then he needed to let her go and give Enzo a shot. What the fuck had that been? Enzo going behind his back.

He played on the fact that the Don wanted to see all of them married. But what Enzo still forgot was that Madison didn't want him. Even if Dante and her weren't serious, it didn't mean Enzo could replace him. It was Madison's choice who she wanted to date.

A choice he realized he took away from her because he assumed she wanted to be with him. He sat in the car next to her in silence, his mind spun until he couldn't take it anymore. He turned toward her.

"I can't believe we're together," Madison said. "I never—Never wanted this. Never could picture being in an actual relationship. Never would have chosen to put my heart in danger like this."

Dante couldn't believe how he'd taken it for granted that she wanted him when it was obvious she didn't.

"I'm sorry for saying that—"

Her face fell from the beautiful full-on grin she had. "Oh. I thought you meant it."

"No, I meant it. Of course I meant it."

"Then why are you apologizing?"

"I didn't ask you if you wanted to date me and go to Lucca's engagement party. I didn't even tell you there would be a party. I never ran any of this by you."

"That's ok. I figured you mentioned the party and stuff in the moment. I could tell something was happening and whatever it was, you would say anything so that Enzo didn't win. I didn't want Enzo to get the upper hand either."

Dante's heart squeezed so hard it could have burst. She didn't want to date him or go to the engagement party. He would have to tell them. Did she want to keep seeing him until the agreement was up, or was she done?

"I can tell them you don't want to go."

"Yeah." She looked out the window. "I think I want to go home. I guess you can drop my stuff off tomorrow at the club. If it's ok you can have Ed bring my money down."

Wow, she didn't want to see him anymore. Not even to get her money. "So I guess you want to get out of our agreement."

"I guess. We can keep going if you want. I thought you were done with me."

"Done with you. No." The band around his heart loosened. Maybe it was just a misunderstanding. "I want to be with you. Like in a full-blown relationship." He held his breath. He was putting it all on the line and she could reject him at any moment.

"Then why did you apologize for saying it?"

He reached across the console for her hand. "Because I didn't give you the choice to say if you wanted to do it, to be with me or not. I always want to give you a choice, and I'm sorry I took it away from you."

She turned to face him. "It's ok." She cupped his face with one hand. "It was too much to hope for. I want what we have together to be real too. Two consenting adults who enjoy being together and are exclusive."

That was a weird way to put it. "Good. Then it's official. We're a couple. Let's seal it with a kiss."

Dante leaned over, and Madison met him halfway. He deepened the kiss and then pulled her across the console and onto his lap where he could have better access to her. He wouldn't have stopped if it hadn't of been for the knock on his window that broke into his fog.

He looked out the window to see Lucca and Gabe stood there.

"I guess this is for real." Lucca leaned down.

"As a heartbeat."

"Congratulations, man. Way to lock a good lady down."

"Thanks, man. We're going to head home. See you guys later."

During the time he was talking to them, Madison crawled out of his lap and sat back in the passenger seat. He could feel the embarrassment flowing off of her in waves from being caught making out. It was cute and why he couldn't get enough of her.

****

Madison was light as a bubble. She was afraid she would pop. Her and Dante were an official couple. She wanted to pinch herself, but instead she pinched him.

"Ouch. What was that for?"

"I wanted to see if you were here with me or if it was a dream."

Dante rubbed his arm where she pinched him. "I

think you're supposed to pinch yourself."

"I know, but if you were a dream you would disappear when I tried to pinch you. Even if I'm dreaming, I'm still there. It seems silly to pinch myself."

She could tell Dante wanted to argue, but he could find no fault in her logic.

"See. I did the right thing."

"You could have tried to test it out some other way." He pulled her close. "Like a kiss."

She leaned into him. "Yes, but I would have been sad if I had tried to kiss you and you dissipated."

"Aww. Don't worry that I'm going to go anywhere." He lowered his head and she met him in the middle. She wanted to feel his lips on hers as much as she believed he wanted to feel hers on him.

Dante walked her backwards but she lost focus as a heavy fog settled around her head and blocked out anything else except the kiss they shared. The back of her knees bumped the edge of the bed, and she tumbled down with a surprised gasp.

He was on her before she could move. He loomed over her body. The sight of him as he hovered over her was arousing. He was all around her and she was warm, safe, and protected.

Madison wrapped her arms around his neck and pulled him closer for another kiss. Dante's hands roamed up and down her body and it wasn't until the cool air hit her chest that she realized Dante had removed her top and bra and kissed his way down her body as he tugged her jeans off and left her panties on.

He placed a kiss to the top of her panties before he kissed down one leg and up the other. He bypassed her special place to kiss back up her body and ended at her lips.

"I know we can't have sex yet. But if it's ok with you. I'd like to make you feel good. If anything bothers you, I'll stop."

Madison knew he would, but she wanted him so bad as long as he left her sex alone she was game for anything. "Yes, it's ok. I want you."

"And I want you too." He said before his head dropped and she found his mouth on hers. He dived into her lips like they were food and he was going to binge before going on a diet. He licked and nibbled his way across her mouth and down her body till he reached her breasts.

He teased her and circled around her breasts without touching her nipples.

"Dante, please."

He looked into her eyes. "How could I refuse you?" He dropped his head and licked and suckled one nipple while his hand circled, flicked, and pinched its twin. He sat in between her legs, and she rotated her hips on his bulge and she wished she could get it inside of her. The pressure from his cock on her sensitive clit and with what he did to her nipples, it wasn't long before the familiar feeling of an orgasm approaching rushed over her.

It crested and broke over her in ripples of pleasure as they eddied through her body in a continuous flow from her center and then out to her arms and legs and ended in her hands and feet.

"Oh, oh, oh, Dante," she keened as he slowed down his suckling and let her ride out the waves.

He kissed back up her body and placed a soft kiss her on her lips. He lay down on his side and pulled her close to him.

"That was nice. Thank you for always being so willing to give me pleasure without taking for yourself."

"I enjoy teasing you and hearing you moan. It's good for me, and gives me pleasure to give you pleasure. Come, let's get ready for bed."

Madison climbed off of the bed and padded to the bathroom to clean up and put on her nightie. She still didn't feel weird only wearing her period panties in front of Dante. They weren't the sexiest, but being with Dante she was sexy in anything. Or at least feel that way.

She paused to look at herself. She looked different. She glowed, but it wasn't just that this was different. It was the feeling of being loved. Well, maybe not loved but cherished.

It couldn't be love this soon, and either way she doubted it would ever amount to love. She figured they would still stay together until Dante got bored and moved on. She would let go when he was ready, but until then she would hold on with both fists.

She changed into her nightgown and panty set. This one a cobalt blue color and left the bathroom. Dante was getting undressed and ready for bed. He slept nude, with his cock on her ass as he spooned her. And her face didn't heat with embarrassment, but from arousal.

She climbed into bed, not wanting to dwell on the fact that she still wanted him with a burning passion. Would it ever die down? Dante went into the bath and came out a few minutes later with a toothbrush in his mouth.

"Did you already brush or do you want to brush together?"

"I already did, but next time I know to wait for you."

"Sounds good." And he disappeared back into the

bathroom, but not without giving her an eyeful of his tight, round ass.

Madison climbed into bed and lay on her side waiting for Dante to come back out. His feet made soft sounds on the tile when he left the bathroom and her body stiffened with tension. The bed dipped and he climbed in and pulled her close to him.

The tension eased out of her body as he kissed her shoulder, then her cheek, and then her lips. What was supposed to be a quick peck turned into something more. Like it had a habit of doing when they were together.

"Let's go to sleep. Good night, Madison."

She snuggled back into the cradle of his hips and closed her eyes. "Good night, Dante." And with that she drifted off to sleep thinking that she was in the running for most-loved girlfriend.

****

Madison and Dante decided to still keep their relationship private from the people at the club. Part of her was happy with that, as she didn't want to fuel the rumors already going around. But there was a part of her that worried if he didn't want a lot of people to know. Dante had to go away on business, so she was back at her place. She worked on her design and was going to go and visit Henry. Dante would be back tonight.

It had been torture being without him. She had become so used to sleeping with him at night that she could not fall asleep on her own. He called her every day while he was away and called before she went to bed without fail to tell her he missed her and for her to sleep tight and know he would come back to her soon.

Madison packed up what she had done on her garment. There was a steady progression and looked wonderful on her model. She loved the way it moved as the model walked. She had some finishing touches to do and some things that didn't look how she wanted that she had to change, but she was in a good place. She stopped and went to visit Henry.

She let herself into his place after she rung the bell and he didn't answer. She was worried he collapsed because she had seen his car and he wasn't one to go for a walk. He would sit outside so he might be on his balcony on the other side and didn't hear the doorbell.

Madison walked in and there were groans from upstairs. Her first image was that Henry had fallen and hurt himself and she ran up the stairs and opened the bedroom door to see something she didn't expect.

Sabrina was there and on top of her brother. It was clear they were in the middle of sex and she turned her back, embarrassed to have caught the scene.

"Oh, I'm so sorry, I heard the noise and figured you had fallen and hurt yourself and I was coming to help. No need to, uh, stop. I'll let myself out and catch up with you guys, uh, later." She closed the door back and ran down the stairs the way she had come closing and locking the door behind her. Her face was red.

Why hadn't they told her they were seeing each other? She wouldn't have minded and was in fact happy for them. She just wished they had been comfortable telling her so she wouldn't have walked in on them.

Madison wasn't a drinker, but she needed a stiff one after that sight. Lucky for her Sabrina had been on top, so she had only seen Henry's arms and legs but the sounds they had made were burned into her brain. She needed to take her mind off of it, so she headed back home.

She figured she would work on some more of her design. She knew Dante was coming home today, but he hadn't told her when. He said he would surprise her. She wanted to surprise him too. Her period had still been there before he had left so they hadn't been able to have sex.

She couldn't wait to have sex as an official couple. Would it be different? She let herself into her place and screamed. "Dante. What are you doing here?"

There were rose petals all over the place and he was in a suit and tie and held a bouquet for her. She ran to him and he caught her in his arms. Their lips found each other and they made out as if he had been gone for years instead of a few days.

She let her legs fall and he let her slide down his body. She could feel his arousal.

"You look handsome." This was a dark gray suit with navy blue pinstripes. It made his eyes look like storm clouds.

"Thank you. You look beautiful as ever. These are for you." He handed her the flowers.

"Thank you, I didn't expect you to be here now or I would have stayed." And not have caught her brother and Sabrina together.

"I couldn't wait to see you so I headed straight here."

"I wish I had known. I went to see Henry and I caught him and Sabrina in the middle of it."

"It?"

"Yeah. You know. It."

"Ohhh, they were having sex."

Her face heated, and the images and the sounds replayed in her head again. "Yeah."

"You're so cute." He kissed her nose. "I can see how it would be uncomfortable to see them like that. It will fade away."

"I hope so."

"I'm going to go home to put my things away and change. You get dressed up. I want to take you out for dinner and dancing."

"On a Wednesday?"

"We can't go another day because we're working."

He had a point there. "Ok. What time should I be ready?"

"Let's say I'll pick you up at six p.m."

"Ok, I'll be ready." She walked him to the door and they stood in the open doorway. She threw her arms around his neck and kissed him. He put his hands on her bottom and lifted her up before he sat her down.

"See you tonight."

"Tonight."

Madison closed her door and went to see what she was going to wear when her doorbell rang. She ran to the door thinking Dante had come back. "Did you forget your key—"

It wasn't Dante, but Sabrina. From the look on Sabrina's face, she was sure she had seen Dante leave her place.

"Sabrina, hey."

"Hey. I came here to apologize for thinking you were sleeping with Dante and for seeing Henry and not telling you, but it looks like you were fucking Dante for the top spot."

It was as if Madison had been slapped with the bitterness in Sabrina's voice.

"I did not. Dante and I got together after I became

the headliner."

"Why didn't you tell me when I asked you?"

"Why didn't you tell me you were seeing Henry when I asked you?"

Guilt and something else flickered across Sabrina's face. "It was new, and we wanted to keep it private."

"It was the same with Dante and me. We are still keeping it private, so please don't tell anyone at the club."

"Why don't you want people to know?"

"Because I don't want it to cause problems with the customers. Eric will think he can do what he wants. Besides, we don't think it's that important for the staff to need to know."

"The staff already thinks something is going on between you guys."

"And that's fine. They will figure it out when they figure it out." Madison looked at her watch. "Sorry I can't catch up with you more. Dante is taking me out tonight. I'll see you tomorrow. Maybe we can set up a time to chat."

"Yeah, I guess we could." Sabrina turned and left.

Madison showered and used her favorite body scrub. Because of the time she spent with Sabrina, she wasn't able to soak in the tub like she wanted but the shower and shower gel would do the trick. She rubbed lotion on her body and slipped into a blue dress. It was midnight blue, close to black. It was something she had designed herself.

She picked out some nude pumps when Dante walked in. He had on a suit and again, he looked amazing in it.

"You look beautiful; maybe we'll stay in tonight."

"Thank you. You look handsome. I love seeing you in a suit and tie, but I think you look hot in anything you wear."

Dante pulled her close and his hands ran up and down her body and he stopped at her breasts. "What's this?"

"Oh, just my ID card and some cash."

He looked down at her clutch. "Why don't you put it in there?"

"These bags are small, plus they are there for show versus functionality. I like to build a hidden pocket into all my creations. It's like a hidden surprise for the customer."

"Is it always in the same place?"

"No, I move it around depending on what the design is."

"Clever. Your own little guessing game for the consumer."

"Yep. Let me finish my makeup, and then I'm ready." Madison walked off to the bathroom and could feel Dante's eyes on her and she added an extra sway to her hips. She could swear he had groaned. Teasing would do him good.

Madison finished up her eyes and then painted her lips a warm red color. She left the bathroom. "Ok, I'm ready."

Chapter 14

Dante looked up to see Madison come out. She looked spectacular. His breath was taken away by her beauty and grace. "Let's go. I can't wait to get you home tonight."

"I can't wait for it either." She leaned in close to him and pressed her chest to hip into him to whisper in his ear. "My period is over." She nipped his chin.

"Maybe we skip dancing."

"We can't; you promised me dinner and dancing."

"You're right, but I'm going to have you for dessert."

Madison's center pulsed, and she placed her hand in his and then left her place. She locked up, and they headed to the car.

At the restaurant, they were quick to be seated. "Wow, this place looks amazing and expensive. You don't need to take me to some place so extravagant."

"I know, but I wanted to. You deserve it. Besides it's also a celebration. We are an official couple." They looked through the menu, ordered the food. This was the third time she had mentioned money, this time it was different though. She was saying he shouldn't be spending that much on her. Which one was it? Did she want him for his money, or did she care even if he didn't have any? What did she do with the extra grand he gave her each night she worked?

"How was your trip?"

"It went well. I made some changes to our food and liquor vendors for il Signore, and that went well."

"Oh that's good. What did you have to do?"

"I finished up our old contract and vetted the new vendors. They wanted me to be there to sign the contracts in person instead of by mail."

"Oh, ok."

"Yeah. I'm happy with how it turned out, even though it kept me away from you." He placed his hand on top of hers. "But enough of my stuff. How is your design going? Where is your pocket in your fashion week dress?"

"It's going well. I built a secret panel into the waist. I'm nervous as to how it will look in the finished project. I've never done one here as I think it's too bulky, but there was no other good spot."

Dante reached across the table for her hand. "I'm sure you will figure it out, and it will be wonderful."

"Thanks."

They went dancing until Dante had enough. "I'm taking you back home."

"I was waiting for you to ask." Madison panted and pressed herself into Dante which she had been doing all night. He couldn't wait to get her home and punish her with his cock. He could feel her beaded tips through the dress.

He wasn't sure if they would make it to his place, or if he would have to release some tension. But he would control himself. He wanted their first time as a couple to be special, and that was why he would wait until they got home and he could show her what he'd done to prepare for them.

He had expected her to still be on her period and planned on them to fool around, and he would be grateful for that. However, now that she was done with her cycle, he wanted to show her all the things he wanted to do to her and the way he was feeling for her that he wasn't ready to put into words.

They stumbled into the house and the closed door, when he had her dress unzipped and pooled at her feet. He helped her step out of it and just stared. She wore a white lace set and the color contrast was inviting.

He was quick replace her top with his hands as he palmed her breasts and found the tips ready for his mouth. She was still shorter than him even in her heels, but he liked her in them and couldn't wait to see them over his shoulders.

They moved as a unit together, and he picked her up and moved to the bedroom where he had rose petals strewn around on the floor and a large heart in the middle of the bed made out of red rose petals.

He placed her down in the center and, in slow motion, peeled her undies down her legs and off and tossed them away. She wouldn't need them anytime soon. He was quick to undress and watched her eyes heat as his body was exposed. He kneeled on the bed and climbed up between her legs.

Her eyes were focused between his legs and she reached for him, but he swatted her hand away in a playful way. He wanted to take his time. He kissed down her stomach and found her center glistening.

He couldn't help himself and he dived in, licking and flicking her clit before he lapped at her folds.

"Oh Dante, yes."

He could tell she was already close, but he didn't

want her to come too soon. The night was young, and they had plenty of time. He gave her one more lick from top to bottom and then turned her over on her stomach. She went to push up to all fours. He knew she was thinking he was going to take her from behind, but he had other plans.

His hand came down before she knew what was happening.

"Oh."

"Have you been playing with my pussy?" He was gentle when he slapped her ass again.

"No, Dante. You're all I want."

Her words were enough to undo him, and it was only by sheer will he didn't tell her he loved her or start to pump into her. "Good." He ran his hand down her ass cheeks and plunged two fingers inside her wet tunnel.

They both groaned. He pumped his fingers in her a couple of times before he pulled out. He licked his fingers clean and then licked her pussy until she came. He turned her over on her back as she came down.

He kissed her body from head to toe and everything in between before he lifted her legs over his shoulders. Seeing her heels still on made him hard as steel. He took his time and lined up with her entrance and with his last bit of control hanging on by a thread he went slow and fed his cock into her tight pussy.

When he was all the way in, he held still as her muscles adjusted and milked his cock. He slow pumped, and he leaned forward to lift her hips higher and kissed her. She kissed him back in a way he knew she was feeling the same emotions as him.

They didn't need to say anything. By the look on her face, he knew she could feel the love, and as her eyes went all dreamy, she kissed him slow and deep letting him know her feelings.

He couldn't hold back anymore and broke the kiss. He stared into her eyes he let her see the love, but he also could see it from her eyes, too. He increased his speed.

"Oh Dante, yes."

He knew what she wanted, and he increased his pace as her boobs bounced with every thrust. He leaned down and took a ripe nipple in his mouth, and Madison whimpered and her body shuddered. She was close again.

"Please. Come with me."

He increased his speed more and released her nipple with a plop to tease the other nipple before he let it go too. His mouth came crashing down on hers just as they both were gripped by a powerful orgasm.

He could see his awe mirrored in her eyes, and he balanced on his knees and released his hands to grab hers. They intertwined their fingers just as their climax ripped through them. She wrapped her legs around his hips and continued to meet him thrust for thrust as wave after wave after wave of pleasure rushed over them.

Nothing like this had ever happened to him before. This was a connected orgasm. They both experienced it together at the same time, but it was different than before when they came separately even at the same time.

This time it was as if the orgasm happened to them as a unit. They were trapped together as the orgasm washed over them. They held each other tight knowing that this was different, and they had crossed over into something powerful.

As the orgasm subsided, he lowered her legs and slid her heels off while they were still connected. He rolled over so he was no longer on top of her and he draped her body over his. Every time before this, they would get up and clean up, but it was by unspoken mutual agreement that they didn't move.

Even when Madison's pill alarm went off, they looked at each other and then snuggled in close while their bodies were joined. His heart swelled. Was she as ready to have a baby with him as much as he had been ready to have one with her?

They fell asleep like that.

Dante woke up to something tight and wet squeezing his cock. He opened his eyes to find Madison still asleep, but her pussy was awake as was his cock. He held still, not wanting to wake her and waiting for her to wake up.

When she did, he took her on their sides nice and slow as they faced each other, her leg thrown over his hip. The orgasm was gentler this time, but there was that same connection between them and their release. It only seemed to get better.

This time they got up to clean up and he took her one more time in the shower, before he decided she needed her rest. They made breakfast together and spent a lazy day in bed and on the sofa and watched tv together. It didn't matter what was on, just that they were together.

Before they knew it, it was time to leave for the club. They both forced themselves to change into real clothes and left. This time he didn't drop her off at the bus stop, but they walked hand in hand and he walked her to the bar. He didn't care what others saw and he didn't want Madison to think he was trying to hide her.

If the girls there wanted to start some shit, he would deal with it. No one was going to bully Madison. Besides he was tired of them sneaking around like what they were doing was wrong or needed to be hidden.

He tilted her chin up and kissed her on the mouth. "See you tonight. Come up after you're done." He ended it with a kiss and then turned and left.

****

Madison turned around, and Zoe stood there. She worried how she would take it.

"Congratulations. You deserve some happiness and love in your life."

"Thank you." Madison didn't want to tell her there was no love between them, but she couldn't lie. Not even to herself. Something had shifted between them. First the intertwined orgasm and then by mutual agreement for her not to take her birth control pill that first night.

Her hand went to her still flat belly. She had taken the pill early the next morning, but she wasn't as unsure about if she would one day be growing life in there. She still wasn't sold on the idea of having kids, but she wasn't as put off by it as before. Time would tell what her and Dante's relationship would be and if they would decide to bring kids into their relationship.

The rest of the night was not so uneventful.

Madison went to the back room to change for her sets, like normal. But unlike normal, all the girls were back there. It was weird because they had never all been in the back room at the same time. Several girls would be on the floor and at least one person would be on the stage.

Madison went to the changing room, but the door was locked. She knocked on the door, and Sabrina answered. "Be out in a bit."

"Brina, do you know how long you'll be? I need to

change for my sets."

"Oh, I think I'll be a while. Why don't you change out there?"

The rest of the girls snickered and stared at Madison.

"Yeah, why don't you change in front of us," Brittney said. "You don't have to follow club rules, so we should get to see what the boss sees in you."

"For now," Gina said.

Madison's eyes widened as she looked at Gina.

"What?" Gina angled her head. "You can't expect that you're going to be together forever. Dante's happy to have a virgin."

"Yeah, he is just having fun with you. He can train you to do what he wants," Brittney added.

"Until he gets bored." Amber spoke up. "My first was like that until he moved on."

"Oh, look at you. You thought you were special. Just because you gave it up doesn't make you special or mean what you have is going to last. I doubt you'll make it three months," Gina inserted.

Sabrina's trademark snort came from the other side of the door. Madison didn't know what to do. She needed to change for her set, but she wasn't going to change in front of them. She couldn't go up to Dante's office to change because that would start more problems between her and the other girls.

She needed to decide what she was going to do, she would be late for her set if Sabrina didn't come out.

"What are you going to do? You're out of time. Might as well change in front of us. Don't want to make boss upset by being late," Brittney said.

"Yeah, it wouldn't look good for the headliner who is fucking the boss for the spot to be late for her stage time," Gina insinuated.

Madison knew now Sabrina wasn't going to come out in time. She undressed in front of the girls. It wasn't as if she needed to change clothes per se. She had her outfit on under her jeans and t-shirt, but she would be more comfortable disrobing in private.

She took off her shoes fast and then slid her pants down her legs before she removed her shirt to show the racer back tank underneath. She sat down on the bench to put her heels on.

"You've got to be kidding me," Gina said. "You wear your outfit under your clothes, and you still want to change behind closed doors. What a prude. I can't see that Dante stays with you for long." And Gina sauntered out. The other girls followed behind her and left the room.

The lock to the changing room door clicked and Sabrina opened the door. Madison didn't know if she wanted Sabrina to say anything to her or not. By now, she knew she wasn't going to apologize, but so far Sabrina hadn't said anything rude to Madison's face.

"They're right, you know. You're not Dante's type, and once the novelty of having a virgin wears off, he's going to dump you. You can't think that you satisfy him. He'll be done with you soon." And Sabrina slinked out.

Madison wished Sabrina hadn't given her opinion. Were they right? Madison knew the other women were jealous and full of it, but their words mirrored her own insecurities and fears. Did Dante only stay with her because she had given him her virginity? Would he get bored of her and dump her soon?

Madison had never been a girlfriend before, so she had no clue if what she and Dante were doing were things every other couple did. And why were the other girls so upset? Had they slept with Dante too?

She didn't think they would be together forever. Dante wanted marriage, but would their time together be over faster than that?

She didn't have time to dwell on it. She pushed it aside and squeezed it into the box where she kept her fears and doubts and went out to perform. She couldn't let what had happened affect her performance, or they would be winning and Madison couldn't let that happen.

The sets went as well as could be expected. Dante was there for them like he always was, but instead of looking for his eyes, she avoided them. This time when she went to the room, it was empty. She used the empty changing room to redress. When she left, Enzo stood inside the room.

"You think because you gave him your virginity that he's going to keep you?"

"Enzo, this isn't something that we need to discuss. If you'll move. I'm needed at the bar."

"I can't believe you gave it up the first time you met him. I guess you're just a slut in disguise. He's going to use you and be done with you. You don't think Ms. perfect Madison can fit in Dante's life forever. I bet he didn't even trust you enough to tell you he's part of the Bianchi crime family." Madison opened her mouth to speak, but no words came out. Enzo chuckled. "I can see that he didn't. I bet you didn't know you were getting fucked by a mobster. Our uncle, Lucca's dad, is the head of the family."

"No."

"Yes."

"That's not true. Dante paid protection money."

"Ha, is that what he told you?"

"Well, no. He didn't say that."

"So that was something you told yourself to make you feel better when you were getting fucked by a bad boy." He moved into her space. Madison stepped back, unsure what he was going to do. She looked around behind him, but no one else came into the changing room. She wanted to push him away, but didn't for fear of what he would do.

"Let's see how long you two last." And he turned and stomped out.

Madison was left standing alone in the room. Things had been so promising this morning, but now she didn't know what to do. If she knew for sure that Dante was in the mob, could she continue to see him knowing what he was? In her heart, she still wanted to. From what the other girls had said, her time with Dante was limited anyway. He hadn't promised her forever and either way he still wanted to be married and Madison didn't. And there was the small matter of kids. She had woken up in the night and taken her birth control pill. Better late than never.

****

Dante noticed that something was off with Madison, but he didn't know what the cause was. Before her set, there had been no girls on the floor which was unusual. During her sets, she did a good job of looking around the room, but when their gazes connected they held for a few seconds, but this time hers danced away, as if she was afraid to look at him.

He hoped it didn't have something to do with Enzo. Enzo had been in but disappeared after Madison was done, and Dante hadn't seen him since.

When Dante got back to his office. He found Madison inside on the couch. Her legs were curled underneath her and she stared off into space, with one hand touching her hair. He closed and locked the door behind him and walked over to her. She didn't react, like she didn't hear him.

"Hey." He reached for her shoulder.

She jumped and looked at him. Fear and wariness crossed her face. He knelt down in front of her and she pulled back.

"What's the matter?"

"Are you part of the mafia?"

Dante was caught off guard with the question, but he wouldn't lie to Madison. "Yes. Why?"

"You said you owned il Signore."

"I do. It's part of the family businesses."

"When you said family, I believed you meant like a real family."

"We are a real family."

"You're a mob family?"

"Well, yes." Dante had no idea what brought this on, but from the look on Madison's face it didn't look good for their relationship.

"So I'm sleeping with a mobster?"

"If that's how you want to put it, then I guess yes."

"What do you mean if that's how I want to put it? You're telling me it's the truth."

"The truth is you're dating me." He put his hands on his chest. "Dante."

"Who is in the mob."

"Yes. I happen to be in the mob."

"I didn't know you were a criminal."

This wasn't going well. "Madison, baby."

"Don't 'Madison, baby' me Dante. I told you I didn't want to be on the wrong side of the law."

"Technically you're not."

"I don't think that would hold up in a court of law."

"Just because you're dating me doesn't mean you are on the wrong side of the law. Where is this all coming from?"

"Enzo told me what your family business is after I finished my sets."

"Of course he did." Dante wanted to find his cousin and beat him. "So what does this mean for us?"

"Why didn't you tell me?"

"Enzo said in high school you, uh, didn't do anything illegal or against the rules, so I didn't know how you would take it."

"Not well."

"I can see that."

"I was sure it was just rumors that the club was run by the mob."

"Well, it's true. I would never put you in a situation where you could get in trouble, and I'm in the process of cleaning things up."

"Yeah, you mentioned that. Was that the reason for your business meeting?"

Dante could feel himself relax. She hadn't run away. Maybe she would stick it out with him. "Yes. I'm cleaning up our businesses so that everything is law abiding." Well, at least looked like that to the feds.

"But you're not doing it for me are you?"

"Well, no. I had this in motion this before we got together. I told you this, remember."

"Yeah."

"And from our weekend at my place?"

"Yeah. You said several times you were working on making changes, and that you were going to do something else." She touched his face. "Ok. I trust you. I trust you'll keep me safe."

He kissed her palm. "Of course I will. I would never put you in harm's way."

"I know that. I believe it here." She touched her heart with his hand. "I'm sorry I freaked out a little. Well, a lot. But I don't know what to believe anymore."

"It's ok. It's understandable. You can trust me. I have a job offer with a brokerage firm that I'm going to take. I'm going to leave the family." If they let him leave.

"I want to be with you."

His heart unlocked, and he leaned forward. "I want to be with you too." He gave her soft kisses that teased.

"Dante."

"I know, baby. Let's go home." He stood up and took her hand and they went to the car.

****

Madison sat next to Dante in the car. He was holding her hand with one hand as he drove with the other. They were headed back to his place. The day hadn't ended like she would have pictured it in the morning, but at least it was better than what it could have been after her run in with Enzo and the other girls at the club.

Dante was right. She wasn't dating the mafia; she was dating Dante the man. The mob tie was like a job and a family he was born into. He didn't choose that life, and he told her he was taking active steps to get out of it on his own. Before he had met her.

Dante hadn't tried to lie to her or tell her she was overreacting, which she appreciated.

"What do you want to do tonight?"

"You want to watch a movie?"

"Yeah. That might be nice."

"I'll play one of my favorites."

"Does it have a lot of explosions in it?"

"I'll let you see for yourself."

Madison smiled. They would be ok, for as long as they lasted. And she would enjoy every moment of it.

****

Madison went back to her place. She needed to put some finishing touches on her project.

They were doing interviews that week, and hers was scheduled for Friday at noon.

Her phone rang. It was Henry. They hadn't talked since the Sabrina encounter. "Hello."

"Hey, I wanted to let you know they scheduled surgery."

"Oh, that's great, Henry. Let me get my calendar and add it to the schedule. When is it?'

"This Friday at ten in the morning."

"Oh no. I have my interview with the fashion house that day. Let me see if I can switch with someone. Either way, I'll be there."

"Let me know if you can't switch, and I can see if they can reschedule."

"No, don't do that. We don't want to push it back. I'm sure they'll understand.

Madison got off the phone with Kristy. They didn't understand. It didn't matter that she was donating a kidney. They told her it was a prime, once-in-a-lifetime opportunity, and that if she didn't make it, it would count against her in the running.

They did say she could switch with someone else if they were willing, but they wouldn't open up any new dates or times for her.

She knew Sabrina would be her best option, especially since she and Henry were dating she would want him to get the kidney and would be willing to switch with her.

"Hey, Brina, Did Henry tell you his transplant was scheduled?"

"Yeah, for Friday. What are you going to do? isn't that your interview date?"

"I'm going to do it. I can't not give him the kidney." That would be selfish if she were to do the interview instead of being there for Henry. What would people think of her?

"Wow. I can't believe you're going to give up the opportunity to work at AS house of fashion."

"Well, I was hoping to switch with you. I talked to them, and they said I'm not out of the running, but it will knock me down if I can't interview. It all counts for points."

"I can't switch. Sorry."

"Why not? It's just one day earlier. If it has to do with work at the club, I can talk to Dante."

"I'm sure you could *talk* to Dante, but it isn't that. This is a competition, and I'm in last place. I need anything I can do to get ahead. Sorry." Sabrina hung up. It had irked Madison more the way she had stressed talk as if she would just sleep with Dante to get him to do what she wanted, which wasn't the case.

Even though it sucked. She got where Sabrina was coming from. It was a competition and it was everyone for themselves, but she figured because her and Sabrina were friends or at least had been friends outside the competition and she was dating Henry that she would do it for her and for Henry. She should have known. Sabrina had already showed Madison her true colors the night she wouldn't leave the changing room. Now it was time for Madison to believe what she was seeing. The friendship was dead.

Chapter 15

They had been dating for over a month. Later that night as they were getting ready for Lucca and Ainsley's engagement party, she shared the conversation she had with Sabrina with Dante.

"Are you serious? You've worked hard towards this, are you going to throw it away?"

"I'm not throwing it away. I'm still in the running."

"This isn't going to make people think less of you because you don't do it."

"Of course, it won't, because I'm going to do it." She clipped her last earring in and turned to look at Dante.

"I don't think it's a good idea to throw your dream away or maybe throw it away to do this. They can reschedule the surgery. I'm not saying don't do it, just not in place of your dream."

"I don't want to keep going over this anymore." This was their first tiff, and she didn't want to have it when she would meet his family for the first time. They didn't need to be snippy with each other.

"Ignoring it won't make it go away."

"I'm not trying to ignore it. I just don't want to have this fight right now."

"Ok." He pulled her into him and kissed her forehead. "I'm sorry. I don't want to fight either. You look exquisite." He moved her away with his hands at her hips to take in her dress.

This one was fire engine red with an asymmetrical neckline with a cut out in the front and a keyhole cut out in the back.

"Where is your pocket in this one?"

She flipped up the hem of her dress to show him the hidden pocket.

"Are you sure it isn't higher?"

Madison looked down and lifted her dress up higher.

"Here, let me help you."

She smacked his hand away. "We're going to be late." She was already on high alert because not only would she meet Dante's parents for the first time, but she was going to be surrounded by people who lived a life of crime. What had she gotten herself into?

****

Dante was nervous as they pulled up outside the restaurant. He hoped everyone got along with Madison. He planned on making her a permanent fixture in his life. She hadn't taken her birth control pills for two weeks now. Was she pregnant yet? If not, it wouldn't be for lack of trying.

But they still had time. They had made it through their first fight, well, second, if you counted the one when she walked home instead of to the club and he had been worried she had been hurt.

Two fights and the mafia talk and they were still together. It wasn't a lot, but they had communicated well with each other and that was the most important part. Dante led Madison into the restaurant's back room for parties and special occasions.

In the room were his parents and Lucca's mom and dad along with Lucca and Ainsley. Gabe and his parents were there, and so were Enzo's parents, but Enzo wasn't there. Dante let some of the tension run out of his body. Maybe he wouldn't show. He hadn't gotten a chance to confront Enzo for telling Madison they were in the mob.

He didn't want Enzo making a scene or doing anything to upset Madison.

Dante introduced her to everyone and then left her with Ainsley. The men were going to a backroom to discuss some things.

"Be right back." He kissed her lips and disappeared.

In the back of the back room, they gathered around a table. They were using the get together to give a status update.

"So far I have just a quarter of the finances left to turn over. Real estate has new books. The clubs and restaurants have new books. I'm having trouble with Enzo's side, and I haven't been able to get in touch with him. I've done as much of the new books as I can without his input." Dante looked around the room.

"That all sounds good. He should be here soon." The Don looked around the room

"Do we know if he found the mole?" Lucca said.

"Not that I know of, but maybe that's why he is late," Enzo's dad said.

"Let's wait for a few to see if he shows. Someone send him a message," said Don Calo

****

Madison stood next to Ainsley unsure of what to say. The older women looked at them, but none approached. They had been kind when she was introduced. Well, everyone except Enzo's parents. Her nerves were out of control to know she was in the presence of the mob.

Did Ainsley know? Madison suspected she did since she was marrying Lucca who was the Don's son according to Enzo.

"So, how long have you and Lucca been together?" She rubbed her hands up and down her arms even though it wasn't cold in the room. There were some rough-looking men standing around. Madison could see their guns, which scared her on a different level. Her hands were clammy, and her heart raced. Her eyes darted around the room and took in everything and nothing at the same time.

Why did they need guns at an engagement party?

"Not long. Around two months."

"Wow, that is fast. I guess when you know, you know."

"Well, my dad lost me in a bet that he was sure he would win, and lucky for me they aren't into trafficking and Don Calo wanted a wife for Lucca and figured I would make a good one and here we are."

"Wow." That was not what she had expected.

Were the guns to keep Ainsley from leaving? "Do you want to be with Lucca?"

"At first no, but now I do. You and Dante?"

"Close to eight weeks." Although most of that was when they had their arrangement with each other. They had only been official for around four weeks. But no one needed to know that.

The door opened, and Madison turned around to see Enzo enter. She had been curious as to where he was. He headed straight for them instead of the back room where the other men were.

"Ainsley, I need to speak to Madison in private."

Madison didn't want Ainsley to go, but she didn't

think grabbing the woman's arm and begging her to stay would be a good look. Even in front of witnesses, she didn't want to be around Enzo.

"Sure, I was just getting ready to head to the ladies' room. Nice meeting you, Madison. Look forward to seeing you around." With that she gave a wave and left the room.

Madison backed up. "Enzo, I don't think we have anything to say to each other."

"Maybe, but I bet you didn't know Dante has been giving you extra money for your services." Enzo, moved into her space.

"What do you mean services? And what extra money? I earned all of that."

"You know, you're lying on your back for him. Or maybe you're on top, or does he take you on all fours?"

Madison went to slap him, but he caught her hand this time.

"He's been adding a grand to your money."

"No."

"He did it that day you guys decided you were dating and not just fucking. That extra ball of money was from his private stash."

Madison tried to pull her hand away, but she knew what he was saying. She had remembered the time Dante had added another bundle to her money but never asked. And she had noticed she was getting a grand extra than what she expected and it was consistent, but brushed it off as it being due to the headliner position. She yanked her hand out of Enzo's grip.

"Even so. I'm still not going to date you."

"What's your price? Two grand and I can get you on your back? Is there a family discount?"

At that moment, the guys came out of the back room.

****

Dante noticed Enzo next to Madison, and then she took her hand from Enzo, and he made a beeline for them.

"What's going on here? Why did you touch Madison?"

"I was telling her how you've been giving her an extra grand for her bedroom services. But I guess you guys don't just keep it in the bedroom. I was asking if there was a family discount or if she is running any specials."

Enzo hadn't finished when Dante slammed a fist in his face.

Madison screamed. "Dante, don't." She tried to pull on his arm. "Dante. Stop. That's what he wants."

Gabe pulled her away from Dante, just as Enzo sent a punch that Dante dodged before he headbutted Enzo and knocked him into the table. Plates and silverware clattered to the floor as the two rolled around on the broken dishes.

Madison tried to get to Dante, but Gabe held her firm. "I need you to stay here."

"Can't you do something?" She looked up at him.

Lucca had waded in and tried to get a hold of the two of them, along with the other men.

"Stay put." Gabe left her to grab Dante.

Ainsley came to stand next to her. "Whoa. What did I miss?"

"Enzo being a dick."

"This is only the third time I've met him, but that tracks."

The men were able to separate Dante and Enzo after some time. Enzo looked worse for wear. Dante still tried to get back to Enzo when Madison ran over to him. "Dante, stop. It doesn't matter what he says. I want you. I choose you."

Dante stopped fighting to get away and looked at her. "Please, let's go home." She held out a hand to him, and he took it. Lucca and Dante's dad released him and they walked out of the restaurant and to Dante's car.

Madison was feeling stupid in the car ride back to Dante's. She hadn't let Enzo get in her head like last time when he told her they were in the mafia, but she knew he wasn't lying that Dante had added money to her cut.

How could she have been so blind? She had wanted to believe that because she was the headliner and doing three sets. Combined with the bartending and tips had accounted for the extra money.

But no. Dante added extra money. She wasn't as dumb as Enzo believed she was though. She knew he wasn't paying her for sex. Her and Dante both enjoyed having sex with each other, and there was no need for payment.

She knew he was trying to help her, and she should be thankful, grateful for it even. She had needed a nest egg and to help Henry with his medical bills plus if her dad needed something and her mom had spent the money she would buy it or pay the bill for him.

But it was her choice to take it or not, and he had taken it away from her. He said he wouldn't do that and he did. She was like an ungrateful baby. She should have stayed and ignored Enzo. She knew what he was trying to do, and she let him win. She followed Dante into the house.

"Madison—"

"Dante—"

"You go first," Dante said. He placed his hands on her hips.

"I'm sorry I let Enzo get in my head, but I'm still upset with you for adding money to my split. I know you were trying to help me, but I want to—No, I need to do this on my own."

"I'm sorry I went behind your back and did that. I won't do that again." He kissed her nose.

Madison slid her hands up Dante's chest to wrap around the back of his neck. "I'm also sorry I ruined the engagement party."

"It's ok. It wasn't ruined. Everyone is fine, we're family." Dante's hands moved to cup her bottom and bring her in closer.

"Yeah, but I'm ashamed that I lashed out and tried to hit Enzo. That wasn't right."

"But you've hit someone before, right."

She looked away. Did he know Enzo came to her place?

"Let's be honest with each other. If we are, no one can come between us."

"Enzo came to my place the night we were going to spend our first weekend together at your place a few weeks ago and tried to kiss me. He wouldn't take no for an answer, so I slapped him and then kneed him out of the door."

"I figured something like that happened. I want you to know you can come to me if something like that happens again."

"I don't want to come between you guys. Even though my family is dysfunctional, I still know family is important. Especially for you.

"That's true, but you're important to me too." He pulled her closer to him. "Don't leave me, ok?"

"Ok."

They kissed and made up. When they came up for air, Dante said, "Let's get you something to eat."

"That's ok. I'd prefer to stay in." She undid his buttons and then tie, she let everything fall off his shoulders and down to the floor when her phone rang. "Sorry, I have to take this. It's Henry."

"What's up?"

"They found a spot on my liver."

"Oh no."

"Yeah. They want me to do a biopsy instead of the kidney transplant first. I might need to do a liver and kidney transplant. It depends on what they find. I looked at rescheduling the biopsy appointment. They can also do it next week."

"No, don't change the appointment, that's fashion week. I won't be able to do it then. This Friday works for me.

"But wouldn't you be downgraded? Besides you don't have to come for it, it's a routine procedure."

"I will, but I can't not be there for you."

"Maybe you should, take the job for me, that would make me happier than you giving me a kidney, or for you to show up for this procedure. You don't have to be there the whole time if you want to come. You can still do the interview and then come when I'm out of surgery. We all need you to get this job. Your bartending doesn't make enough to cover Dad and me."

"I can't do well in the interview if I'm worried how you're doing. No, I don't want to hear it. Dante already told me what he thinks. I don't need your opinion either. I'm doing this, end of story." Was the only reason he wanted to change it was because he wanted to help her secure the job that would net him more money from her?

"Fine, come over so I can give you the pre-surgery instructions. I'll need you to take me for the liver biopsy so that you can drive me home and take care of me."

"Sure, of course. So it will still be this Friday at noon?"

"Yes."

"Ok, we'll be right over."

"We?"

"Dante will bring me."

Dante lifted an eyebrow at her, but she knew he would agree.

"Thank you. I want to meet this guy who is going to be taking care of you. Also Dad and your mom will be there."

Madison's jaw tightened. Dante was still in his suit pants from the engagement party. She could tell it was expensive and her mom would know too. She hoped her mom didn't embarrass her. "Great, we are on our way."

She hung up and then looked at him.

Dante redressed himself, but he left the tie off. "Come, you can tell me how to get there."

"Do you want to maybe change clothes?"

"Why? Are you going to?"

"No, but that doesn't mean you can't change."

"I'm not going to change. We're wasting time. What is this have to do with anything?"

"Ok. I have to warn you my parents will be there too, and my mom might ask you for money, just so you know."

"I think I can handle myself."

"I don't think you can't. I just wanted you to know and know that I don't expect you to give it to her if she asks. I would prefer if you didn't or she will keep asking."

"Noted. Let's go."

****

Dante arrived at Henry's place and followed Madison up the apartment steps. Henry's place was better than what Madison was living in thanks to Madison. It made Dante sick how her family took advantage of her and played on her sense of duty.

He hadn't seen one of them offer to help her with anything. But she was out there busting her butt and willing to give up her chance at what she wanted most for her brother, who had given up what for her?

She knocked on the door. He remembered her being embarrassed at catching him having sex with Sabrina and figured to be on the safe side she wasn't using the key. He couldn't resist teasing her though.

"I think if your parents are there you won't catch him doing anything."

Her face darkened, and she looked at him with widened eyes. "Thanks for reminding me, not. I'm not using my key so my mom doesn't know Henry and I have keys to each other's places. If she did, she would make a copy and come into my place when I'm not there."

The door opened, and there stood a tall bald black man. It made sense that Henry was tall because he had been a pro basketball player.

"Hey, glad you could make it." He gave Madison a hug and then extended a hand to Dante. "Henry."

"Dante."

"It's nice to finally meet the man that is making my sister so happy. Come on in. Our parents are back in the living room."

Dante trailed behind. He didn't like others walking behind him. He liked to be in the back so he could take everything in. He might not enforce or get his hands dirty, but he still had the family way ingrained in him.

The living room was furnished with black furniture and blue accent pieces. It was neat. A pet peeve of Dante's was messy places. On the sofa was an older gentleman. He knew he was tall even though he was seated. As far as Dante could tell, Henry resembled their father.

Madison took after her mother and he could see why Madison's dad gave her everything she wanted to the detriment of his daughter. She was shorter than Madison but still had a trim figure. Her hair was the same reddish brown that Madison's was and her eyes were hazel, which explained Madison's gold flecks.

He knew her dad was sick so he walked over and leaned down to shake his hand. "Hi sir, I'm Dante."

"Madison's boyfriend. You know she's never had a boyfriend before. I hope you're treating her well."

Dante looked at Madison. He hadn't known he was her first relationship. But he believed she had been saving herself.

"Dad." Her eyes were big and imploring. "Way to embarrass me."

"I just want to make sure he knows and doesn't try to take advantage of you. I know how these young fellows behave."

"Milford, that's enough." Madison's mom stood.

"I'm Elaine. It's nice to meet you."

Dante went to shake her hand and she stepped inside his arms and gave him a hug that was too friendly. Dante had an idea as to why Madison never had a boyfriend.

"Why not a hug?" She looked up at him and tried to rub against his crotch area. He stepped back, setting her away from him.

"We're close to family." She patted his chest, unwilling to take the hint. "You smell nice. Is that newest high-end cologne from France? The name eludes me."

"Yes."

"And you're wearing a suit from that new designer that's been in the news, is that right?"

"Yes."

"Madison, let me take a look at you. Did he buy you this dress? It's a nice design. I haven't seen anything like it. I don't recognize the brand."

"It's one of my own."

"Oh. Well, maybe he will buy you something nicer. Can't have my daughter wearing handmade clothes." She moved back to sit next to her husband.

Dante couldn't believe she had the nerve to put down Madison's hard work. He looked around at the hurt expression on Madison's face.

"Lots of people would be willing to wear Madison's handmade clothes. Some of her designs will be shown at fashion week."

"Yes, we know." Madison's mom tugged at the bottom of her dress. "I got the tickets, Madison. We will be there to see the latest and greatest."

"And Madison's work as well." Dante spoke up.

"Of course, we will try to stay to the end for the amateur hour."

Dante realized there was no point in saying how hard Madison worked and that it was more than just amateur hour as she put it.

"I still need to find something to wear." Her mom smoothed her hands down her dress again while giving Dante the eye.

"Mom, I have a design that I wanted you to wear."

"Something you made?" Madison's mom didn't even bother looking away from Dante to answer her.

"Yes."

"No, thank you. You know I only wear designer pieces."

"I am a designer."

"Not famous, dear. Anyway, enough of this. Henry, what did you call this meeting for?"

Henry cleared his throat but said nothing about what Madison's mother had said. "I brought you here to discuss the biopsy. Even though I'm stronger and they scheduled me for this Friday, there is a risk that I won't make it or that they find something else. So I wanted you to be prepared if I don't make it out of surgery."

"Don't say that. Every surgery has that risk. Same with me." Madison pointed to her chest.

Dante's heart constricted at the image of Madison dying while giving something to her ungrateful family.

"I didn't come here for an 'I might die' conversation." Madison's mother looked at her watch.

"It's something that we need to be aware of and also the fact that because of the risk, you might not want to follow through on the kidney transplant, and miss your interview slot. I mean I'm not sure on the recovery time for you. Will you still be able to show your design? Could it go on without you? We need you to get this job."

Henry looked around the room. "Also, there will be nothing for you to do while they are doing the biopsy. So you could drop me off, use my car to do the interview, and then come back and get me once I'm out of the recovery room.

"I'm not changing my mind."

Dante wished she would. He would talk to her when they left.

"An interview, dear. What for? I'm sure your nice young man will take care of you. No need to get a job." Madison's mom winked at him.

"Dante isn't here to take care of me. The interview is for the fashion house."

"Oh, that. Yes. I'll be happy when this is over and you move onto something else. I want to be able to say something other than my daughter is a seamstress. What do you, Dante?"

"I work in finance."

"Nice. Keep him around, Madison, and keep him close or he might find someone more experienced."

"I forgot I have an early appointment tomorrow."

"On a Sunday?"

"Money never sleeps. It was nice to meet you." He turned around and reached for Madison. She walked over, and he wrapped an arm around her, and she leaned into him. He kissed the side of her head.

"Don't worry. I always have you." And he would for as long as she let him be a part of her life. He would be there for her.

Chapter 16

Madison followed Dante out. Why was she never good enough? Only Dante had stood up for her against her mom. He might have only did it because he appeared to feel sorry for her. No matter how hard she tried or what she did, it wasn't enough.

Even if she won the competition, her mother would have something to say. At least Dante didn't fall for her mom's tricks. Her mom assumed she was too stupid to know that any boy she brought over or who asked her out ended up sleeping with her mom.

Her mom was the reason she never had a boyfriend and was a virgin. She looked over at him as he drove them back to his place. She could tell he was upset. She put her hand on his thigh and squeezed it.

She supposed that he was mad for her until he took her hand off his thigh. Then she realized he was mad at her, but why?

"Why are you mad at me?"

"What makes you think I'm even mad, let alone mad with you?"

"Well, one, your jaw is tight and you're gripping the wheel like you want to kill it. I think you're mad at me because you moved my hand. You never don't want me to touch you. Even when you're mad. You say I calm you down."

"Do you think maybe I don't want to calm down?"

"Why not?"

"They disrespected you and no one said anything."

"It was only my mom."

"No, your brother and father just let her put you down."

"Thanks for not taking my mom up on her advances."

"You knew?"

"Yes. I'm not as stupid as you all think I am." Or maybe she was. "Besides, the guys told me they slept with my mom. So maybe I didn't know at first, but everyone made sure I knew after the fact." There was pity in his eyes. "Nope." She held up her hand. "Don't. I don't want to hear it."

"Then didn't what Henry said change your mind? He might die. Do you want to give up your chance to get what you've been working so hard toward to do something for someone who can't even stand up for you. I would cut them off."

"Did you cut Enzo off?"

"No." His jaw clenched again.

"Why?"

"Because he's family." Came out between gritted teeth.

"Exactly. It can't be only family counts for you."

"You're right." He came around the car and opened the door for her like he always did and pulled her out and into his arms. He wrapped her in a hug. She wanted to cry. But she didn't.

"He even said you could still do the interview. You don't need to be there the whole time. Will you consider still doing the interview?"

"I just want to go inside. I'm ready for bed."

Madison followed Dante up the steps. She didn't think she and Dante would work out. They were just too different. And the most important thing was he had different rules for her than for himself and expected her to follow those rules.

She wasn't a child, and she didn't appreciate that he treated her as such. Madison slipped off her shoes. She would leave after she gave his money back. She knew today had been an emotional day and that she didn't want to make any decisions, but in her heart she knew she needed to walk away. She was glad she went back on her birth control after the first night.

"Are you sure you don't want something to eat?"

"Yeah. I don't think my stomach can handle anything right now."

"You feel sick?" His voice was hopeful and his eyes dropped to her stomach.

"No, it's just the stress of the day."

"Do you want me to run a bath for you?"

"No, thank you. I think I'll just take a quick shower and go to sleep. It's been a long day."

"Ok." Dante walked up behind her and wrapped her in a hug. He kissed the side of her head.

Dante wasn't making her a better person. He agreed with that small part of her that was wrong and selfish and didn't want to give Henry the kidney or be there for him during the biopsy and go to her interview instead.

They had a routine where they would undress each other and he followed her to the bedroom. With her back still to him she moved her hair to the side and he unzipped her and placed kisses along the exposed skin.

She knew no one would be any nicer or act like she mattered any more than what her family did now, which was nothing. She tamped down the voice and reaffirmed her commitment to give Henry the kidney and to being there for him during the biopsy instead of showing up after her interview. They were starting to become friends, and she was sure this would bring them closer.

"Thank you." She turned and was efficient as she helped him out of his suit jacket and unbuttoned his shirt. She kissed his chest before she slid the shirt down his arms.

Maybe she had to ask Henry to stand up for her. Maybe he didn't think she wanted him to speak up about her mother's behavior. She would tell him after the surgery and hope that she would have atoned to a higher power for wishing she didn't have these responsibilities in secret.

She stepped out of her dress and then unbuckled his belt, undid his pants, and went to push them and his boxer briefs down his legs when Dante stopped her.

"It's ok, you don't have to. Go and take your shower. I'll be out here. I have a couple of things to do."

"Thank you." It was normal for them to shower together, but he was giving her much needed space to think.

She wished that she could be young and carefree like her friends or what friends she did have. Her and Zoe had grown closer, and she hadn't pushed Madison away when she found out she was dating Dante. Not like how Sabrina had.

She still hadn't been able to address Sabrina's feelings. She knew Henry had said Sabrina was jealous of Madison, but Madison had no idea it ran so deep. Madison figured it had to do with frustration from the competition.

It had Madison on edge, and she was in first place. She couldn't imagine how Sabrina was feeling, and Madison needed to remember that and be more mindful of how Sabrina was experiencing things.

Madison got ready for bed and lay down on her side like normal. Later, Dante came to bed and pulled her close like they had always been sleeping together. But it was different. She was stiff in his arms.

She didn't want to end the last of her time like this. So like anything else she pushed it down and did what she believed was right in the situation and not what was best for her. She relaxed. She couldn't bring herself to have sex with him, not that he had asked.

She couldn't because she knew it wasn't going to be make up sex, but goodbye sex. At least for her and she wanted to have the good times fresh in her memory and not this sad one.

She cried.

"Shh, baby. It's ok. Let it all out."

His words only made her cry harder. Dante rocked her to sleep. Her last memory was as if her heart was breaking. It had become more and more obvious; she was body, heart, and soul in love with a mobster. And she needed to walk away.

****

Dante noticed the change in Madison. He had given her some space and had held her when she cried last night. He had empathized with her and wished he could take away her pain, but he couldn't do more than that. Not if he didn't want to make her more upset.

But she had been stiff in his arms, and her speech was disjointed the next morning. He could see her brain working out a solution, and he hoped he won out. But by lunch, he knew it wouldn't happen.

"I need to go back to my apartment to work on my project. I have some last-minute finishing touches to make. Besides, I need to prepare for Friday."

"Are you doing the interview?" He sounded hopeful, but he knew what the answer would be.

"Dante. You know I can't do that. I need to be there for Henry. He needs me."

"What time is the surgery again?"

"It's at noon, but there is no reason you need to be there. I know you don't approve, and I don't want that negativity between both of you."

"Even though I disagree, it doesn't mean I won't be there to support you."

"Well, just so you know. I don't expect you to be there. So if there is something else you need to do, you can do it. I won't be upset. Besides, I'll be sitting and waiting, so there won't be much to do."

Dante was hurt. After all they had been through she didn't want him by her side when she might need him the most. She was giving up on them, and he couldn't allow it. "What is this? There is something that you're not telling me." He knew now, or at least was ready to admit that he loved Madison. He wanted her in his life for as long as she would stay.

"I guess it's nerves for my showing at fashion week. I need to win."

He just hoped this wasn't the end.

****

On Thursday, Dante showed up at the club. Would Madison would call out? They had texted and talked on the phone while they were apart, but it wasn't the same.

So he was surprised when she came in and came up

to his office like their routine.

"Hey." He moved his chair away from the desk so that she could come and sit in his lap like was their routine, but she didn't move from just inside the doorway.

Regret flickered across her face before it was gone.

"I just came up to bring you the money back. I don't need the extra, and please don't add anything to tonight's either." She walked toward the desk and then went back and closed and locked the door. She placed the money on the desk but didn't move around it to sit in his lap.

"What's up?"

"I'm sorry, Dante. I can't do this right now. With all the things going on, I don't have the time to devote to a relationship."

"That's bullshit, and you know it. Things are slowing down for you. Fashion week is next week, and then you will start your new job."

She looked away.

"Just tell it to me straight. You're not a good liar, and I think I deserve the truth."

"I don't want to be in a relationship with you anymore. My time here is up, and I think it's best if we just make a clean break. No hard feelings. It just didn't work out."

"You mean you didn't want it to work out."

"That's not true."

"Whatever, Madison. I don't have time for your games. I'm too old for this shit."

"We're just too different. Besides I realized I'm not comfortable with your, uh–" She touched her neck. "— background."

Instead of having her leave, he got up and walked

away. He unlocked the door and left her in the office alone. Dante didn't stop until he reached his car and then he got in and drove.

He drove for hours. Past the time of her sets until he knew she would be gone and then he headed back. She had a key to his place. Would she be there when he got back? But when he came in the house was empty. In the bedroom, her things were gone. Where had she left the key, or did she keep it in case she changed her mind? He found the key under the mat in an envelope that had "sorry" written across it.

He wanted to punch something. To scream and rant and rave. He wanted to convince her to give them a go. To tell her how much he loved her, but she didn't love him back and didn't want to try and grow to love him.

How was it that less than a week ago he had introduced her to his parents for the first time and now they were no longer together. Life sucked.

****

Madison took the bus to Henry's house that morning. She would drive them to the hospital in his car and then drive him back. She was going to stay the night with him and see how he was in the morning. This was the new plan since the surgery was just for Henry and no longer required her for this part.

She knew Dante had wanted to be there for her so she didn't have to be alone. Who knew if her parents would show up. She brought a book to keep her company and keep her mind off of the fact that she would miss her interview.

She didn't know how it had happened, and she never would have expected that she would fall in love with a mobster. Sure he wasn't hardcore, but he was still part of the mafia.

Instead of her usual mode of trying harder, she had gone to the other extreme and had run away from him and her feelings. It was too much. It wouldn't work. She couldn't believe she had believed it was a good idea to bring a baby into their relationship.

She was glad that something had made her decide to start taking her birth control again. She knew she should have discussed it with Dante as he didn't know she was back on her pills. Sometimes she would see him eyeing her stomach.

All it took was one time. She hoped she wasn't pregnant. Although she frowned for thinking so. She wished she had a part of Dante that she could keep and love and that would love her back unlike the baby's father.

Her period was late, but it could have just been from the stress of everything. She was pretty regular and even with not taking the one pill on time, she didn't think it would change her cycle.

She had taken a pregnancy test, but it had come back negative. It could have been too early. She knew they would give her a pregnancy test before the transplant so she guessed she would find out soon enough. If it still hadn't come before they rescheduled the transplant, then she would buy another test.

Chapter 17

There was still time to get to her interview. She knew with the way things ended with Dante, that he wouldn't take her back. And did she even want him to take her back? Sure, he treated her nice, better than nice. But he was a criminal from a criminal family. A long line of criminals. And not only that he wanted a wife and kids. Things she didn't want. Nope. It was for the best. Like she told him, they were just too different.

Henry went back to get prepped for surgery. Then a nurse came out to get her to wait with him until they took him back.

"How do you feel?" She reached for his hand.

"Good.

"It's time for you to go back, Mr. Bryant," the nurse said.

Everything happened in a blur and before she knew it he was being wheeled away from her. Another nurse directed her to where she could wait for Henry. She found a window seat. Her parents had come, but they were too late to see Henry before he went back.

"Hi, Mom, Dad. Henry just went back. I just came out to find a seat."

"Where is your young man?" Madison's mom looked around.

"I told him he didn't need to come." Madison didn't bother to tell them that they had broken up. Her mother would make a snide remark that Madison wasn't able to keep a man.

"Well, how long are we supposed to wait?" Her mom looked around the room, already uninterested in the real reason she was there.

"I don't think it's supposed to be more than two hours." Madison pulled a book out of her bag.

"What's that you have there?" Her mother grabbed it from her hand. "Oh, a romance. I wouldn't think you need to read those anymore now that you have someone. He would be more appreciative if you read a sex for dummies or something like that."

Madison's face heated. She would say she couldn't believe that her mom would say this in front of Madison's father, but nothing fazed her when it came to her mother anymore.

"Well, I had already scheduled a hair appointment with the same salon Glenda uses. It took me forever to get off the waitlist, so I'm not giving it up." Her mom handed Madison the romance novel back and looked at her father. "Milford, do you want to stay here and I pick you up after I'm done? Or if Henry is done before me, Madison can drop you off."

Madison looked at her dad's face. She could tell he was unsure if it was a good idea to let her mother go off on her own and being torn wanting to wait for his son.

"I'll stay here and wait for Henry to come out."

"Suit yourself." Madison's mom kissed her dad and side eyed Madison as she left.

"Here, Dad, let's find a place where we can sit together." Madison moved away from the window seat and found them two chairs next to the TV. Her dad gazed up at the screen, so Madison pulled her book out and went back to reading. She had just reached a hot scene that made her think of Dante and she looked up to find him at the nurse's station and he looked in her direction.

What was he doing here? He walked towards her and she couldn't take her eyes off him as he approached. Her center pulsed and her nipples beaded against her shirt. She shifted under his gaze. She was getting wetter and could feel her slickness between her thighs, as her folds rubbed together. Nothing new when Dante was around. She didn't know what the connection was between them.

She didn't have time to deal with it now. Her dad had fallen asleep. She didn't want her conversation with Dante to wake her dad so she got up to head him off, but he was already there.

"Hey."

"What are you doing here?" She didn't mean to sound as harsh as she did and softened her voice. "I didn't think I would see you again." She looked around. There were not too many people waiting for patients so that was good, but they had drawn some attention. Her dad stirred and she tried to move Dante away from him.

"I went to pick you up. Weren't you doing your interview?"

"I told you I wasn't going to do it." She lowered her voice.

"What did you have to lose? Henry isn't even out yet." He made as if to touch her and then let his hand fall away.

Madison angled her body to block Dante's view of her dad. "Yeah, but I was with him before he went back."

"Your parents could have been with him for you."

"They were late and didn't get to see him before he

went back." She looked over her shoulder at her dad still snoring.

"You can't be everything for them."

She crossed her arms under her breasts. "I'm not going to be nothing either."

"Excuse me. You're here for Mr. Bryant?"

"Yes. Is he out?"

"The doctor wanted to speak with you all. I can show you to the room."

Madison got her dad up and Dante inserted himself and grabbed her bag.

"If you all will follow me, I'll show you where you can wait."

"Is Henry not out yet?"

"The doctor will be with you in a minute." The door clicked closed behind the nurse.

Before Madison could voice her worries, the door opened and the doctor came in with a priest and another person.

"I'm Doctor Benjamin. You are Mr. Bryant's family?" He looked between them all.

"I'm Henry's father. This is his sister and her boyfriend."

"Ok."

"I can leave." Dante spoke up. "I'm just here to support Madison."

"Right. No, stay. She will need it." He looked back at Madison's father. "I'm sorry to have to tell you that Henry didn't make it through the surgery."

"What?" Madison looked between her father and the doctor.

"No." Her father slid down into the chair Dante had pushed behind him.

"What happened? Can we get him some water please?"

"Sure, I'll be right back," said the woman next to the doctor and left.

"There was a complication. He went into cardiac arrest, and we couldn't save him."

"No." Madison's emotions bubbled to the surface and rushed like waves. Henry was gone. What did that mean for her father? How would he survive without his only son? She watched her dad crumple up in the chair with the realization that his only son was dead.

Madison tried to process what was happening, but there was a rushing sound in her ears and she looked between her dad and Dante and then things went blank.

****

She awoke to Dante sitting next to her. She tried to sit up. "What are you doing here?"

He released her hand and got up to help her. She looked around. "What happened? Where is Henry?"

Dante reached for her hand. "Madison—"

"No, don't. Don't tell me that." It all came rushing back to her. "This was routine surgery; he couldn't have died."

"I'm sorry. Madison, baby. Don't cry." He wiped the tears from her face.

"Where are my parents?"

Dante's jaw tightened and she looked away.

"My mom didn't come back or she did and they left?" She didn't know which was worse.

"They left."

"Right. Of course." They didn't care. Dante came. Why? She still wasn't sure.

"Can I see him?"

"I'm not sure, but I'm sure we can ask a nurse and she might be able to tell us."

Madison looked up at the ceiling and swallowed the big lump in her throat. Henry was gone. Her parents had left. Her mom would make it all center around herself. They hadn't even stayed for her to wake up.

Would they send a counselor around? They had sent a priest, so Henry must've put down Catholic on his forms. Maybe a priest or nun would come back. She was in disbelief and denial. She knew she would need help to get through this on her own.

Without Henry, she had no one. Dante and she were no longer together, and she didn't want to burden Zoe with her grief and make her the sole dumping spot for her sadness and pain.

"Come, let me take you home." He reached for her hand.

"I can take myself home. I have Henry's car. Thanks for coming. I appreciate it." She looked out the window. She couldn't look at him because her mind had played tricks on her and it looked like Dante had a hurt expression flash across his face. And that couldn't be.

Why would he be? He had told her how temporary their relationship was. Was he upset that he hadn't been the one to end it?

"I'm already here, I can take you. Besides, you fainted. I don't think you should be driving."

Shit. He was right. "No, thank you. I can call Zoe. Oh no. I have to tell her what happened."

"I can tell her for you. I'm sure she will understand that I'm going to take care of you. You need someone to stay with you. You shouldn't be alone."

"I'll be fine. Can you please pass me my phone? I'll

let her know what happened to Henry."

"Madison. I have Zoe's number. I can let her know. You shouldn't be worrying about this right now. Let me help you get up and we can go home."

"I'm not going home with you." She knew he would try and take over and treat her like a child again. He assumed he knew best.

A nurse came in behind Dante. "Is there a problem?"

"No."

"Yes."

Madison and Dante spoke at the same time. The nurse looked between the two. "Sir. I'm going to have to ask you to leave."

"Madison, baby. Let me take you home."

"No. Zoe will come get me."

"Sir, you heard Ms. Bryant. Please leave."

Dante looked at Madison. "Fine." He held up his hands. "I'll leave, but I'll come and check on you when you're back home." He turned and walked out of the door.

She watched him walk out. He didn't have to tell her. She knew he would come to look for her at her place. If she had to, she would get a hotel room for a couple of days until he got the hint.

"Here, hun, let me help you get up. Someone will be in to see you from our counseling center. They will be able to give you more information."

Madison let the nurse help her then she sat on the edge of the bed and waited.

—Zoe: I'm so sorry. Let me know if you need anything. Even if you just want me to sit with you."—

—M: Can you pick me up? I don't have a ride. Well, I have Henry's car, but I don't think I should be driving

right now. Unless you have something you need to do. I can do a rideshare. I know this is all last minute.—

—Z: It's not a problem. I got a message from Dante telling me about what happened and that he was going to take you home. I wanted to check in with you.—

—M: I told him I don't want him to take me home. If it's ok, can you still please come and pick me up.—

—Z: Sure, I'm on my way—.

While Madison waited for the counselor and priest she stared at her phone. Of course Dante would have gone behind her back. He always treated her like a child and presumed he knew what was best for her. It was another reason why they wouldn't work out.

She listened to the counselor drone on, but she was a bundle of emotions and everything bounced off.

"Here are some pamphlets and resources we have available for you to use. And again, I'm sorry for your loss." The counselor handed her the folder with the information and left. She looked at the priest.

"Let us pray."

Madison let the tears fall as she listened to the father's prayer. Henry was dead. If she had done the interview instead, he still wouldn't be here, but she would have had a better shot at her dream. It had been a reaction to the anesthesia, and he went into cardiac arrest and they were unable to save him.

"Amen."

Madison wiped her tears and looked up. "Amen. Thank you, Father."

"Here is my card if you need anything." And then he left, and she was alone again.

Everything went by in a blur. Zoe came and the nurse wheeled her down to the front door while Zoe pulled the car around. They didn't talk and it was awkward, but Madison couldn't focus.

She couldn't go back to her place and pretend not to be there. Dante had a key and he hadn't given it back. She bet he waited for her there now.

"Zoe, can you take me to Henry's place instead." She had collected his things and had his keys.

"Are you sure?"

"Yes."

Madison told Zoe how to get to Henry's place and she dropped her off.

"I can stay with you if you want or go to your place to get you some things." Zoe helped Madison carry Henry's and her bags inside.

"No, that's ok. I think I want to be alone."

"All right, I understand. Let me know if you need anything and I'll come over."

"I know and thank you. I appreciate it." Madison went to close the door. "Oh and when Dante asks, you can tell him you dropped me off at a hotel or something."

"Will do."

"Thank you."

Madison closed the door and sank down to the floor, with her back against the door. Her head rested on her knees. She was screwed. There was no way Dante was going to let her go. He was going to keep hounding her and thinking he knew best. He would want to take over everything.

It didn't seem bad. He would be trying to help, but she needed to do it on her own. She was so used to doing everything that she didn't know how to let someone else do something for her.

That had been one of the nice things that came with

being with Dante. He was always doing sweet little things for her, giving her things and experiences that she wouldn't have had without him.

But that was in the past. Besides, the more time she sat with it, the more she didn't know her true feelings on being with a mobster. Part of her believed it was hot. But that wasn't the logical rational part of her. That part knew it was dangerous and that she shouldn't have moved past a booty call with him once she found out. But by then she was already in too deep.

She realized the tears had stopped flowing and she picked herself off the floor and looked at what she needed to do. She needed to dip into her savings for Henry's burial. She would need to win at fashion week. With the surgery and fashion week the next week, she and Dante had decided for her to stop dancing so she could recover and focus on the competition.

Now that they weren't together, she didn't want to go back to il Signore even just to bartend, so that was out for her. She needed this job to be able to survive. Madison looked at her phone. She had texted Sabrina, but hadn't gotten a reply back from her.

She ignored the missed calls and messages from Dante asking where she was. There was nothing from her mom or dad. She needed to call and at least speak to her dad to see if he had anything he wanted done for Henry's funeral.

She dialed his cell. "Hey, Dad."

"Madison." Her dad sounded tired. She worried this was too much for him.

"I was calling about Henry. I was going to make the arrangements, and I, uh, wanted to know if you wanted anything special done?"

"I hadn't…I didn't think I was going to be burying my only son." Her dad choked out on a sob.

"I know, Dad. It's ok. I'll take care of everything."

"Thank you. I'm just not in a place to do anything right now."

"I know, it's ok."

Madison's mother's voice was in the background. "Milford, ask her for some money. I don't have an LBD to wear to the service and you'll need a new suit."

"Dad, do you need me to buy you something?"

"We do need help with a few bills."

"Ok. I'll come over tomorrow."

"They're"—he coughed— "going to cut the power."

"Dad, this is serious. You should have told me sooner. I'll be over to pay the bill and see what else is outstanding."

Madison ended the call. This was another reason why she shouldn't have been with Dante. He had become her whole world and she had forgotten her real responsibilities, like making sure her dad was ok. She set Henry's things down and left to catch the bus. Her parents lived farther out so she would need to take the metro and then another bus to get there.

She sat down and the bus moved but stopped and opened its doors. A man in a nice suit got on. Madison noticed that it wasn't just the style of the suit, but the cut of it was well done. Like it had been tailored for this man's specific measurements. And it looked expensive too. He walked past her and she looked at his face. What was his story? She had seen him several times before. She remembered thinking the same thing when it came to his suit.

She figured he had spent all his money on clothes

and had to take public transportation to get to and from
his job.

Chapter 18

Madison stood outside her parents' place and waited for someone to open the door. She didn't know why they kept this big place. Well, she did, because her mom wanted to. But they needed to downsize. A cute condo would work well for them and be less expensive than the four-bedroom three-level house. They didn't even need the big yard.

"There you are, dear. We've been waiting ages for you to show up."

"Mom, you know I don't have a car. Besides it didn't take too long."

Her mother looked behind her. "Where is your nice young man?" Her mom slid her hands down her body-hugging dress. "I assumed he would bring you so I dressed up. Don't want him to think everyone in this family doesn't take pride in their appearance and wears handsewn clothes."

"Mom, all clothes are either hand or machine sewn. Everything is handmade."

"Yes, but it depends on the hand that makes it. One wants an important hand."

Madison didn't bother responding. "Where's Dad?"

"In his study with the bills. Glad you could find time in your schedule to make it over to take care of them. I guess your young man has been keeping you busy in the bedroom. I'm sure it's intensive, having to teach someone everything."

"You would know." Madison turned and walked away, ignoring her mother's gasp. She had never spoken up for herself before and doing it felt damn good.

"And just what is that supposed to mean?"

"I know what you did with any guy who was interested in me."

"I only showed them the ropes. How was I to know they would prefer me to you? I was trying to help you out. Two virgins together never make a good experience."

Madison's eyes widened at her mother's words. "So you're saying you were training them for me?"

"Or the next woman who came along. I'm sure they were appreciative of the lessons I taught them."

"So you admit that you cheated on Dad."

"He likes it. I go out and have fun and come back and tell him. It's our thing."

"You know, you are something else."

"That I am and don't you ever forget it." Her mom slinked away.

Madison continued on to the study to find her dad at his desk.

"Let me take a look." She sat down on the opposite side of the desk. "Dad, some of these haven't been paid for months. Why didn't you tell me? I would've had helped you."

"You weren't working, so I didn't want to take too much from you. I had Elanie go and get some money out from our joint account, but I guess she didn't pay the bills like I told her to."

"It was you? That was my savings. She took the whole thing."

"Sorry, sweetheart." He patted her hand. "She promised me she would just take enough to catch us up."

"Well, she didn't. And why would you trust her? She hasn't paid a single bill with the money you've given her. In fact she has just went out and made more bills. How can you live like this? You know you need to sell the house."

"I know, but your mother doesn't want to."

"But what about you? What do you want?"

"To keep your mother happy."

"What about your happiness? You can't tell me you're happy living like this."

"It suits me."

"You know she cheats on you, right?"

"Yes."

"But you still want to keep her happy?"

"That does keep her happy. If it hadn't been for this stroke, we would have been fine."

"I don't get it."

"It works for us."

"Right. Ok." That was way more than she needed to know. "Let's pay these bills."

****

Dante waited at Madison's place for Zoe to bring her home, but she didn't show. He tried contacting Madison, but she wasn't answering her phone or any of the texts he sent. He called the guys he had tailing her to learn where she was. He realized she wasn't coming home and he left. He needed finish things up before the sting operation. He would have to talk to Madison later. As long as he had eyes on her and knew she was safe he was ok. For now. It wouldn't last long.

****

Madison got dressed for the funeral. It would be at the funeral home since Henry hadn't been part of a church. They had been able to do things fast. Madison still hadn't had any contact from Sabrina, although she had texted her the information for Henry's service. She wasn't sure if she would show.

Zoe had offered to pick Madison up, but she didn't want to burden her. The service was going to be small, because things had happened so fast, some people hadn't been able to attend. It would just be Madison and her parents and some friends.

Madison stood beside the coffin. They had done a nice job. If she squinted, she could pretend that Henry was asleep. She still didn't believe it. But she had no time to grieve. Her dress would show at fashion week this weekend. She still needed that job and the steady income it would bring.

Not only that, but this was her dream. The one thing that she had and loved and that she had pursued even when her mom had suggested something else for Madison. She stayed the course. Even at eighteen she knew that doing what her mother wanted wouldn't get her her mother's love. She didn't have enough left for Madison.

The door opened, and Madison turned to see who was coming to the service late. It was Dante. Their eyes met, and there was that pull, that spark, that joy at seeing him and she broke eye contact and faced the front.

She couldn't believe he had shown up. How had he found out? Had Sabrina told him? And where was she? The service was bordering on being over. Madison could feel Dante's eyes on her back, and her nipples hardened and she squeezed her inner thighs together. This wasn't the time or the place, but he had that effect on her.

The service ended, and they filed out of the building to head to the burial site.

"Oh look, your nice young man is here. Let's ride with him." Her mother walked over to Dante and hugged his arm to her chest.

"I have room."

Of course he would. Zoe stood beside her. "Great, then you guys can go with Dante and I'll go with Zoe." She grabbed Zoe's arm and dragged her away before anyone could say anything.

"Did you invite him?" Zoe asked.

"No. I have no idea how he found out. I didn't tell my parents that we broke up. So many things have happened. But don't leave me alone with him."

"I won't."

They drove to the cemetery where the grave was dug. Zoe stood next to Madison. Dante stood on the other side with Madison's parents. They watched the coffin being lowered, and they threw some dirt into the open grave. Madison tossed some flowers in.

She looked up to see men in black carrying guns and running towards them. They were coming up behind Dante

"SWAT. Hands up. Put your hands where I can see them."

Dante turned. "What the fuck?"

Madison was confused. Why was the SWAT team at her brother's funeral? It had to be a mistake.

"Dante Giovanni Bianchi, you're under arrest for money laundering, tax evasion, and racketeering."

"What? I haven't done anything wrong."

"Tell it to the courts."

"Dante?"

"Go home with Zoe. I'll be out soon."

"I wouldn't be so sure of that," said a member of the SWAT team who dragged Dante out.

"Madison, I—"

And then he was being dragged away.

But everyone didn't leave. A female agent walked over to Madison. "Ms. Bryant, I need you to come with me."

"What? Why?" Madison looked around at her parents and Zoe. They were all standing there frozen as if their minds couldn't process what was happening

"Standard procedure. Come this way."

"Madison, dear. What is your young man into?" Madison's mother pushed to the front.

The agent took a firm grasp of her arm and led Madison away. She got down the hill in time to see Dante shoved into the back of a car. When he turned around, he could see Madison was coming.

"Don't take her. She doesn't know anything."

"That's for us to decide," said the lead guy.

Madison was placed in the back of an unmarked car. The lady agent slid in next to her and closed the door.

"You're not under arrest. We just want to bring you in for some questioning."

Madison was scared. This was only her second time seeing a gun in real life.

"Right."

The rest of the car ride was quiet and uncomfortable. Inside she was taken into a room and left alone. She didn't know what to do. The room was cold, and Madison shivered and looked around the stark room.

She sat on one side of the table and on the other side

were two empty chairs. She shouldn't have trusted Dante when he said she wouldn't get in trouble. They had broken up and she was still taken.

She didn't know how long she sat there until the lead agent and the female agent from earlier came into the room.

"Sorry to keep you so long, Ms. Bryant. I'm Agent Bravo and this is Agent Daniels. We just have some simple questions for you." They sat down in the other chairs.

"Ok. I'm not sure if I have the answers that you are looking for." Madison shifted side to side.

Agent Bravo leaned in, "And why would you think that? You don't know the questions yet."

"Well, I don't know anything that pertains to Dante's… family."

"That's fine. How long have you known Mr. Bianchi?" He leaned back and placed his hand on a folder.

"Less than three months."

"And how long have you known he was part of a crime family?" Agent Bravo drummed his fingers on the folder

"Less than a month, I guess."

"Less than a month. But you work at il Signore, which is run by them." He held his hand up in a questioning gesture.

"Yes, I worked at il Signore. Dante told me he was the owner."

"Well, maybe that's true. But it's still part of the crime family's holdings." He cocked his head.

"I have no knowledge of that." Madison shook her head.

"Of what exactly?"

"Anything that has to do with the crime family."

"See that's where I think you're wrong. I think you know more than this little innocent act you're putting on." He tapped the folder with his index finger

"I don't. Dante and I almost broke up over it."

"But you didn't?" He put his elbows on the table.

"Well, no."

"Why not?" He leaned forward.

"He told me none of this would touch me, and, uh, that he's going to do something else."

"You can see that was a lie."

"I see that now."

"So, can you add anything more to the something else?"

"I don't know. He just said he was changing things up. I know he had a meeting that had to do with it."

"See, and you didn't think you knew anything. I think you know plenty."

"Agent Bravo, go easy on her. I think she's telling the truth," Agent Daniels said.

"I don't think so, but I know how to make her talk. When we go to court, we will subpoena you. And if you lie, or hold back you'll be sent to jail for contempt."

"Jail? But I don't know anything."

"You didn't hear him say anything like he was cleaning up?"

Madison stopped breathing. Was that something to do with what they wanted to know?

"See, Ms. Bryant. You know more than you let on, but a sit in jail will get it out of you."

"Am I being arrested?"

Chapter 19

"No, you're free to go. For now. Agent Daniels will walk you out."

Madison had no idea what had happened. It was as if she woke up in the twilight zone. Henry was dead, Dante would be in jail, and she was alone, with the possibility of going to jail too. Madison didn't know what to do. She wasn't sure if she should call anyone. The only person's number she had who could help Dante was Enzo's. There was no reason for her to have Gabe or Lucca's numbers since she only dealt with Dante and Enzo. Less Enzo now that she and Dante were dating. She didn't want to talk to him, but she would do it if it helped get Dante out of jail.

At home, Madison used her phone to call Enzo. She didn't think it was a texting situation.

"Hello?"

"Hi. It's Madison."

"I know."

"Oh. Ok. Well I was calling to tell you that—"

"You're now interested in dating me now that Dante's been arrested."

"What? How do you know?"

"I knew you would see the light when Dante was out of the picture."

"Ew, no. I mean how did you know he was arrested? That's why I was calling you to get help for him."

"Of course you would. He gets a phone call."

"And he called you?"

"No, he called the lawyer."

"Who told you?" Madison was still confused. He wasn't explaining how he knew.

"No. Look it doesn't matter how I found out. I'm willing to take you back. Dante will be in federal prison for a long time."

"You can't take me back. You never had me." She hung up.

What a weirdo. She had no idea Enzo was so unhinged.

She was resting on the sofa when her front door opened. She jumped up. Had they come to get her? The only people who had a key was Henry who wasn't using it, and Dante who was in jail.

"Enzo, if that's you, leave now or I'll call the cops."

She looked around the room for something to use and picked up her phone.

"Madison."

"Dante?" She turned around.

He came into the room.

"Dante. What are you doing here? Why aren't you in jail?"

"I got out. Why did you think I was Enzo?" He stopped in front of her.

She rubbed her hands up and down her arms and kept them crossed. "I just called him to get help for you."

"I got a call."

"I know he told me. You called the lawyer. I didn't know how he knew."

"We always get a call or at least we can say I want a lawyer and they have to stop. Enzo would know that."

Madison nodded. "Yeah, I guess. I was just surprised with things happening so fast that he would know you were in jail."

Dante's face took on a confused look, but cleared up.

"Why are you here?"

"I had to come here after they took you in."

She opened her arms for him. "I was so scared. I didn't know what to do. I still don't know what to do. They said they could make me testify and if I don't tell them what they want to know they will put me in jail."

"You don't have to worry. You don't know anything." He cupped her face in his hand.

"Well, you told me that you were changing things up."

"Right, but you don't know what."

"But they think I do. You said this wouldn't touch me."

He kissed her forehead. "I know, and I'm sorry. The only way I can protect you all the way is for us to get married. Then you could invoke spousal immunity, and they can't make you testify."

Madison pulled back. "I don't know if I want to do that. Is there another way? I never wanted to be married."

"It's the only way I know of that is quick, and that I can guarantee you protection."

"Ok, then I guess I have to do it."

"I'll go and make the arrangements."

And then he was gone again. Madison had no idea what was going on anymore. She didn't know which way was up. She floundered and had nothing to hold onto except for Dante's promise to protect her, through marriage.

How did that even work? She looked it up and once they were married on paper, she wouldn't have to testify. Dante had been right. It was pretty straightforward.

****

Madison was sketching at the table when her doorbell rang.

She opened the door part way and peeked out. "Lucca?" It was Lucca and his father, who Madison now knew was the head of the family.

"Can we come in?"

Madison was nervous and afraid to have a mafia don in her place. Especially after what happened to Dante. And he was coming to see her for a reason. It couldn't be good. She didn't know if she could take any more bad news. "Come in. You can sit down in the dining area."

"Thank you, we won't take much of your time. Dante told us you're grieving. We are also sorry for your loss," Lucca said.

"Thank you."

"We've come to get you for the marriage," Lucca said.

"Already? That was fast."

"Dante wanted it done fast to protect you as soon as possible," the Don said.

"Oh. Ok. What do I need to do?"

"All you need to do is come with us," Lucca said

"When they interviewed you, did you say anything?" the Don asked.

"No. I don't know anything to tell them."

"We have a judge. He'll marry you two, and there you go." the Don said.

"Ok." Madison looked around. "Right. Well, I don't want to go to jail, so if this is the only way to avoid it, then I'll do it."

"Great choice. We will take you to the courthouse to meet with the judge who will be marrying you two," the Don said.

"Great."

Madison excused herself and went to change. She guessed she should wear something other than lounge clothes to be married in. She picked a slate gray piece she had made after her and Dante had been having regular sleepovers.

It reminded her of his eyes and how they looked when trained on her. She hadn't worn it before. She had been saving it for something special. It was fancy with a ruffle skirt to make it flirty.

What was more special than your wedding?

They hustled her to the car, and she didn't have time to ask how spousal immunity worked besides what she had read on the internet. She was nervous to see Dante again. They still hadn't spoken since he had come to her apartment. Before that, she had been able to avoid him. That was why his arrival at the service surprised her. All too soon they arrived, and she was ushered into some judge's chambers.

Dante was there in the same suit from the morning. Her eyes scanned over him, and he was as handsome as ever. Their eyes met, and the familiar spark ignited. The tug at her center that was there the first time they had met across the bar at the club.

Was it the same for him? Had it disappeared for him? Or even worse, had it never been there and was just a line he had used to get into her pants?

Dante walked over to her. "Hi."

She gave a wave. "Hi."

"I'm glad you could come." He reached for her hand.

Madison let him take her hand. "I kind of didn't have a choice."

"This is for the best and the only way I know to protect you." He pulled her towards the judge.

The ceremony was brief and quick. Dante slipped a ring on her finger and before she knew it she was married.

"You may kiss the bride."

Madison turned her face for the peck she assumed to receive when Dante's mouth came down hard on hers as if he was punishing it. And then his lips were gone.

Dazed, she looked around. The men left, and she followed behind like a dutiful wife should. They handed her off like a package as if they were playing hot potato and no one wanted to be caught with her.

Dante handed her into the car like he always did when they were dating before he went around the car. She touched her lips. They still burned from where his had scorched hers.

Madison assumed Dante was going to take her back to her place and was confused when he passed the exit for her place. "Where are we going?"

"Back to my place."

"Why?"

"We're married."

"Yeah, I know."

"So we live together."

"Why?"

"That's what married people do."

She turned to look at him. "What?" They needed a marriage license. It didn't change anything, and she believed that things would go on as they had been. Why did they need to live together?

"Bianchi men marry for life."

"Oh." She wanted to bang her head against the window. What had she gotten herself into? She was not only going to be married to Dante for life, but she would have to live with him. Stuck in a one-sided marriage. She should have clarified what the marriage was going to be like.

She assumed it would be like the fake ones in her romance novels. Not a forever marriage.

She didn't believe in divorce. That was why she never planned on getting married. Could she get an annulment? How long would she be at risk for going to jail?

"What does that even mean?"

"Bianchis don't divorce, so we're together until we die."

Great, so not only was she stuck with him, but it was obvious to her that he would be cheating on her. Did he have a mistress already?

"We also don't cheat. We are loyal, so you don't need to worry. We both have work, so we won't be under each other all day. If we need to, we can look for a bigger place."

Madison took a sharp intake of breath when he said they wouldn't be under each other. They had spent a lot of time like that. In the bed, shower, anywhere they could. "Great. Can we do an annulment? How long is the statute for your charges?"

"Four years for civil and five years for criminal. I'll have someone pack your apartment and bring everything over. I need to go out to meet with the lawyer, so make yourself at home."

Madison looked around Dante's place. She didn't know how she ended up back here. The day was like something out of a nightmare or horror film. She had buried Henry, been interrogated, went home, married a mobster, and was sitting in his place to avoid going to jail. She didn't know how things could get any crazier.

Madison walked around the house in a daze. She still couldn't believe Henry had died. She couldn't talk to Dante. She didn't want to hear him say I told you so. Her only hope had been Sabrina, but she was ignoring it, or at least ignoring Madison.

She walked into the bedroom. It smelled like it always did. Of Dante. She looked at her hand. She was married. To Dante. For at least four years. Then she could dissolve it like it never happened, and continue with her life.

She collapsed on the bed. Dante's house had several bedrooms, but none was set up like a guest room or bedroom, so she would have to sleep here. With him. Every night. For four years at least.

Well, that wasn't true. He did say they could look for a bigger place so that should leave a room to be set up for her. So she would just have to make it until they found a place. How hard could that be?

Would he do it without her or would they go together? She should have some input as she would be there for at least four years. Ugh it was like a broken record in her head. Four years. Four years. Four. Years.

It was like she had received a prison sentence. She guessed it was better than being in a real prison, but by just a little. That was the last thing she remembered as she fell asleep.

****

Dante came home to find Madison asleep on the bed. She was still wearing what could be called her wedding dress and it had inched up her legs as she slept. He remembered those legs wrapped around his head, waist and over his shoulders. He ran a hand through his hair and let out a shaky breath.

He had gotten what he wanted. He was married to Madison, but from the way she responded it seemed like it would only be long enough to dodge a prison sentence. But it gave him something he didn't have before.

Time. Time to show Madison how much he loved her. Time for her to come to terms with who he was. Time for her to love him back. Now to convince her to stay married to him.

Dante went into his walk-in closet to take his suit off and threw on jeans and a henley. He left Madison in the bedroom to sleep and headed to the kitchen. The day had been nuts, and he doubted she had eaten so he would prepare something light for her.

He got set to get the things ready to make her toast and scrambled eggs. When he had spoken to Tony, Dante told him to move some holdings under Madison's name. He had also added her to his credit card accounts. New cards were being mailed for her. In the meantime, she could use his. He didn't want her to not have whatever she needed or whatever she wanted.

Dante had a feeling Madison didn't do little extras for herself, and that was something he was going to do for her during their time together. He sensed her presence and looked up to find her standing at the edge of the living room where it met the kitchen.

He couldn't stop his eyes from scanning over her

body, and his dick hardened. He wanted her. But like when they had first slept together. It was going to have to be her choice. She would have to make the move.

"Hi," she whispered.

"Hi."

"I guess I fell asleep." She shivered under his gaze and ran one hand up and down the opposite arm as if to warm herself up and to keep him away.

"Yeah, no worries. It's been a day for you. I was going to make you something to eat once you woke up."

"You don't have to, I could do it myself."

"It's no trouble. I have to make something for myself."

"True. But it doesn't mean you have to make extra for me."

"That's true, but like I said, it's no problem. I want to."

"Ok then. I guess go ahead. I'll go change out of this." She tugged at the hem of her dress."

"That's nice. Is it one of yours? I don't remember seeing it before."

"Yes." She looked away. "I was keeping it for something special."

That gave Dante hope, that she chose something special to wear for their wedding. "Where is the pocket in this one?"

"Here." She flipped up the bottom and showed him the pocket. Well, he guessed she showed it to him. When she had lifted her dress to show the pocket, she lifted it higher than she would need to in order to show it. It revealed her lace panties to his eyes. These ones in a light brown color that hinted at what was underneath.

He could smell her arousal from across the room and

her nipples became more visible in the dress. Had she been aroused by him looking at her?

He looked at her face, and it was flushed. Her eyes looked darker, and there was longing, arousal and something else flicker across her face before it disappeared.

"I better go change." Her voice came out breathy. She was quick to turn around, and he watched her ass as she ran for the bedroom.

She still wanted him in a sexual way. But that wasn't enough for Dante. He wanted her heart too. He wasn't opposed to starting their physical relationship up again, but he wanted their friendship back.

She came out a few minutes later. He was scrambling the eggs and the toast had popped up.

"Here let me help you. I don't expect you to do everything while we're married." She came into the kitchen and grabbed plates. She put the toast on each one and went to the fridge for the butter, jam, and honey.

The honey had been something they had picked up at one of their farmer's market trips. She remembered he liked it drizzled on his toast. She took it all to the table as he served the eggs onto both plates and brought them to the table, where she had already taken a seat.

He placed a plate in front of her and then himself. He looked at her, but her eyes darted away and she picked up a fork and shoveled eggs in her mouth. But then she looked up at him and moaned.

"What did you put in the eggs? They're amazing." She went back for more.

Dante was glad he was seated, because when she moaned his dick stood to attention.

"I put in crème fraiche."

"I'm going to have to start doing that when I make eggs from now on." She pointed in his direction with her fork. "These are spectacular."

It wasn't long before they had finished eating. "I'll help you clean up." Madison pushed her chair back and stood. She leaned over to get his plate, and her oversize shirt slid down her shoulder, revealing golden skin and the strap of her bra. Also light brown in color. But what drew his eyes more was her rounded globes hanging from her chest. This time he was sure her nipples hardened, and he looked at her face and it was clear that she knew it happened too.

"Madison." His voice sounded rough. "We should discuss how our marriage will work."

She stood up and moved to the sink. "Ok that sounds good. Let me finish cleaning up here, and I'll meet you in the living room.

Dante went to wait for her and rubbed his hands down his thighs. They were clammy. He was worried about this talk. Because of who he was, and what he was a part of, there were certain criteria that needed to be met for his house. They also needed more space. He would talk to her tonight, but he doubted she would want to share a bed with him, in a platonic way while they looked for a place.

There was nothing that met their needs in the Bianchi holdings so he would need to spend time looking for something along with dodging the charges on his plate.

She came into the room. "Sorry, I went to get socks. I forgot how cold the tile can be sometimes." She sat down at the other end of the couch and pulled her legs under her.

"Yeah. I can, uh, turn up the heat if you want." He stood, but she put a hand out to stop him.

"No worries. Wearing socks won't kill me." She wrapped her arms around her body. "Ok, so what did you want to say to me?"

"I guess we need to discuss how our marriage will go. Like I said earlier Bianchi's don't divorce or annul marriages. We stay together through the good times and the bad. But I won't make it difficult for you if you want to go with either one." Hurt passed over her face before it disappeared. It was so quick he knew he had to have imagined it.

"So what were you thinking then?" She shifted on the cushion.

"That we treat it like a real marriage."

"Yeah, but real marriages have love."

It was like an ice pick pierced his heart. She didn't love him. "True, but it's been shown with time you can grow to love someone."

"Maybe, if you say so." She rubbed her eye. "Ok, a real marriage. I'll have to think on this. I don't want to be married, real or not, even if there is love. I think I want to go back to sleep again." She unfolded from her spot and walked away.

"But sleeping?" Dante asked her back.

She stopped. "We can sleep in the same bed together until we find a bigger place. A bigger place would be better. I could have my own room." And with that, she walked away.

Dante was fucked. He had hoped to nail some things down like what they each would and wouldn't be doing, but it looked like the conversation was over without any real questions answered.

****

Madison lay in bed. She was lucky that the mob was efficient, because while Dante had been out, her stuff had arrived. She had seen it when she ran back to the room after she got wet in front of Dante. Could he smell her arousal? She was worried she was going to have to wear some of his clothes until hers arrived, but there they sat in a corner of the closet.

She knew she should ask for the annulment when the time came, but she knew she wouldn't. At least not right now. She held out hope, because she loved Dante and was hoping maybe he would come to love her like she did him. Maybe down the line. But how long could you go and still get an annulment? How long would it take for him to fall in love with her? If he was, wouldn't he have fallen in love with her by now? Was he going to come to bed with her? Or would he wait until she was asleep.

She should have stayed out there to listen to more of what he had to say and what a real marriage meant to him, but it was too late for tonight. She went to shower, but the tub called her name. It had been a long hard day and she wanted to just soak it away.

She slipped into the water and let it lap over her. The heat relaxed her shoulders and she rested her head back on the lip of the tub. She remembered their time together how she and Dante had spent some time making love in the tub. She couldn't make herself call it fucking.

It had been hot and a couple of times they had spilled water on the floor when they were in there together. It had been fun. Her nipples hardened at the memory. She wanted to touch herself, but she wouldn't. She had been in there long enough. She didn't want Dante to walk in on her, so she drained the tub and got out. Since she had all her clothes, she could wear lounge wear to bed instead of her usual. But she liked night dresses. She didn't like to wear pants or shorts to sleep in.

But she could suck it up for the time it would take for them to find a bigger place. She knew she and Dante could restart their physical relationship, but she couldn't. It would only draw her in deeper. She knew he wouldn't push her to either. But what she had told him was true. She didn't want to be married to the mob, although she now was.

But that was something else. He had said she wouldn't get in trouble. But look where she was now. Married to a mobster to keep from being put in jail, even though she didn't know anything. She had been right not to trust him. So there was not going to be any accidental sleep sex between them. She would wear a tank and pants. Because she couldn't trust herself.

That decided she dressed for bed and went to sleep.

Madison woke up to find Dante's hard cock pressed against her ass. She worked her hips on it to try to help it find her entrance. Ugh, why did she have these stupid pants on? She reached for his cock and could feel the weight of it in her hand. With her other, she tried to pull her clothes off.

Why wasn't Dante helping? It was normal for him to pull her panties to the side and plunge in. He couldn't because she had pants and panties on.

"Dante." It had been like routine that when she said his name, he knew what she wanted and gave it to her, but this time was different.

Dante peeled her hand off his cock and moved her over to the opposite side of the bed.

Right, that's why she had on pants and panties. So this wouldn't happen. If it had been someone else, they wouldn't have stopped her. But that was one thing with Dante. If there was anything iffy or if there wasn't clear consent, he wouldn't move forward.

Even in the middle of the night, he would make sure she was awake and wanted it, before he acted. He rolled over, and she lay there embarrassed. She wanted to cry herself to sleep, but that would go against everything she was trying not to do. She didn't want him to know she was awake. She lay there until she fell asleep.

It happened several times that night, because in sleep, they would be drawn together. Each time Dante moved her over. She guessed that that was the last straw because he just got up and left the room and then she did let soft sobs take over until she cried herself back to sleep.

****

Madison woke up alone. She wasn't sure if Dante was still home or not. She needed to meet her model Becky that afternoon. She would have to tell her the location had changed. Or maybe she would just do it at her place. They packed it up, but she still had the apartment for the month.

She dressed and went out to find Dante in the kitchen.

"Good morning."

"Good morning, thank you." She took the coffee he held out for her. She didn't know where to look, she could only remember him rejecting her over and over and over during the night. He looked tired. Where had he gone to sleep when he left the bedroom?

"What are your plans for the day?"

"Nothing much. Fashion week is this weekend, so it's just the final touches. I meet with Becky today, and tomorrow the fashion house is letting me do the interview."

"Oh, that's great."

"Yeah. They were more sympathetic once they learned Henry had died."

"I can see you beating yourself up, but you didn't know. You were doing what you believed was best in the situation. We can always see the better path after you've taken a different one." He sat his coffee cup down. "Come here, please. You look like you need a hug."

And she did. Her legs didn't listen to her brain and walked her over to Dante's embrace. It was comforting being in his arms again.

"I wanted to talk to you about a couple things before I left for the day."

"Ok, sure." She stepped back. Her body reacted to being near to his, and she needed to put some space between the two of them.

"First, I looked for a house in our holdings, but there is nothing that fits what we will both need. So I'll work with Lucca to find a place."

"Ok. How long do you think that will take?"

"I'm not sure."

"How long did it take you to find this place?"

"It took a couple of years to find it, and then I needed to renovate it, so it was close to three years before I moved in."

Shit. She couldn't go on like last night for three years. She didn't know how she would make it a week.

"Second, I've assigned men to follow you, just to make sure you're ok."

"Why?"

"Because of my ties, people might think that by getting to you they can get to me."

"So I'm in danger again."

"It's possible. But my guys are good. You won't notice them unless you need them, and this is more a precautionary measure than anything else. There haven't been any threats made."

"But it's still early, right?"

He tilted his head in acknowledgment. "True."

"Ok. Is there anything else?"

I think that's it. I have a meeting, so I'll be out for most of the day."

"Ok."

"I'll be going." Before she knew what hit her, he dropped his head and put a quick peck on her lips. The touch was electric, and she moaned and Dante deepened the kiss. She fisted his shirt and tried to get closer to him. He broke away from her.

"See you tonight." And he was gone.

Chapter 20

Madison was surprised when Sabrina called her the day after Henry's funeral

"Hey, sorry I've been MIA. It was hard to process so many things at one time."

"I understand." And she did. It was hard for her to believe that yesterday she buried Henry and got married.

"I wanted to talk to you."

"Sure."

"In person."

Brows knitted together. "Why?"

"Well, part of what I want to show you I can't over the phone."

"Can you take a picture of it? I'm supposed to meet Becky in a few hours." She had already done her interview with the fashion house.

"Well, I wanted to give it to you to keep. You might want it."

"Ok Sabrina, this all sounds mysterious." Madison didn't want to hear anything else that had to do with rumors or to see pictures of her and Dante together.

"Fine. I'll tell you over the phone. I'm pregnant with Henry's child."

"What?" Madison couldn't believe it.

"Yes, they had me on bed rest because I was bleeding when I found out Henry had died."

"Oh, Sabrina that's terrible." Madison's heart

squeezed, and she believed she was in the wrong for thinking Sabrina didn't care for Henry, or even care enough for him as a person enough to show up. "Oh, this is so exciting. I'm going to be an aunt. What did you want to give me?"

"An ultrasound picture of the baby for you and your dad."

"Oh, Dad will want that. Where are you? I'll come meet you now."

"Great."

****

Madison showed up outside the cafe to find Sabrina and her brother Randy waiting. "Hey." She gave them each a hug. Sabrina was stiff in her arms. "I can't believe this is happening. Dad will be so excited when I tell him."

"Did you tell anyone where you were going?"

"No. Why? Should I have?"

"It's going around the club that you and Dante got married. Must be nice."

"Uh, yeah. Ok." Madison didn't know where things were going, but she wouldn't discuss her marriage with anyone. How did they even learn they had gotten married? "Can I get the ultrasound? I need to get back to meet Becky."

"Randy, show her what she's won."

"Won?" She looked between them.

"What if I tell her?"

Something pushed into her low back and she turned to look over her shoulder. She froze. The man towered over her and he had tattoos on his neck and ran up his face. Maybe they went lower, she didn't want to imagine it. He let her see the gun he pushed into her side. "Mrs.

Bianchi, you'll come with us," the guy said.

A black SUV pulled up to the curb and they pushed her in.

"Wait, what is this? What do you want? Sabrina what are you doing?"

"They are going to take you for a train ride. A double train and you get to be the engine."

Madison's body went cold ,then hot, then cold. She had an idea of what Sabrina had meant. Madison fought against the new guy, but he was too strong for her. She stomped on his instep.

"You're going to pay for that." He tightened his grip on her.

She looked up at the shouts calling her name and there was three men in suits headed towards her, but they were too far away. And out jumped some other guys.

The last thing she could see was them pull out guns before she was pushed into the truck and followed by the big tattooed guy. The other door opened, and Randy slid in. Over his shoulder, Sabrina smiled.

"You hate me." It was a question, but came out like a statement.

"Yes."

"Were we ever friends?"

"When we were younger, but the friendship ended on my side a long time ago."

The door closed and then the car sped off. Madison sat there and tried to process her fate.

"I'm going to have fun with you." The tattooed guy rubbed a hand over her thigh and her skin crawled, and her stomach cramped.

He looked over her head at Randy. "Too bad we can't keep her. But even used, she will bring in a lot of money."

Madison's stomach dropped. This wasn't just a way to make her miss the fashion show. Sabrina wanted to get rid of her. For good.

She looked at Randy. "Sabrina hates me this much?"

"I bet it's more than this."

"Then why was she friends with me?"

"You know how the saying goes. Keep your friends close, and your enemies closer."

"Did she ever like me?"

"When you were little girls, you guys were friends, but once you guys hit middle school, it was a competition between the two of you."

"I didn't know."

"Doesn't matter. But one you were in just the same."

Madison turned to face Randy. "This is crazy. Randy, you've known me for so long. Please don't do this to me. If it's money for you guys, I'm sure Dante would pay whatever. You don't have to do this."

"It's already been put in motion. If we don't follow through, we will be seen as weak."

"But Dante will go to war to get me back."

"And that's fine. We're prepared to handle that."

"How can you do this to me? I know Sabrina must have told you I lost my virginity not that long ago."

"That's where the big money is coming in." Vince spoke, bringing Madison's attention back to him.

"So what's going to happen to me?"

"Someone said you know how to work the pole, so we're going to take you to the Donnettis' club, have you dance for us, and we'll place bets to see the order that we're going to sleep with you."

"And Sabrina knows this?"

Madison cried. She couldn't believe that Sabrina had known she had been a virgin before Dante and would want this to happen to her. She was going to be sick. Her stomach rolled like it was on the world's twistiest roller coaster. She was sure she would pass out, the walls of the car closed in on her and squashed between the two men, she was like a child.

"She wanted us to run a double train on you, but like you said, you were a virgin not that long ago, so I decided not to do that." He looked over her head. "Right, Vince."

"Not the first time anyway. Did Bianchi take that ass or no?"

Madison's eyes got wide, and she sucked air in through her nose.

"I guess not. Let's see who gets first pick."

"This is going to be fun."

****

Dante picked up the phone after the fifth ring. "I said I don't want to be disturbed."

"Boss, we lost her."

"What?"

"They took her."

"Shit." Dante's first instinct was that she had slipped the tail that he had put on her, but this was even worse. "What the fuck were you guys doing?"

"She went to meet her friend. We didn't expect the Donnettis to be waiting. It was an ambush boss. Even if we were closer, they would have still taken her."

"Where are they taking her, and better not tell me the fuck you don't know where my wife is going."

"We have the friend. But I doubt the lackey's sister is going to get us a trade."

"What do you mean lackey?"

295

"One of the footmen for Donnettis. We got his sister."

"And the friend? Did they take the friend too?"

"No boss, we have her."

Her, not them both. It was one and the same and that could only mean one thing. Sabrina.

Dante would give them whatever they wanted before they even asked for it to get Madison back safe and sound.

"Where did she say they're going?"

"She won't talk."

"Bring her in. I'll meet you guys there."

"What's going on?" Lucca looked up from his phone.

"Donnettis took Madison. Did you check on Ainsley?"

"Yeah, Rocco just got back to me. They have eyes on her, but they will move in closer. I'll send some extra guys. Do you think they're going for her next?"

"I don't know. I doubt it. Sabrina is the one who helped them get Madison, so I feel like she is all they want. If they had wanted both, they would have had teams to take both at the same time."

"True. But this is the Donnettis. They aren't the brightest. and they are low down in the game."

"We will find out soon enough. I'm headed to HQ. Put a call out; find out what they want and that I'll give it to them to get her back." Dante grabbed his stuff and left. Lucca was right behind him.

"What are you doing? Finish the meeting."

"And let you go out there alone? Hell, no. We're going together. I'll call Gabe." Lucca headed for his car.

All Dante could see was red. The Donnettis dealt in

trafficking which was below the Bianchis. They didn't do drugs or human trafficking or even guns. They were strict to keep their hands in white collar crimes with some blue-collar tendencies. He knew what they would do to Madison.

He had to get to her. He didn't have a lot of time.

Dante called Gabe himself.

"The Donnettis have Madison."

"What? Why? How?"

"Doesn't matter. I need you to meet me there with some guys."

"Where?"

"I guess they took her to their clubhouse." Dante didn't carry guns, but they did have them. "Bring me something to use. I'm sure we are going to have to take her back by force."

"On my way. I'll round up some of the enforcers and then we will be there."

"Get there as soon as possible. They're going to hurt her."

Dante got in his car and took off. He used his Bluetooth to call a dirty cop.

"Meet me at the Donnettis' place and bring backup."

"What's going on?" Mike asked.

"They have my wife. She's been gone for close to a half an hour now. I'm on my way, and I'm bringing backup." Dante disconnected and sped towards the Donnettis' side of town.

****

The SUV stopped outside the club. Randy opened the door and pulled Madison out. She still had her pin cushion attached to her wrist from the finishing touches she was doing before Becky came for the final fit. It wouldn't make a good weapon. Turning the men into pin cushions wouldn't stop them. She also didn't know if she could stab them deep enough for it to be effective.

She also didn't have enough pins for everyone. As she tried to process everything, it made her want to pass out. Dante's men had seen them take her; but did they know where she was being taken?

Sabrina had done this to her, so she knew where Madison was and wouldn't send anyone to help her.

Madison tried to drag her feet to keep them from pulling her inside the club, but Vince picked her up and threw her over his shoulder. From her view she could see the ground and his and Randy's feet moving her closer toward the door.

"Yes, you guys brought her back."

"Get in line outside the backroom. You can place bets and line up in order of highest bidder."

"She looks good."

There was a hand on her bottom, and she wanted to vomit. No one was going to save her. She would need to save herself. As she was carried past a line of men, she stopped counting when she reached ten.

Her stomach bottomed out, and she could feel the bile rise in her throat. She wanted to scream, but she knew they would feed off of it. They would want her screams. She couldn't fight off all these men, but if they came one at a time, she might have a better chance.

A door opened and she was unceremoniously dropped onto the bed. She scooted back as far away from them as she could.

Her eyes scanned the room and looked for a way out. There was one window, but it was up high. Besides the bed, there was a shoddy nightstand and that was it. It was clear the room wasn't for someone to stay in.

il Signore had rooms like this. She had seen the inside of one, the one time she and Dante had snuck into the room that was for entertainment in a more private setting. It had been much nicer than this.

They closed the door and left her in the room alone. But she could hear the men outside taking bets. From what she could hear. Someone named Donnetti would be first, and then the rest of them would pay for the positions after Donnetti.

She was in some type of sex auction, and they were fighting for the lowest numbers. Madison didn't want to know how many numbers were up for auction. She looked around there was nothing in the room to use as a weapon.

It did make her laugh to see a Bible in the top drawer of the nightstand. She was sure none of the people who had been in that room had read the Bible including herself.

"Make her strip, Donnie, want to see what I'm paying for."

"Ok, take her clothcs off and bring her out. You know what, bring her out, and we can take her clothes off. Maybe cut them off."

There was a lot of laughter, and Madison ran her hands down her leggings and sweater. They were both her designs, and she found in one hidden pocket where she had put her butterfly seam ripper when she was taking in her creation at the waist.

It was forked, and one end was longer than the other. She figured if she stabbed someone in the neck with it, it would stop them. But could she do it? And it wouldn't work for all of them. Someone would come and take it away from her.

She watched the doorknob turn in slow motion. She didn't want to use it too early, but she couldn't keep it hidden in her clothes. If they were going to take them off of her.

She stuck it in her hair which was tossed up in a messy bun. It had a decorative butterfly handle and the seam ripper part was the antenna. They wouldn't know the difference, and it would be easy to grab and use.

"Time to come out, princess, and show us what we're getting."

"Yeah, it must be good if she was Bianchi's."

Madison was dragged out of the room and onto the stage. She wasn't sure what they would do next. She didn't want to count the number of guys there. It would only make her panic more, and she needed a clear head.

But if she was to have a good plan she needed to take stock of the situation. Before things got out of control. She looked behind her. The stage was in the back of the club in a corner which was kind of good for her. No one could sneak up behind her, but that meant to get out she would have to go through them.

"Nowhere to run."

"Make her strip," was followed by choruses of "Yeah" and fist bumps.

"You heard the crowd. Do it or we will do it for you."

Madison didn't know which was worse, having to take her clothes off on her own, or them doing it. One guy made a move forward, and she took fast action and grabbed the hem of her sweater.

She decided it was best to do it herself. She didn't want them to get close and touch her. She was sure they wouldn't just take her clothes off, and she didn't want their grimy hands on her.

Madison was happy that she had thrown another shirt on under her sweater and that she hadn't removed her sweater even though it had been hot outside. She could drag this out.

She closed her eyes and pretended Dante was there and she was stripping for him. She would tease him slow.

Madison took her time and pulled her sweater up.

"She's getting into it. Put some music on."

Maybe she could buy herself some more time. There was a pole on the stage and now there was music. She could drag it out until someone got there.

But no one was coming to save her. If Dante's men knew where they had taken her, they should've been there by now. She was on her own. She wouldn't give up. Maybe Dante's guys had let him know she was taken, and he was getting back up. But how long would that take? Whenever that was.

Hope faded that someone would get there before she was raped. She would be there for days, if not weeks.

She only had herself to depend on.

Finished with her sweater, she went to her pants. Madison told herself it was just like she was swimming. She was just stripping down to her swimsuit. That's all she was doing.

It didn't matter that she would wear a one piece and no one had seen this much of her body besides Dante. It was just her stomach and that was fine. She was ok.

Madison wouldn't take off any more than that. She hoped her pole skills would keep them mesmerized. She started a routine.

Chapter 21

When Dante got to the club, Lucca, Gabe, and some men also pulled in. All hell was going to break loose. Gabe handed him a gun and then he charged into the club. It was dead inside as not a lot of people were going to be there on a Wednesday afternoon. Inside, the bar looked empty and was dark, but there was a line of guys that led to a back room.

When he got closer, he could see they surrounded a stage, and Madison was on it, dancing.

The guys were distracted by Madison's show and didn't notice more guys coming in.

He went up to a guy at the back.

"What's happening?"

"A show before the train ride. She was supposed to be stripping, but she hasn't taken anything else off." The guy didn't even look at Dante. His eyes were trained on Madison who had her eyes closed.

He wished he had gotten there sooner. He knew how private she was with her body, and he was thankful for the privilege to see her body every time she chose to show him. And now these guys were getting to see what was his, or at least had been until he fucked it up.

"Take the rest off."

"Yeah, I want to see your tits."

"And that pussy."

That was never going to happen, but before Dante

could say something, one of the men rushed the stage and pulled Madison off the pole and yanked at her bra.

Dante knew he wasn't going to get there in time, but it wouldn't stop him from trying.

The only problem was that as Dante also moved toward the stage. Other guys rushed the stage too.

In slow motion, the first guy pulled Madison down and reached for her top, and then like a scene out of a movie, Madison pulled something from her hair and shoved it into his neck. Blood spurted out, and Madison took off running.

That's when it got crazy. One guy caught Madison by the hair and smacked her. That was the last thing the guy did, before Dante's fist introduced itself to the guy's face.

The guy's head snapped back, and confusion shown on his face and then he was down. Dante could hear fighting all around him, but all he could focus on was Madison.

She ran into his arms and he wrapped them around her. "You're safe. It's ok, baby. I'm here. I'm here now."

Madison shook in his arms. He picked her up and cradled her close to his chest.

"I need you to hold on while I get you out of here."

Dante trusted his guys to have his back as he took Madison out and put her in his car. "Keep the door locked while I go back in. Don't open it for anyone."

Madison grabbed on to his arm. "Don't leave me. Please."

"I've got to make sure my guys are safe. I promise I'll be right back and I'll never leave you alone again." Dante ran back into the clubhouse, but his guys were all coming out. No one looked hurt so he turned and got in his car to take Madison home.

When he got back in the car, he gave her his suit jacket so that she could cover up.

"Thank you."

"You don't need to thank me, Madison. I should be apologizing that I wasn't there for you when you needed me." He was gentle when he touched the back of her neck. He noticed in her hands she still had the thing she stabbed the guy with clutched in her hand.

He looked at her face and could see the bruise forming, and he wanted to turn the car around and punch the guy who hit her again. "I'm sorry I didn't get there in time."

"You did. They didn't touch me." She was careful when she touched her face. "Well, besides this."

They stopped at a red light and she turned and looked at him. "How did you know where to find me? I know Sabrina didn't tell you."

"My men. I also have connections and once I knew it was the Donnettis, I figured that was where they would take you."

"Good thing you had guys follow me today."

"Yeah." Dante had never told her that he had her tailed since they first decided to sleep together. He should tell her, but he didn't think now was the right time. He would tell her later. "Why did you go to meet her? You said you were done with her."

"I was, but she called and told me she was pregnant with Henry's child and she had a picture for me to take to my dad."

"I can see how that would get you out of the house." Dante pulled up to his place and helped Madison out of the car.

"I'm going to take a shower." She pulled the jacket tight around her and walked past one of his men in a suit, and then back to the master bath.

****

Madison entered the house and headed straight for the shower. The feeling of being dirty was there, and she wanted to get out of her clothes and into something else. She couldn't believe how the day had gone. It seemed to have lasted forever. There was something that had triggered a memory in her, but it slipped away before she could grasp it.

Her fingers started to look like raisins, so she figured it was time to get out of the water. She didn't want to face Dante or anyone else. She just wanted to lie in bed and forget everything that happened, but she couldn't. She climbed in the bed and looked at her phone. Dante had given it back to her.

She had missed calls and texts from Becky. Madison had missed the final fitting and the chance to see her dress walk in the rehearsal. She would get time to tweak it on the day, but it wouldn't be as long. She'd also missed the chance to see the competition.

Dante walked into the room and sat on the edge of the bed.

"How are you doing?"

"I guess I'm fine. I still can't believe how these last two weeks have gone." Her and Dante had gone from being together to breaking up, Henry's surgery, and then finding out that Henry had died. And then this week with the funeral, being interrogated, getting married, and then being kidnapped, and she still had to present at fashion week in three days. It was a lot.

"Yeah, it has been a hard time for you." He rubbed

the back of his neck. "And I'm sorry for what happened between us."

"I wish I could go back in time." She closed her eyes and leaned her head back on the headboard. "I would do the interview. I wouldn't be near you to have to be taken in for questioning. This thing with Sabrina would have still happened somehow, though."

"What do you mean you wouldn't have been near me? We would have still been together."

"No, we wouldn't have."

"Did you plan to dump me all along?"

"No, but what I said when we broke up is still valid. We're too different, and it's clear I can't trust you to keep me safe, and I'm still uncomfortable with your family background." Madison touched her hair.

"You're part of that family now."

"Not because I wanted to. It's because your family's criminal dealings spilled onto me, when you said they wouldn't."

"So you don't want to be married to me?" Dante placed his hands on his thighs.

"I told you that before we broke up. I don't want to be married to anyone. I don't see how you're latching on to that and ignoring the fact that you broke your promise to me." Even though she wasn't one hundred percent sure she wanted to be married, she was eight-five percent sure she wanted to be with Dante.

"No, I didn't."

"Yes you did." She leaned forward. "You said this stuff wouldn't touch me and it did."

"But I protected you from going to jail, by marrying you."

"Whatever, Dante. You won't admit it, but we both

know the truth. You broke your promise to keep me safe and untouched by this part of your life. And you know I didn't want to be married, or at least was unsure if I wanted to get married." She sat back on the bed.

Dante turned more to face her. "Ok, you're right. I messed up, but I'm doing the best I can to fix this. I've set up some appointments to look at some places that fit our needs."

"What are our needs? You haven't asked me. I'll be living there too." Madison smoothed the sheets down and avoided Dante's eyes.

"I know, and I'll make sure that we find something that you like. It's just being a Bianchi, there are certain…restrictions on what is needed in a home."

Her head snapped up. "Right. Of course. Your 'family' life comes first."

"Well, if you're only going to be living there for four years, it won't be that bad. I mean what is on your list?"

He had her there. She didn't even know. Anything would be better than having to keep sleeping with him. She was worried she would embarrass herself in bed with him one night. As if she hadn't already last night. "You're right. It doesn't matter. I just need a room that's not yours."

Dante placed his hand on her thigh. "I'm not trying to make things difficult for you on purpose."

"I still don't understand why I can't stay in my apartment?" Madison picked at the top sheet.

"We're married."

She crossed her arms over her chest. "Not for real."

"Yes, it is. A judge signed off on it and everything."

"Whatever. What are you going to do with this place?" Madison spun her hand around.

"Keep it for after you're gone."

"Wow. You said you wanted this to be real? Now you can't wait to get rid of me." Madison's head tilted to the side.

"I never said that. You're the one who said you wanted to leave in four years."

"Yeah, but you said Bianchi men marry for life, but you would give me a divorce or annulment if I wanted." Madison leaned forward and poked Dante in the chest.

"Well, you said you also don't believe in divorce, but asked how long this marriage lasted for." Dante leaned into her space.

Madison threw her hands up in the air. "Because I didn't think it was real."

"Well, it's real. So what do you want to do now?"

Madison shook her head. "No, real marriages have love between the partners."

"Bullshit. There are arranged marriages that work out well. That's what this is like. Look at Ainsley and Lucca."

"Yeah, but Ainsley said she loved Lucca and I guess he loves her back, or she is fine with him not loving her back. I'm not fine with that."

A smile came over Dante's face. Why was he grinning? What had she said?

"You love me."

"I didn't say that."

"Yes, you did."

"No, I didn't."

"You said Ainsley loves Lucca."

"Yes. She told me that."

"So you love me."

"I don't see how you're coming to your conclusion.

I just said I wouldn't want to be with someone who I loved and who didn't love me back."

"Fine. I stand corrected. But Ainsley didn't start out loving Lucca."

"Ok, that's fair. What does a real marriage mean to you?"

"I think you know, but I'll spell it out so there is no confusion. We sleep together. We communicate. We make our own family. It's simple. What do you say?" He leaned back into her space.

"I don't want to make any decisions today."

"Ok. I'm going to get ready for bed."

Madison rolled over on her side. After the day she had, she hoped she passed out and stayed asleep on her side of the bed.

****

Dante slipped into bed next to Madison. He had noticed she changed her sleepwear from what she wore when they would sleep together. Instead of a scrap of lace she had been wearing, she had on lounge pants and a tank with a shirt on top. She made it clear there would be no physical contact. He believed he could handle it, but after having to remove her hand five times from his cock, he had decided that he didn't need any more sleep. Tonight, he had put on loose sweats over his boxer briefs.

He didn't want her hands on his cock again. Not until she was ready to be with him. He lay on his back and waited. It didn't take long before she came over to his side. He let her rest her head on his chest.

It wasn't normal for them to sleep like this, but had on occasion after rounds of sex when she was on top. He took in her scent and let her breathing lull him to sleep. It didn't last for long when her hand slipped down his thigh and found him hard and waiting.

He hadn't bothered to try a cold shower, because just being around her could get him hard and he didn't jack off because that wouldn't help. Nothing would stop him from getting hard for her.

Her hand traveled back up his stomach and before he could catch her hand, it had snuck in under his pants and boxer briefs and grabbed hold of him. She gave him a hand job, while her beaded nipples pressed into his chest.

"Madison, baby." He stopped her hand.

"Dante."

The hairs on his body stood up when she said his name. When they were together he would have taken her once she was awake, but now, he hoped he could get her hand off and her back on her side of the bed without waking her.

He had listened to her cry when he left the room last night. He hoped she didn't think he didn't want her anymore. But he wanted her without reservations. If she couldn't accept his background, then they would have to divorce. He couldn't live like this. Even if they found a place where she had her own room.

What kind of marriage would that be? Not one he wanted to be a part of. Neither of them would be happy. But he was firm on the fact that they wouldn't sleep together until she was ready to accept him in all ways. That was what he needed and he wouldn't back down.

Dante had most of her fingers off of him when he knew she had woken up. Her body went from pliant to stiff. He froze. Did she want him to keep removing her hand or did she want to take it back herself? What would be less embarrassing for her?

"Dante." This time her voice was resigned. She took her hand off of him and out of his hand. "I'm sorry."

"It's not a problem."

"You're wearing boxers and pants?"

"Yeah."

"And it still happened."

"Yeah."

"There is no way we can go on like this." She rolled back to her side. "Why can't I just stay at my apartment until we find a place? It would be better than this."

She had him there. "After what happened with the Donnettis, I don't feel comfortable not having you here."

He could see she wanted to argue. "But that was Sabrina."

"True, but others might hear and try to do the same. Besides, we don't know if Sabrina is going to stop."

The color drained from her face, and her eyes widened.

"Don't worry. I've increased security, and I've hand-picked one of the guys to be your bodyguard."

"Excuse me if I still worry. That didn't help the last time."

"I didn't have as many as I've assigned now. I told you I would keep you safe."

"You also said I was just dating Dante the man and that I wouldn't get in trouble with the law. So I'm withholding my trust."

That wasn't good for Dante. He needed her to trust him. To believe in him. "I'll do whatever I can to show you that you can trust me."

"I'm going back to bed. Can we try extra pillows in between us?"

"Sure. You go to sleep, and I'll be back. I need to

check on some things."

Dante went to his office. The brokerage firm Stanley and Richards had sent a follow-up email. He hadn't sent back the completed job-offer package. He had signed it but not sent it out. He still hadn't talked to Don Calo yet. He might have signed his own family away; and then he wouldn't have the job or Madison, if he ever had her.

He would go through the proper channels to secure a meeting with his uncle.

****

Madison woke up somewhat rested. The pillows had helped. She hadn't climbed over them. Dante had no problems staying on his side. Had he come back to bed after he left? She got up and went to the bathroom.

The redness from where the guy had backhanded her had faded. She had been able to get a make-up meeting with Becky. Dante had said he had something to do, but he would send the guy who would be her bodyguard to come meet her. Madison wasn't clear on her feelings of having a bodyguard. Well, no, that was a lie. She knew and she wasn't for it. It would be strange to have someone follow her around. Especially if they carried weapons, which she guessed they would be.

****

Dante entered his uncle's compound. It had been quicker to get the appointment than when he was planning it out. It helped that he was actual family. He walked past enforcers and foot shoulders in his uncle's compound.

He was shown into the office, where he found Don Calo at his desk.

"Don–"

"No need." He looked at the other men in the room.

"Leave."

Once the men had left and closed the door behind them, his uncle gestured him to come closer and to sit.

"Now what is it that's so important you needed to see me right away."

Dante took a breath. He could be sealing his fate. "I have an offer."

"Is that so? From who?"

"From a brokerage firm."

"And they want to partner with us?"

"No. They want me to work for them."

"You want to do both?"

"No."

"I see. So you want to leave."

"Yes. I haven't been happy with my position as accountant. And even though our marriage is legal, she is still nervous with who we are."

"That's a part of you. Won't change if you leave."

"I know, but it would make her feel more comfortable."

"And that's what you want? She's caused a lot of problems in the family between you and Enzo."

"Those were Enzo's problems. Madison has always made it clear she didn't want Enzo."

"Right. I remember her words at the engagement party."

"Yeah." Before he had fucked it up.

"So you want to leave because of her?"

"No. It's just this life isn't me. I got picked for this role because I was good with numbers, but I want to run businesses and invest. Not spend my time keeping two sets of books for everything and looking over my shoulder."

"I see."

Don Calo stared at him hard. "I knew this life wasn't for you. That's why I let you not only go to college, but overrode your father so you could get your masters. You're a learning person. I can see why Stanley and Richards want you."

Dante was shocked. "You knew?"

"Of course. Nothing happens in the town or especially with this family that I don't know. Take the offer, and I'll release you from your duties. But you will still always be family. You may go home and tell your wife."

And just like that a huge weight was lifted off his shoulders. He was free, and he had Don Calo's blessing to leave and the knowledge that he and Madison would be safe.

"Thank you."

"No need to thank me. What are uncles for? Come."

He motioned for Dante to come over and his uncle clapped him on the head and then hugged him. "You can go in peace. But I still expect to see you at family functions."

"Yes, of course."

"Now get outta here. I have an empire to run and a new accountant to bring on board."

Dante left the office and closed the door behind him. He could go home and tell Madison the feelings he had for her. He didn't want to put pressure on her, so he would wait until after she had fashion week.

****

Madison was glad when the time to walk the runway was here. Her design was ready; her model was prepped. She just had her last-minute changes to do to make sure her creation fit the model to perfection and showed off the design and movement.

She knew she had aced the make-up interview and was still in the top. Her design would either keep her there or not. She crossed her fingers and toes and hoped granny was looking out for her.

Behind the stage everything was chaotic. Models were undressing and being dressed. Hair and makeup were either being done or retouched. Madison was waiting for her model who was in hair and makeup. She had her pin cushion and her trusty butterfly seam ripper with her in her hidden pocket.

Once this was over, she and Dante would look for a bigger place. And she couldn't wait. Dante had been avoiding her, which she guessed was fine. But it seemed more awkward that he always happened to never be around or always leaving when she was coming in.

She shook her head, now wasn't the time to be concerned with it. She looked around, her model was done. "Perfect. How do you feel?"

"Good, nervous." Becky looked at herself in the mirror.

"Me too. Let's get you dressed."

Madison helped Becky into the dress. In the end, the hidden pocket at the waist hadn't worked like Madison wanted. She had changed the design to include two invisible pockets in the side of the dress and she had figured out how to do a hidden pocket in one of the folds of the dress that wouldn't mess with the look when not empty. What was the use of a hidden pocket if you couldn't use it or it changed the look of your dress.

Becky looked amazing. Madison made some final last touches, and then they went over to the runway for her turn to walk. She hadn't gotten a chance to see Sabrina's design, but her other competitors' designs were ahead of her. They were going in reverse order, from bottom to the top. As the other two designs went to walk, Sabrina's design came off.

Sabrina had been standing on the other side of the runway waiting for her model. She gave Madison a smug look. Madison was taken aback at the fact that Sabrina's model wore a substandard version of Madison's design. Sabrina had somehow stolen a copy of Madison's design.

But there was nothing she could do. It was time for Becky to walk. There were gasps as Becky took to the runway and the murmurs of this being like the first dress to walk, only better.

Sabrina's smug smile faltered, and she shot daggers at Madison. Becky was at the end of the stage and showed off the pockets which got a round of applause. By the time Becky had finished walking, Kristy from HR was behind the stage. They were supposed to pick the winner during the show, but Anastazia made an announcement that they would do it at the end of the fashion show tomorrow.

"Madison and Sabrina. I'd like to see you and your models over here."

Madison and Becky followed her, along with Sabrina and her model. When they got to the room, Anastazia was coming in.

"It seems someone copied someone else's design. Since there is no way to prove whose original design it was, you both have been disqualified."

Madison's heart dropped. She had lost the thing she most wanted due to Sabrina. Madison doubted Sabrina had expected her to show, if Sabrina's plan had worked. So disqualification hadn't been her end goal. She had wanted to win the position at the fashion house.

"She stole my design," Madison and Sabrina said at the same time.

"That is a strong accusation coming from both of you. It's a 'she said, she said' with no actual proof."

"It's also the truth," Madison said. "I can prove it's mine."

"I'm not sure how you will prove this," Kristy said.

"I have the sketches, and my model will back me up."

"That all could have been faked after you looked at my design. Your model would lie too because she would get the top spot in the magazine spread," Sabrina said with a smug look on her face.

"She has a point."

"I can prove it's mine because I put a hidden pocket in my design. I did it for all my designs as it's my signature. If you look at my previous designs, you will find the hidden pockets. I can tell you where to find them along with the one in this design."

"All right then. Sabrina, where is the hidden pocket?"

"There isn't one; she is making up excuses."

"Show me where the pocket is."

Madison walked over to the design and showed Kristy the hidden pocket in the bottom fold of the dress.

"It looks like she is right; there is a hidden pocket."

"She could have added it after she took my design." Sabrina spoke up.

"That could be true, but I'm having one of the interns bring in the work Madison's done for us during her internship."

Madison's shoulders relaxed. It seemed Kristy believed her or at least was open to the idea that this was Madison's design.

She showed the hidden pockets in all of the items that she had made.

"It looks like the hidden pockets is in fact Madison's signature. Unfortunately, there is nothing that says Sabrina's wasn't the original and Madison added a pocket on to it." Kristy looked between the two of them.

"Stealing someone else's work is unethical and won't be tolerated. There was a chance that the other designers could be picked up by other fashion houses, but no one will touch either of you now, knowing that one of you stole another competitor's design and tried to pass it off as your own."

"Even when comparing the design execution, Madison's is still superior to Sabrina's and has better features. Madison, I'm curious if she stole your design, why doesn't hers have the pockets?"

"On my sketches I sign my initials where the pocket would be. Let's look at the sketches."

"It looks like here in Sabrina's that is on the waist."

"Yes, that was my original idea, but I like the pocket to be functional and able to hold credit cards and cash without bulking out the design and I just couldn't get it to work so I went with the invisible pockets on the side and the hidden pocket in the fold."

"I see. Can we see your sketches?"

"Of course. I keep them all together to show the evolution of the design as I work on it."

"Yes, it's all here."

"I'm curious as to how Sabrina got your design."

"Well, we were friends outside the competition. At least on my part, we were. She came to my place several times, but I think how she got that earlier version was through my brother who passed away."

"Oh, and how is that? Since he's not here to corroborate."

"They were seeing each other and he has—had a key to my place. I believe Sabrina used that to get in and take a copy of my original design."

"Why didn't she just steal your dress?"

"I was keeping it at my, uh, boyfriend's place as I was spending more time there."

"Ok, well that makes sense to me. Sabrina, what about you? Why do you think we should believe that it was Madison that stole your design?"

"My designs are good, maybe not as well executed as if Madison had done them, but the concepts are there and out of the box."

"That is true, your ideas are what helped you make it to the finals."

"But my ideas are just as good. It's not like execution is the only reason I'm in first place."

"That is also true."

"Well, Madison has a history of stealing from me."

"What? That's a lie."

"No it isn't. She took the headliner position at a strip club that we work at."

"Is that true, Madison?"

"No. The boss caught my set when I subbed for Sabrina and asked me to work there. I didn't know he was going to give me the headliner position."

"Yeah, because she was sleeping with him to get the position."

"That's not true. We were seeing each other after I started working there."

"Well, this is all getting kind of messy. We can't tell who is lying. Unfortunately, we will have to stick with our original decision to disqualify you both. I don't know if another fashion house will be willing to touch either of you.

Sabrina lunged for Madison. "You bitch. Why did you have to get away?"

Madison hadn't been expecting Sabrina's outburst and wasn't prepared for Sabrina to put her hands around Madison's neck.

"You ruined everything. I hate you."

Madison tried to push Sabrina off of her.

"Oh dear, someone get security."

Two security officers stood nearby and headed over to pull Sabrina off of Madison. Sabrina yelled as she was dragged out kicking and screaming. "This isn't over. I'm going to get you."

"We wish we could make an offer letter for you to look over and accept."

"I understand." Madison teared up, but she held her emotions and her tears back. "I'm thankful for the opportunity to compete and to have been able to intern at Anastazia's House of Fashion. I'm grateful for all the knowledge and the exposure to a real fashion house."

"You're welcome. I'm sorry things had to end this way. Thank you for your work, and sharing your creativity with us. Your skills speak for themselves. Enjoy the rest of your day." And she walked out leaving Madison and Becky alone. Sabrina's model had followed her out, knowing she wouldn't be getting the coveted magazine spread.

Madison turned to Becky. "Sorry."

"You don't need to apologize to me. You did nothing wrong. I'm sorry it had to end this way. What are you going to do now?"

"I think I'm going to go home and rest. You?"

"I'm going to go out with my family to celebrate. Even though I didn't get the cover position, I made it to the finals and lots of people were there to see me walk, so I should get some agency calls."

"Oh, that's great." Madison wasn't even sure if anyone had come for her. Dante had been out when she left, so she wasn't sure if he made it. She had seen her parents, but she doubted her mom had stayed.

Madison helped get Becky out of the garment and packed it up along with her things ready to leave.

"Sir, you're not allowed back here," a guard said.

"That's my wife."

Madison looked up to see Dante trying to get to her. "Dante, you made it."

"Of course I did. I wouldn't miss it for anything."

She looked at the security guard. "It's ok. I'm ready to leave." She picked up her things and walked over to Dante.

"What happened?"

"Sabrina stole my design. I'm ready to go home."

"Oh, baby, I'm sorry."

"It sucks. In the end, I couldn't prove it was mine, and I lost the job. Not only that, but no other fashion house will touch me, since it wasn't proven who stole from who."

"That's terrible." He hugged her and kissed her forehead. "Do you want to go out and take your mind off things?"

"No, I don't think so. Not right now anyway. It's been a stressful few hours. Are my parents still here?"

"I'm not sure. They were out there when I came back here. They were headed in this direction."

Madison and Dante walked out from the back to see her mom and dad waiting.

"Mom, Dad, you guys stayed." Madison gave her father a hug.

"I wish I hadn't. I told people my daughter was going to be a famous designer, and it turns out she copied someone else's work. I'm going to be a laughingstock."

"Mom, I didn't cheat. Sabrina copied my work."

"Either way, dear, you're not famous now, are you?"

"No."

"Milford, let's go home."

Madison watched her parents walk away.

Dante had a protective arm around her and squeezed her tight. "She's not worth it. Let's go home."

Chapter 22

Dante could see the stress and a kaleidoscope of emotions on Madison's face and in her body when they got home. "Why don't you go and take a bath? When you're ready, I have some news for you."

"I don't think I can take any more news."

"Don't worry, it is good news."

"Can you tell me now?"

"Let's sit down."

"Ok."

He took her hand and led her over to the sofa. "I took the offer with the brokerage firm."

"Oh Dante, that's great." She wrapped her arms around him. "I know you wanted that. How did everyone take it? Have you told your family?"

"I spoke to Don Calo, and he gave me his blessing. I haven't spoken to my dad yet. I know he will take it hard."

"I can understand that."

"I know you had some valid concerns with regards to my previous job, but now that that is over, are you ready to make this a real marriage?"

"Dante, that is good, but I'm still not comfortable with your past. They are still your family, and there is still the threat of you going to jail. What will I do if you're gone? I don't have a job to go to and support myself right now. I have nothing."

"You have me. Anyway, I'm going to beat the charges. Tony and I have something in the works. It looks like I was set up and false information was leaked."

"Ok, but I don't know if I want to be part of your family."

"Madison, we're married. You already are."

Madison touched her neck. "I guess you're right, but it's not for real. And if you already have something worked out, there is no need for me to stay here and I can go back to my apartment."

"And our marriage?"

"We can stay married I guess, but we don't need to live with each other."

"But Sabrina isn't in jail. She could still come after you."

"I guess that's true. Ok. I guess I have to stay." She turned to go. "But there was that guy you were going to have be my bodyguard? Can he just watch me?"

"He can, but I'd feel more comfortable with you here."

"And I'd feel more comfortable at my place."

"Madison, there is something else I wanted to tell you." He took her hands in his. "I love you."

Her face softened. "Oh Dante, I love you too, but it doesn't mean we have to live together. I know we're married, but you want the wife and kids and I don't know if I do. My mom has taught me one thing, and it is that love is finite, and there isn't enough for everyone. I don't want to stop loving you, but I also don't want to bring a kid into the world that I can't love, or can't provide as much love as they need."

"Ok, I guess I understand your feelings, but there is enough love for everyone." He pulled her into his arms.

"That might be true, but it also might not be true."

"But if you love me, why don't you want to stay?"

"I don't know."

Dante seized on her confusion. "I love you, and I want to be with you. I understand you didn't plan on being married, but now that we are, is it such a bad thing?"

"Well, no. I guess not. But kids?" She looked up at him. "You want them."

"I do, but I want you more. If you decide you don't want kids, then I will respect that, but I don't want to live my life without you."

"Oh, Dante. Are you sure?"

"I'm sure."

He bent his head to kiss her, and she rose up to meet him. The instant their lips touched, everything else fell away. Even though it had only been less than three weeks since they had last been together, it had the feeling of being like forever. His hands slid up and down and reacquainted himself with her body.

Dante was quick to remove Madison's shirt and bra and left her top bare to his eyes. He palmed her breasts, using his fingers to toy with her nipples.

"Dante." Her voice was breathless, and she pulled away to breathe.

"I know, baby." He dropped his head and captured one peak in his mouth, while his fingers continued to work its twin. Madison's hands lifted up his shirt to touch his chest, before her hands slipped down and undid his fly.

She dropped down to her knees and held him in her hand and stroked him while she looked into his eyes.

"I've missed you so much." She swirled her tongue

around his cockhead and then took him in her mouth. She moaned and he slid in deeper. He didn't want to come too fast, so he pulled her off and picked her up in his arms and took her to the bedroom.

He laid her down on the bed. "Let me show you how much I love you. He lowered his head to her glistening folds and took a broad lick up to the bundle of nerves at the top. Her hips arched off of the bed, and her nails dug into his shoulders. He welcomed the bite.

"Dante, please. I don't want to come without you."

He rose up on his knees and lined himself up with her entrance. He hovered over her body and brushed her hair behind her ear. "Madison, I love you so much. You are all that I want." And then he plunged into her body.

Madison cried out. "Dante, I love you."

He wanted to be gentle and slow and show her how much he cared. But he couldn't hold back. He had missed this connection with her, and he pounded into her body.

"Oh, yes. Shit. Dante." Her tits bounced in his face. "Ahh, I'm sorry, I'll never leave you. I'm sorry, Dante, don't stop."

He could feel she was close, and so he leaned closer to capture her lips in a searing kiss. She had known, what he hadn't until she said she was sorry for leaving. He was punishing her for leaving him. He didn't know until that moment how much he needed her in his life.

Madison climaxed around his dick, and he shot his load into her body. It was like a reawakening, and the connection between them was as strong as if they hadn't spent anytime apart.

Was she still taking her birth control pills? He knew she hadn't taken them that one night, and he hadn't remembered her alarm going off or seen her take them when they had been together, before they broke up.

He rolled off of her and pulled her to lie across his body. "I forgot to ask before we had sex if you were back on your birth control. I didn't use a condom."

"It's ok. I'm back on the pill."

"When did you go back?"

"After the first night."

"I didn't know."

"I know. I changed my alarm and times. I guess I was afraid to tell you, because I knew how much you wanted kids and I still wasn't sure."

"Hey." He tilted her chin up to look into her eyes. "I don't want you to ever be afraid to tell me something connected to your body and what you're doing with it. I respect your choice."

"Thank you."

Dante still needed to tell her that he was having her followed, but he didn't think it was a conversation best had in bed. He would talk to her after his shower, and he hoped it would be before Angelo, the bodyguard he had assigned to Madison, got there.

****

Madison left the bedroom to make her and Dante something to eat. Dante was going to take a quick shower. She headed to the kitchen and he called out to her. "The bodyguard is on the way, so you can meet each other. Can you get the door if I'm not out yet?"

"Sure." Madison went into the kitchen to see what they had that she could make for them. She had just opened the fridge when the doorbell rang. She went to answer it. She was a little nervous to meet this person. Was he going to be big and burly and have weapons on him? Ever since she was kidnapped at gunpoint, guns made her more wary than before.

She opened the door to find expensive-suited guy stood there. What was he doing here?

"Hi, Mrs. Bianchi. I'm Angelo. Mr. Bianchi wanted us to meet. I'll be escorting you around."

"Right. Come in. Dante is in the shower. He should be out soon."

"Thank you. It's good to be able to introduce myself to you. Will you still be taking public transportation? I think Dante mentioned having a car for you."

"Uh, yeah." Madison was dazed as her brain tried to process what was happening. The guy she had seen many times on the bus and metro wearing expensive tailored suits worked for Dante. So what had he been doing? She didn't want to believe it, but had he been having her followed all this time? And what for?

"Dante says you're one of the best guys he has."

"Thanks. That's nice of Mr. Bianchi to say. I've been with him for a while. I'm glad he is pleased with my services."

"Right." They still stood in the doorway. "Oh, come in sorry, my mind is somewhere else."

"No problem. I understand."

"What did you mean you were glad to be able to introduce yourself?"

"Well, Boss had me following you, which was pretty difficult on public transport."

"Right. And how long has that been going on?" She wanted to see if what she remembered was the same as what he would say.

"Oh, I don't know the exact date."

"That's fine but if you had to guess, was it one week?" She didn't know the exact date either, but she had an idea of the time frame.

"No, I've been tailing you for close to three months for Boss."

"Right." Everything crashed down around her.

Dante entered the room. "Angelo, glad you could make it."

"Yeah, no problem. I was just telling Mrs. Bianchi how long I've been tailing her."

"Oh, shit. Madison, baby it's not—"

"Not what? Not what it seems? That you've been having me followed since our arrangement."

"Well, that's true, but it was to make sure you were safe."

"It wasn't that you didn't trust me? That you had it in your head that I was cheating on you still. Like when you had me investigated?"

"Madison, I had to be sure."

Tears welled up in her eyes. "Right. Are you sure now—"

"Yes."

"Is Angelo for my protection or so you can keep tabs on me?"

"Madison, baby, it's not that I don't trust you. Angelo is here to keep you safe."

"Right, and you trust him to do that?"

"Yes."

"Then he can keep me safe in my apartment." Madison turned and left the room. She wouldn't cry. Did he even love her or just want to control her? She packed a bag with her things. Dante's footsteps enter the bedroom.

"Madison—"

"Don't. I don't want to hear it. There isn't anything

you could say to make this better."

"Please, stay. Let's talk."

"There is nothing to say. I'm leaving. You can have them send my things back to my place. I'm sure you're going to still have Angelo watching me."

"Yes."

"Right. Even if I said not to?"

"Madison, I love you and I would die if you were hurt; and having someone like Angelo there could save you. So yes, even if you don't want him. I will still assign him to you."

"Ok. I don't have it in me to argue. I just want to leave."

She walked around Dante and found Angelo still standing in the living room.

"Do you have a car?"

"Yes."

"Please take me to my apartment."

He looked over her head.

"It's ok. Do as she says."

"Thank you," she said without turning around and she walked out of the door.

****

Madison sat with Zoe in her apartment. Zoe had come over for a ninety-day watch party.

"That was so good. It's nice to watch other people's hot messes. It makes mine seem not so bad." Madison picked up her drink.

"Yeah, but some of these people made their own messes." Zoe shifted on the sofa. "I know you don't want to discuss it, but it's all over the club that you and Dante got married, but you're living apart. What's up with that?"

"Well at least this time it's right. We only got married so I wouldn't have to testify, so there is no need for me to live with him."

"But you two were for all intents and purposes living together. I know you guys were having a fight when I picked you up, but I figured you guys made up after the funeral and that's why you got married."

"No, we're still broken up. Just with a marriage license."

"So what went wrong?"

"He's in the mob."

"But I told you that before."

"Yeah, but I didn't think it was true."

"But you had to have found out it was true sometime before this."

"Well, yeah."

"So why was it fine then and not fine now?"

"You are supposed to be my friend. Why are you going so hard on this?"

"I am your friend. That's why I'm asking. You don't seem happy. Not like when you and Dante were together."

"Yeah, but it was all lies."

"Were they lies he told, or ones you told yourself?"

Zoe had her there. "I believed I could handle it, but I can't."

"But word is he left."

"Yes, that's true."

"So then what's the problem?"

"They're still his family."

"He didn't pick them. None of us choose our families."

"I guess that's right." Madison wouldn't have

picked her parents if she had a choice. "But he was having me followed. How can he say he loves me and have guys follow me around to see where I'm going? He doesn't trust me."

"Yep, that wasn't cool. He should have told you sooner. But it did help with that Sabrina situation."

"Yeah, but that wasn't what they were there for. It was only by chance they turned out to be useful. It's not like Dante knew Sabrina was plotting against me. They were following me everywhere, just to report back to Dante my every move."

"He didn't do it the right way, but you can see where he was coming from."

"I can, but why didn't he stop it once he knew?"

"I bet he forgot. I don't think he got special reports on you. With the amount of time you two spent together, you would have seen them coming or some reports or something coming through.

"I guess that's true." There were the "where are you texts" he sent when she went back to her place the first night they spent the weekend together and again after the surgery.

"He even changed the uniform rules for the girls."

"He did?"

"Yeah. You know you love him and he loves you. You guys aren't happy apart. Maybe you should do something."

"Yeah, maybe."

"I'm going to head out. I have an event."

"Oh ok, no worries. See you later.

****

It had been two weeks since Madison found out Dante didn't trust her. Angelo didn't have much to do.

She sat in her apartment after the first week, when she went out looking for jobs.

Kristy had been right. No one was willing to take her on, at least not in a designer position and she needed more income than a seamstress. She needed to see her parents but hadn't had it in her until today.

Angelo drove her to her parents' house. "I don't know how long I'll be. Do you want to leave?"

"I'll wait, Mrs. B."

"Ok, if it gets too cold, let me know..." It had taken her this long to get Angelo to stop calling her Mrs. Bianchi for everything, but he still refused to call her Madison. She guessed Mrs. B. wasn't so bad. At least she could pretend the B was for Bryant and not Bianchi.

"Will do."

He got out of the car with her and walked her to her parents' house and took his position standing outside the front door.

Madison rang the bell. Her mom answered.

"Madison, there you are. We haven't seen you since you lost that silly job. Who is your new young man?"

"He's my bodyguard. He works for Dante."

"Oh nice. Is he coming in?" Her mom made a move toward him.

"No, thanks, ma'am. I'll wait outside for Mrs. B."

"Who's Mrs. B.?"

"Mrs. Bianchi." Angelo pointed at Madison.

"You got married without us? I'm sure your father would have liked to walk you down the aisle." Madison's mom turned and walked farther into the house. "Milfred, did you know that Madison married that young man without us?"

"Mom, we went to a judge. We didn't do anything

big that we didn't invite you for." Madison made a face at Angelo and then closed the door, before following her mother into the house.

"Are you pregnant?" Her dad's voice was hopeful.

"No." She didn't want to be pregnant. So why did she feel nauseous at not having Dante's baby? Shouldn't it be the other way around?

"Let me see your ring." Madison's mom grabbed for her hand. "Seems plain. How much did it cost? You know he should spend three months of his salary on a ring. How much does he make?"

"Mom. I don't know how much he spent or how much he makes, and even if I did I wouldn't share that information with you."

"Well, you should know. It's important to know what your financial situation is."

"Do you know yours?"

"Yes, of course. I know how much Milford made and what his pension is."

"Then why do you keep going over it?"

"Now, Madison, don't talk to your mother like that."

"Why not, Dad? I think something needs to be said. I can't keep bailing you guys out all the time. In fact, that's what I came here to tell you." She placed the papers on the table. "I've paid your bills so you are current, and that is the end of my help. From now on you're on your own if you choose to overspend, then that is now on you."

"Really, dear. You get married, and you're going to dump us for your new family."

"Mom, that's not what I'm saying. I'm still your daughter. I'll still come and visit and do all the other things I've always done. I just won't pay your bills anymore."

"Milford, talk some sense into her."

"Madison, with my stroke, we've depended on you to help us. You know with Henry now gone, you're all we have left."

"And I'll still be here, Dad, just not as an ATM, but as your daughter."

"That's not acceptable. Do you know what we would have to do to live without your help?" Her mother stomped her foot.

"Yes, and it's not anything that can't be done. Downsize and stop buying so much."

"I will not. Milford, I won't stand for this."

"And that's fine. I think this conversation is over. If you want to speak to me you have my number. Just know I will not be able to help out in a financial way anymore. I'll let myself out."

Madison got up and walked out. She wouldn't let them see her cry. That was all she had been to them was a walking wallet. Did they ever love her or was it just her money that they loved?

"Mrs. B., you ok?"

"I'm fine, why?"

"You're crying. Did you get bad news. Is it your pops?"

"No, he's fine. They're both fine. Just take me home please."

"Sure, no problem."

Madison sat in the back of the car and leaned her head against the window and let the tears fall. She knew Angelo would tell Dante, but she couldn't stop.

She walked into her place and was relieved not to see Dante. He still had a key, and she had believed he would show up. She didn't want to have to put on a brave face or act like she expected more from her parents or see his pity.

She just wanted to take a hot shower, eat some chicken lo mein, and drink herself to sleep. First step to her plan was to shower. She didn't have any wine on hand so she would need to go out and get some. Something else for Angelo to report back to Dante. But she couldn't help it. She needed a drink.

****

Dante looked at the text from Angelo that Madison had cried after she left her parents' house. He had figured something like that would happen and he wanted to go to her, but knew she wouldn't want that.

But something had been bothering him from the time he went to see Madison after he was released on bail. The fact that she had called Enzo, and he knew Dante had been arrested. No one but their lawyer should have known that, and he wouldn't have called to tell Enzo.

Something didn't add up. He didn't want to believe it, but all signs pointed to Enzo as the mole. Now he just needed proof and that was why he met with his lawyer.

"What do you have for me?" Dante turned his chair to face Tony.

"I had a guy check and it looks like someone hacked the system and moved money around to make it look like you were not only laundering money, but were also embezzling money," Tony said.

"Who would do that and why?" Dante looked off to the side.

"It seems like someone wanted you out of the way. The feds want to talk to your wife. I can brief her on the no comment and of course sit in the interview with her."

"Ok, set it up for a few days. She's been through a lot." Dante leaned back in the chair, still thinking who could do this.

"Can do."

"I know a guy." Dante placed his palm on the table. "I'm going to reach out to him to see what he can find."

"Are you sure? Isn't this something Enzo can handle? We don't want to involve too many outsiders." Tony gathered his folders.

"Enzo is too busy looking for the mole to add this to his plate. I'll take care of it and don't mention it." Dante pushed back from the table.

"I won't."

"Great. I need to head out." Dante stood.

"Of course." Tony shook Dante's hand and he left.

Dante sent out a text to a guy as he left the building.

****

Dante let himself into Madison's place. On the way he had stopped and picked up chicken lo mein from her favorite place and a couple of bottles of Moscato. He set them down on the kitchen table and went to look for Madison.

Angelo had told him she hadn't left so where could she be? She hadn't come out when he came in. He strode down the hall, but the water was running. He didn't want to scare her, especially while she was in the shower, so he went back to the kitchen and got the food and wine ready.

He could feel her presence.

"What are you doing here?" She had on an oversized shirt and leggings. Her arms were wrapped around her waist and she looked around and avoided eye contact.

"I came to bring you some stuff that I hoped would make you feel better. Angelo told me things hadn't gone well at your parents."

"You didn't need to come."

"I know, but I wanted to."

"Why?"

"Because I love you. I can't bear it that you're in pain."

She looked him in the eye. "Even when you cause it?"

"Especially when I've caused it. I never meant to hurt you. It wasn't so much that I didn't trust you, but that I didn't trust myself. I didn't trust my gut that was telling me you wouldn't cheat and that I was enough for you." He moved closer to her. "I had believed the same with respect to someone else, and it turned out to be false."

"I'm not her."

"I know you're not, and I'm sorry for not realizing that sooner." He moved closer to her.

"So where does that leave us?"

"Nothing has changed for me. I still want our marriage to be real and for you to come back home. If you can accept the fact that even though I left the mob, they are still my family."

"I understand that now. We didn't pick the families we were born into, and they will always be a part of you."

"Can you accept that?" Dante held his breath. This was the make it or break it moment and would determine if they had a future together or not.

"I can. I love you so much, Dante, that it hurts and I'm scared. I don't want to turn into my parents."

"Oh, baby, come here." He wrapped her in his arms,

and she rested her head on his shoulder. "You could never be like them." He cupped her face in his hands so he could look into her eyes. "You're already so different. You were taking care of them, which is more than can be said for them."

He wiped the tears from her eyes with the pads of his thumbs. "Look at your friendship with Zoe and the way you cared for Sabrina, even though after a while she didn't deserve it."

"Yeah, turns out she hated me."

"Not everyone is going to like you. All that matters is that you like yourself."

"I'm nervous to have kids."

"We don't have to have them right away. We can take our time, and you can decide down the road how you feel."

"Are you sure? I don't want you to resent me if I decide I don't want them."

"I won't. I'd prefer to have you than someone else and kids."

"Oh, Dante." She kissed him.

Dante deepened the kiss and then pulled back. "Let's get you something to eat. I know you have to be hungry."

"I am, but for you."

"Me too, but we have the rest of our lives for that. Let's eat and talk. I missed our talks." He reached for her hand, and she slipped hers in his and it was right.

****

Dante needed to call a meeting. One that he would invite Enzo to later. Would Enzo show up or just skip it and ignore him? He was using a meeting room in one of their office buildings where they kept offices for real estate and their financial firm.

The men filed in some one by one, others in groups until everyone was there except Enzo. The family lawyer was there as well. Dante waited for his tech guy to show up. When Hunter came in, Dante began the meeting.

"The reason I called everyone here is because Hunter found out who hacked the accounts and set me up."

"Who?" said the Don.

"Hunter, if you want to go ahead and give your report again."

"Sure. It took me several days to uncover the culprit. He was good at hiding his tracks, but a new piece of spyware technology has come out, and I was able to use that as it was so new. The hacker didn't have access to it yet."

"That's all nice and well, but who is it?"

"It's Enzo."

The room was so quiet you could hear a bullet drop.

"Enzo. How can it be?" Enzo's dad asked.

"He's family," said Don Calo.

"Yeah, are you sure someone isn't setting my son up like they did Dante?"

"I'm sure. Once I told Dante, he believed the same thing, so I hacked farther into his computer and I found evidence."

"Like a manifesto. That sounds too convenient," Don Calo said.

"No, it was checking browser history and purchases. He had scrubbed his computer well, but as I say with new technology coming out every day, I was able to piece it all together. If you want to look at the screen, you can see the images that I took."

"Why would he do this?" The Don asked. "We're family. We stick together."

"Dante has something Enzo wants." Enzo's dad hung his head. "I didn't think he would stoop to this, but he is obsessed."

"With what?" the Don asked.

"Madison," Dante and Enzo's dad said at the same time.

"All this over a woman?"

"Yes."

"I guess when he found out Madison and Dante were together, it set Enzo off. I remember when he came to me and asked for me to step in. We can't get an annulment for the wedding. She's made her choice."

"This history goes back several years. So he planned to do this before Dante and Madison were together. There is information to suggest Lucca was next."

"How?" Don Calo's voice was hoarse.

"Real estate fraud and license revoking was something he had been looking up. This around the time Madison first was working at the club."

"Why?" Enzo's dad looked around.

"He wanted to be selected to take over the family business. He believed with Dante out, who I love like a second son, and my own son he would be next in line. Gabe is too young. I would never have picked him," the Don said.

They all sat around the table lost in their own thoughts.

Enzo walked into the meeting room. "Was it not at one PM?"

"We opened early with a presentation you didn't need to be here for. We found the mole."

Enzo's eyes got shifty and then he tried to make a run for it, but his dad blocked the door.

"How could you do this to your family?"

"It's the Don's fault he never let me use any of my skills that I learned in college to help out. I wanted to take over and I knew he wouldn't choose me, unless I got rid of the competition."

"So this wasn't concerning Madison?" The Don asked

"After they were sneaking around together, I knew I had to do something. She was mine." He looked at Dante. Rage on his face also radiated off of his body like tsunami waves that crashed on the shore. Ready to destroy everything in its path.

"She was never yours." Dante shook his head.

"She would have been if you hadn't interfered with what was happening between us. She was almost ready to date me."

"She wasn't. She was never interested in you, Enzo. I didn't take what you didn't have."

"Enzo, no," Enzo's dad said.

But it was too late. He was across the room and sucker punched Dante in the face, who was at first stunned but then began pummeling Enzo.

They had to pull Dante off of Enzo, and he looked like he had a broken nose and a busted lip and there might have been a black eye forming. Blood was pouring from Enzo's nose, but he wasn't trying to stop it. He just kept rocking back and forth, mumbling, "She was mine," on repeat.

Dante had called the feds to be ready pick Enzo up. They came in and hauled him away. They had been in the other room listening to the meeting. Their lawyer,

Tony had gotten Dante immunity to get Enzo.

With his confession of what he had done, he was going to a federal prison. They were going to at least isolate him so that was a comfort to Dante. He didn't want to think of Enzo being hurt in jail. After all, he was still family. Even if he was a traitor.

****

Madison sat at home unsure of what to do. She had taken several tests, and they all came back positive. She knew she had to tell Dante. She waited for him in the living room with one positive test and a new one because she was sure he was going to want her to do it again with his own eyes.

She knew he was at a meeting. He had told her that he might be home late. She didn't have anything else to do, but practice in her head what she was going to say and to think how much her life had changed.

She wasn't working at AS house of fashion or any other fashion house and all she had was time on her hands. She had no idea what she was going to do. She kept playing the conversation she had with Zoe in her mind. She was right. Too often Madison went with what other people wanted and what made them happy that she had lost sight of who she was. Before Dante, she wasn't given choices, she was just expected to help out. But with Dante he showed her what it was like to make choices on her own and for herself and what she wanted.

He had given her two beautiful gifts that she would always cherish. Madison awoke to gentle shaking.

"What? Oh sorry, I must have fallen asleep waiting for you."

"I think I know what you want to tell me." He held up the positive pregnancy test.

"Yes, that was part of it."

Dante looked over her shoulder and she knew the exact moment her packed bags came into view.

"You're leaving? Why?"

"Dante. I have to. I don't want to bring up a baby like this."

"Madison, wait. You're not telling me everything. Come on, be honest with me. What's the real reason you're leaving? Because you don't love me?"

"Oh, Dante. How could I not love you? I love you and everything connected with you. I love how you hold me at night and tuck my hair behind my ears. I love watching basketball games with you and just sitting on the couch talking."

"Then why are you leaving?"

"Because one thing I love is that you give me choices and I'm choosing to move back in with you."

He walked closer to her and cupped her cheeks. "I love you. But I'm going to have to punish you for making me think you were leaving me. But I promise to spend the rest of my life saying it to you and showing you how much I love you."

"Are you sure?"

"Yes. I had even bought this for you." He reached into his pocket and pulled out a box. He knelt down on one knee.

"I was drawn to you the first moment I laid eyes on you. Not only your beauty on the outside, but also your beauty on the inside. How you would do anything for those you loved, even though they didn't recognize your efforts. The care you put into your designs. The way you could see the real me. The man behind the money and the mafia name."

"Oh, Dante."

"Madison Blair Bryant, will you marry me again? This time for forever."

"Oh yes, Dante. I will marry you."

Dante opened the box to reveal a two-carat diamond with a halo of diamonds around it.

"Oh, it's beautiful."

Dante stood up and slid it on her finger. "You're beautiful." He picked up her hand and kissed the top of it, before he lifted her palm and kissed each finger before he entwined it with his. He did it with both hands and then kissed her lips and picked her up.

Dante carried her to the bedroom and laid her down on the bed as if she was a precious piece of glass.

He took his time as he removed each article of clothing from her body. He placed kisses on the skin as he exposed it. When he got to her belly he paid special attention to her stomach. With one last kiss he said, "I love you already and promise to always protect you and your mother.

He kissed down her legs and skipped the spot that called to him. It had been so long since they had been together in this way.

This was familiar, but somehow different and new at the same time. When she was bare to his eyes, he backed off the bed and stood up.

"Simply beautiful."

Madison watched as he took his time to remove his suit jacket. Then unbuttoned each button in what felt like slow motion. He revealed tan skin and hard muscle.

Once the shirt was unbuttoned, he left it on but open, and then his hands moved to his pants. He undid the button. Then slid the zipper down. And with a shove, his pants slid down his angular hips. Down muscled thighs to she guessed pool at his feet.

The bed blocked her view, but that wasn't what she was looking at. Her eyes were drawn to what lay between his legs. Even his body highlighted it. The angles of his hips narrowed to a V that highlighted what caught her attention.

It was thick and long and seemed to grow before her eyes. Like a snake it rose up, and she rose as well to her knees and waited for him in the middle of the bed. Arms out. She waited to welcome him home.

Because that's what they were, at home. With each other, they would always be connected. They had made love with their bodies and hearts knowing they were in love. This would be the first time of many that they would make love with their minds knowing they were in love.

Dante climbed onto the bed, and Madison moved toward him. They met in the middle as if magnetized. Their lips met, followed by their chests to hips. Knees kissing.

The kiss was electric. Dante nipped her lower lip before he dived in, his tongue entering her mouth to meet hers. They danced together in a playful way, before he pulled back to kiss her eyes, nose, chin, and cheeks before his lips found hers again.

They tumbled on their sides to lie face to face. Dante placed her leg on top of his and entered her already slick hole nice and slow. They moaned together, like one person. Dante moved inside of her unhurried as he stroked her back at the same time. Madison had wanted this so bad, and her release was quick, like a wave. Overpowering and calming at the same time.

This was what true love was like.

****

Madison climaxed around his cock. He didn't join her. He wasn't ready yet. He wanted to reacquaint himself with Madison and as the slow shudders traveled through her body, he rolled her over to her back taking care to be gentle. He sat back and ran his hands over her stomach.

They had made a baby together that they would both love and cherish. He wanted this coming together to be gentle. To show her how much he cherished her. To show her how much she meant to him. To show her how much he would love her. Forever and a day.

He didn't want to hurt her or their baby. He still couldn't believe he was going to be a dad. He kissed her stomach, and her hands caressed his head and she ran her fingers through his hair.

"You can't hurt me or the baby. Don't treat me like glass but like the woman you love." She opened her legs and ran her hands down her body and tweaked her nipples before she moved to the spot between her legs.

Dante watched her touch herself. She ran a finger down her folds before she parted them so he could see the pretty pink center, and then she dipped two fingers inside her tunnel. Her back arched off the bed as she looked him in the eye and bit her lower lip.

Her eyes darkened, and her hand moved faster. "I want this to be you. I want you to fuck me like you love me."

"I do love you. Take those fingers out of my pussy and let me lick them clean."

She jumped to do what he said. They both groaned as his lips sucked her fingers into his mouth and his tongue licked at her fingers. He took them out of his mouth and then he placed both of her hands on the bed by her head. He laced his fingers with her and plunged inside of her.

"I'm going to show you and my pussy how much I love you."

"Oh, yes."

He used his hands to lift her legs up onto his shoulders before he relaced his fingers with hers and pumped into her. The motion was quick. He pounded her harder and deeper as her tits bounced with each thrust. He held her hands firm to stop her from lifting them and dipped his head to catch a nipple in his mouth.

He knew what she wanted. She loved to have her nipples played with and sucked, and how could he deny her?

"Ahh, Dante, yes."

His hips sped up, and he pumped deeper into her. He was close, and he knew she was too. He released her nipple and then captured her mouth just as the swirling feeling in his center spread outward, like a hurricane that ripped through him.

He knew she was feeling it too as she dug her nails and heels into his shoulders and back. They held on tight to each other as a calmness came over him. Inside, the love he had for her spread out until it was so intense, it was as if he would pass out from the pleasure that was swirling through his body.

It seemed like it would last forever and he was stuck in space with Madison and he wouldn't want to be anywhere else. But in time, they came down. He rolled over, pulling Madison close and then covered them with a blanket.

Epilogue

Three weeks later the charges against Dante had been dropped. Madison stood outside the doctor's office and waited for Dante. He had taken the position with the brokerage firm. Madison was more comfortable now that she knew Dante had a regular nine-to-five. She knew they would always be his family and in turn her family, but she was happy to be removed from that aspect.

Madison checked her watch. Dante was never late, and she didn't have any messages on her phone. She took a deep breath. He wasn't late. She was just nervous. This was their first prenatal visit, and she was excited to see their baby.

She looked around her surroundings. To everyone else today was a normal day. Dante had given her the start-up money for her own fashion house, and she had been busy with that and getting things set up. She and Dante hadn't spent as much time together as they wanted. She had done a half day of work, and Dante had taken the rest of the day off from work as well. They were going to spend the time together. They had both been busy.

Home for a quick dinner and then fall into bed together. Madison was in charge of the wedding planning, and Dante was in charge of finding them a new place to live. Between that and their real jobs, they had not a lot of time left over.

"Hey."

Madison shrieked a little. "You scared me."

"Sorry, you were lost in thought."

"Yeah, I was thinking. We're already married, and I don't need the big fancy wedding. So what if we just go on honeymoon instead since we never did that?"

"That's a wonderful idea, Mrs. Bianchi. Let's do it."

"Thank you, Mr. Bianchi. Now let's go see our baby."

And they walked hand in hand into the office.

A word about the author…

Tabitha Devine crafts steamy romance novels featuring strong, vulnerable Black women finding love on their own terms. With a science background that informs her meticulous plotting and a lifelong passion for romance stories dating back to her middle school days, Devine brings both heart and heat to the page. When not writing, she embraces her multicultural family life with her Sri Lankan husband and their children, expresses her creativity through crafting, and feeds her adventurous spirit through travel. A self-proclaimed "list maker" with an affinity for vintage pin-up styles and fast cars, Devine combines precision with passion in both life and literature. She promises readers no cliffhangers—just satisfying love stories that linger long after the final page. Connect with her online and become one of her "Devine Divas." www.tabithadevine.com

Thank you for purchasing
this publication of The Wild Rose Press, Inc.

For questions or more information
contact us at
info@thewildrosepress.com.

The Wild Rose Press, Inc.
www.thewildrosepress.com